Tough
TENDER

by **Max Allan Collins**

A HARD CASE CRIME NOVEL

A HARD CASE CRIME BOOK

(HCC-153)

First Hard Case Crime edition: March 2022

Published by

Titan Books
A division of Titan Publishing Group Ltd
144 Southwark Street
London SE1 0UP

in collaboration with Winterfall LLC

Print edition ISBN 978-1-78909-143-4
E-book ISBN 978-1-78909-144-1

Design direction by Max Phillips
www.maxphillips.net

Typeset by Swordsmith Productions

The name "Hard Case Crime" and the Hard Case Crime logo
are trademarks of Winterfall LLC. Hard Case Crime books
are selected and edited by Charles Ardai.

Printed by CPI Group (UK) Ltd, Croydon CR0 4YY

Visit us on the web at www.HardCaseCrime.com

Acclaim For the Work of
MAX ALLAN COLLINS!

The beautiful young woman in her mid to late twenties sitting next to Rigley didn't seem the least bit shaken. Pissed off, yes; shaken, no. She was tall, probably five-ten or more, with dark brown hair that curved around her face in a way that reminded Nolan of the way women wore their hair in the forties, the what was it?—pageboy. She had big eyes, huge damn eyes, as brown as her hair and as beautiful; all of her features were beautiful in an exaggerated way. Her mouth was overly large, but nicely so—a sensual mouth that seemed to Nolan designed for any number of erotic pastimes—and her nose was nearly too small and put together so perfectly, it seemed unlikely God could have done it without help. She was full-breasted, small-waisted, lavishly hipped. She wore a matching sweater and pants outfit the color of the rusty brick fireplace; the shadows from the fire were licking her, and he didn't blame them.

Nolan went over and took the shotgun from Jon, and it was in his arms as he looked at Rigley and said, "There are two alternatives for dealing with blackmailers. Go along with them. Or kill them. I can't see going along with you..."

**HARD CASE CRIME BOOKS
BY MAX ALLAN COLLINS:**

SKIM DEEP
TWO FOR THE MONEY
DOUBLE DOWN
TOUGH TENDER
MAD MONEY°

QUARRY
QUARRY'S LIST
QUARRY'S DEAL
QUARRY'S CUT
QUARRY'S VOTE
THE LAST QUARRY
THE FIRST QUARRY
QUARRY IN THE MIDDLE
QUARRY'S EX
THE WRONG QUARRY
QUARRY'S CHOICE
QUARRY IN THE BLACK
QUARRY'S CLIMAX
QUARRY'S WAR *(graphic novel)*
KILLING QUARRY
QUARRY'S BLOOD

DEADLY BELOVED
SEDUCTION OF THE INNOCENT

DEAD STREET *(with Mickey Spillane)*
THE CONSUMMATA *(with Mickey Spillane)*
MIKE HAMMER: THE NIGHT I DIED
(graphic novel with Mickey Spillane)

°*coming soon*

Introduction

For a long while *Hard Cash* and its sequel, *Scratch Fever*, were the toughest of the Nolan novels to find. Their first editions as Pinnacle paperbacks remain among the toughest M.A.C. collectibles to locate.

This is because Pinnacle Books, threatened with legal action by Don Pendleton, caved and published the two novels in small print runs, without the name "Nolan" on the cover...despite the fact that the series was a hit. This capitulation was part of the out-of-court settlement over the absurd claim that Nolan was a Mack Bolan imitator.

If you have any sense of the paperback field in the 1970s and '80s, you know just how many *real* Mack Bolan imitations were out there. Nolan was a crime novel series, not a mob vigilante one, but...Nolan rhymed with Bolan.

As I've noted elsewhere, Nolan was actually the third name for the character, settled on after "Cord" had been discarded and replaced with "Logan." I had changed the latter to Nolan because an obscure paperback series (I believe from Belmont Books) about a character called "Logan" prompted me to find a different if similar name for my professional thief.

This had much less to do with me and more to do with how much Don Pendleton and Pinnacle Books hated each other. Nolan, fittingly, got caught in their crossfire. So *Hard Cash* and *Scratch Fever* went out as novels about "Jon's pal." That's like calling Batman "Robin's pal."

Eventually the books were combined into a single volume, *Tough Tender*, published by Carroll & Graf, back in 1991. It's an easier out-of-print volume to locate than the original two paperbacks, and now Hard Case Crime is including *Tough Tender* in their project of reissuing all the original Nolan novels in two-in-one volumes (*Two For the Money* collected *Bait Money* and *Blood Money*; *Double Down* collected *Fly Paper* and *Hush Money*; and next year *Mad Money* will collect *Spree* and *Mourn the Living*).

Hard Cash continues my propensity to write novels that grow out of novels–this one is, in part, a sequel to *Bait Money*, the first published novel in the series. It also marks the return of everybody's favorite crime-fiction hillbilly clan, the Comforts. Well, my favorite, anyway.

But what I had most in mind in *Hard Cash* was to combine the caper novel with the James M. Cain sex melodrama. I love Cain–particularly *The Postman Always Rings Twice* and *Serenade* –and relished the opportunity to perform this genre splice. In so doing, my femme fatale proved memorable enough to appear in the direct sequel, *Scratch Fever*.

Scratch Fever holds a somewhat unique position in my Nolan series. The first five novels were written in the late sixties through the mid-'70s. But only the first two, *Bait Money* and *Blood Money*, were published in the seventies (both in 1973). The others, because of a merger between publishers Curtis Books and Popular Library, went into that terrible limbo called inventory. Promises of publication were made but not kept. And around 1980, I got the rights back.

With astonishing speed, Pinnacle Books picked up the five books (three of which had never seen publication, remember). I did some rewriting and updating, and suddenly Nolan was again back in business. But Pinnacle was something of a relentless publisher when it came to crime–they offered me a six-book contract.

Which meant that, after seven or eight years or so, I would be returning to the series, with the express instructions that the jump from '70s book to '80s book be seamless.

I think it is. Probably this is my favorite of that first batch of Nolan novels (even if it is, sort of, a one-book "second batch"). I was really getting the hang of writing low-life villains who retained a recognizable humanity, and both Nolan and Jon were getting nice and round, which in particular for Nolan, a genre type if ever there was one, was a good trick. But in *Scratch Fever*, you meet a Nolan with a genuine relationship going on with his girl Sherry (and to him she is a "girl"), not to mention real concern for his partner-in-crime, Jon. You also will find out what happens when somebody fucks with Nolan's dog, and I don't mean the terrier next door.

Two things particularly please me about this novel.

The character Julie, returned from *Hard Cash*, is a particularly good femme fatale, I think. I can say this looking back at the novel since I hardly remember writing the thing, and can take it on its own terms. (I do remember that the two hitmen in this novel were inspired by an apparently gay pair of killers in the classic Joseph H. Lewis film, *The Big Combo*. If you are a real buff, you'll realize that this pits Lee Van Cleef against... Lee Van Cleef.)

The other thing is the presence of rock music in the plot or anyway the ambience. I have played in rock bands since high school, starting around 1966. There have been occasional stretches where I haven't been out there playing, but mostly I have, right up to the present.

The Barn, the venue where Jon and his band the Nodes are appearing, is based on a now-defunct joint called the Pub, where my band Crusin' played every other weekend for at least two years. This is a very accurate rendition of that club. When I wrote the novel, I had just quit the band, who went on without me as a trio playing New Wave under the name the Ones. I returned before long, but in some sense, writing about Jon as a rock musician and this particular venue was a kind of valedictory. Premature as it turns out, but nonetheless *Scratch Fever* marks the most major convergence between my two worlds—writing crime novels and playing rock music—and, for that reason if no other, it holds a special place in my hardboiled heart.

All of my early novels were written when I was a working rock musician. For several years, playing rock was my major source of income...particularly the fallow writing period between when I wrote the Nolan, Mallory and Quarry novels, and landed the Dick Tracy comic strip. Pinnacle publishing Nolan would follow soon, and Mallory finally seeing print at Walker, and Nathan Heller coming to life at St. Martin's Press and changing my career.

Somewhat ironically, *Scratch Fever* is the first book of that second, much more successful time...so it's no wonder it's my favorite of the first seven Nolan novels.

I hope you like it, too.

MAX ALLAN COLLINS

BOOK ONE
Hard Cash

I

Breen's first reaction, when he saw the gun, was to laugh.

A nervous laugh, to be sure, but Breen had an ability to look at himself in a detached, ironic sort of way in stress situations, and the thought of him getting robbed tickled his perverse inner funnybone.

He sat up, jarring the naked barmaid on top of him. He eased her off to one side. She was a cute, plump, German-looking girl with lots of yellow hair. Her lips were a blush-pink color. So were her nipples. She tried covering herself with the little black skirt she'd climbed out of moments before; it was like hiding behind a stamp. Breen was naked too, but he didn't bother covering up. He got a carpet burn on his butt, though, sitting up so fast, surprised.

And the only thing he could see, at first, was the guns—one of them a .45, the other a shotgun, Jesus!—and the long black woolen overcoats, filling the doorway of the back room like two long shadows. The faces of the men were lost, for the moment, in the darkness and the turned-up overcoat lapels, but Breen remembered them immediately, remembered seeing the two men come into the bar an hour or so ago. Remembered the full-length dark coats and turned-up lapels and remembered how stiffly one of the men had walked, almost limping. Limp, hell—that had been the goddamn shotgun strapped to some-body's thigh.

Which explained why the pair hadn't bothered shrugging out of their heavy, wet coats to hang them up as they came in; why they retreated at once to the rear of the place, to a back booth near the men's can, out of Breen's sight.

And he hadn't gotten a close look at the pair, either. The yellow-haired barmaid and another waitress, a sexy brunette who had resisted Breen's advances and just worked there, took care of the customers in the little bar, while Breen just stayed back behind the counter mixing drinks, making occasional conversation. He'd had no contact with the two men, and probably wouldn't even have noticed them particularly if it hadn't been such a dead night.

Tonight, the late December freezing rain that had begun to turn to snow around seven was keeping everybody at home. The bulk of drinking done in Indianapolis tonight would be guys sitting in their kitchens with a bottle and glass, or in an easy chair with beer and pretzels and the boob tube for company. The night was so slow, in fact, the snow looking so blizzard-like, that Breen had closed up early, just after midnight. He was losing money staying open, it was so dead, and besides, that would give him two full hours with that Playboy Bunny of a barmaid and the wife none the wiser.

Women were a weakness of Breen's. Not his worst weakness, but an easy second place. Gambling was his first love, of course —or lust, rather: Breen was a gambler the way a nymphomaniac is a lover, never quite getting out of it what was put in. But he'd kicked the habit, or anyway hoped he had; he hadn't indulged in anything even as harmless as a penny ante poker game these past three months or so. The trick, of course, would be if he could resist the damn horses. It was easy enough to go cold turkey in December, when there was nothing doing but damn harness racing, which wasn't racing at all, in his mind. But what about next summer, when the Chicago tracks started up, and he'd have the old itch to drive in on the weekend? December, sure, but what about fucking May?

Anyway, he was paid up. Didn't owe no bookie no nothin'. Thanks to Nolan, Breen had been able to pay off those four gees he owed that pig bookie of his, and catch up on some of the back alimony and child support he owed his first wife, besides. Things were looking good. The world was spreading its legs for Breen. So was the yellow-haired barmaid, when the guys with guns came in.

She'd been on top of him. Doing her Linda Lovelace imitation and not a bad one at that, after which she'd started settling that sweet German ass down on him, and that's when those fuckers came in.

Thieves, no less.

And he laughed.

Couldn't help himself.

For a second, he laughed. Man bites dog. Thief gets ripped off.

That was Breen, that was what he was: a thief. A stocky, forty-two-year-old, black-haired, crew-cut, fleshy-cheeked, twice-married thief. Who ran a bar in Indianapolis with his brother-in-law Fred (the nights Fred had off were the nights Breen had on—on the plump, sexy waitress, that is) and lost more money on the horses than any bar, let alone one small, quiet, out-in-the suburbs neighborhood bar, could take care of. The only way Breen the gambler could survive was if Breen the thief got out and hustled.

And in the old days, the fifties, even on into the sixties, it hadn't been so bad. It had been good, as a matter of fact, very good. He had worked with the best: guys like Laughlin, Metesky, Randisi, Nolan. Especially Nolan. Nolan was the best organizer in heisting, a real leader, somebody you felt confident working with. But things had started going to hell these last few years. Laughlin and Metesky and a couple of other good men were killed in Georgia little over a year ago, in a back roads chase like something out of the movies, only no happy ending: the damn car went off the side of the road, rolled, blew the fuck up. And Randisi, Christ, he'd just heard about Randisi the other day:

shot through the throat, dead before he hit the ground, and the sad part was Randisi was robbing a fucking liquor store. A guy like Randisi robbing a liquor store, shit. That alone was enough to make you sick.

Christ, for a while there, seemed like everybody in the business was either shot or in stir or otherwise out of commission. Even Nolan.

A couple of years back, Breen and Nolan and some others had been in Chicago (Cicero, to be exact) getting a bank job together, when some syndicate guy shot the job right out from under them. Nolan had had some trouble with the Chicago Family years before, but everybody—including Nolan—had thought that to be past history. Well, it wasn't, it was here and now, and Nolan and Breen and the rest of the string found out the hard way. Luckily only Nolan got tagged with a bullet, but the job went blooey, and Nolan was out of action for a time.

Initially Breen figured Nolan for dead, and so did about everybody else in the business. When Nolan turned up alive, several months later, no heist man worth a shit was willing to come near Nolan, who might as well have stayed dead. Even Breen had stayed clear of his old friend. The risks of the profession were great enough already without including somebody who was wanted by the Family on a job.

Breen had always worked with Nolan as often as possible, but with Nolan and so many other good people out of circulation, Breen had to take what he could get.

And what he could get, it turned out, was the Comforts.

That was what Breen called *really* hitting the bottom. About as bad as Randisi and the fucking liquor store. Stealing nickels and dimes, that's what Breen was reduced to. Literally. Heisting goddamn parking meters with the goddamn Comfort family.

Crazy old Sam Comfort usually worked exclusively with his two sons, Billy and Terry, but Terry drew a short term for statutory rape a while back, and Comfort asked Breen to fill in till the boy got out. Breen had gambling debts to pay, and back alimony and such, and even though he knew old man Comfort had a reputation just slightly shadier than a two-dollar whore, Breen accepted Comfort's offer. When you're desperate, you're desperate.

Actually, he had to give old Sam credit: the parking meter angle wasn't such a bad one. Comfort had worked out a route along Interstate 80, of good-size cities with poorly lit sections of town where parking meters were ripe for picking; Breen and Billy Comfort wore khaki green uniforms with the words "Meter Maintenance" stitched on the back, and Billy would go around emptying meters with keys old Sam provided, bringing back buckets of coin for Breen to empty into the trunk of the Buick, behind the wheel of which sat Sam Comfort, monitoring police calls on a citizen's band radio.

It had been a solid month of six-days-a-week hard work, and when he went to the Comforts' rented farmhouse in Iowa City to collect his share of the nearly fifty thousand bucks that the unofficial meter maintenance team had taken in, Breen had discovered that all the bad things he'd heard about the Comforts were true, and more. Old Sam paid Breen his share by shooting him.

Once in the side, once in the leg.

But Breen had managed to get away, despite the pain and inconvenience of the two wounds. The Comforts, in their quaint, folksy manner, had gotten drunk before Breen showed up, which made evading them no great trick. The trick had been not getting killed by those first unexpected blasts.

Breen had scrambled to his car and got it going, while behind him the back windshield had turned into a big lacy glass doily, thanks to the hole punched in its middle by Sam Comfort's handgun. He had driven the car to Planner's, Planner being an old heist guy who was a good friend of Nolan's. It turned out that Planner had died not long ago, and Nolan and a lad named Jon were presently staying in Planner's place, getting the estate settled or some damn thing.

Anyway, Nolan helped Breen get on his feet, or rather on his back, providing a bed and patching him up and letting him stay there and heal a while. Furthermore, it turned out that Nolan's troubles with the Family were really over this time, and Nolan was evidently thinking about getting back into circulation. On hearing of the Comforts and the double-cross, Nolan offered to get the money back for Breen.

Breen hadn't been too hot on the idea. He was never one for revenge, placing his ass first on his priority list. Fuck, he was grateful just to be alive. Let bygones be bygones. He didn't hold any grudge against those goddamn fucking asshole Comforts. *But at least*, he had told Nolan, *if you do rip them off, kill them too. If you don't,* he'd told Nolan, *you might as well kill me now, because the Comforts are going to figure me for this and come around and feed my balls to me, à la fucking carte.*

But Nolan was hard to sway once he got an idea in his head, and Breen stayed behind, resting up in bed, while Nolan and Jon went off to the Comforts' home territory—a farm in Michigan, near Detroit—and got the parking meter money back. Breen's share and all the rest of it, too.

And the really nice thing was the Comforts—Sam and Billy anyway—had been killed in the process.

It wasn't Nolan's style, killing people, or anyway, it wasn't his style to kill people needlessly. But here there'd been a need: the old man and his son got wise to the heist and came out with guns. So Nolan and this kid Jon had killed them both.

Or anyway, that was what Breen had been told.

Because now, several months later, as he sat naked on the floor of the cramped, closetlike back room, on the soft carpeting he'd installed with cute, plump barmaids in mind (a German-looking, yellow-haired example of which was next to him, huddling in wide-eyed fright against stacked boxes of booze, a young girl as naked as he was and trying to hide behind an inch or so of black cloth), after he'd laughed momentarily at the thought of being caught with his pants down, of being a professional thief about to be robbed by some petty cheap-ass punks, Breen wondered if there was such a thing as ghosts.

Because one of the men aiming the ugly round, hoglike nostrils of a shotgun at him was a white-haired, gray-eyed old man with sardonic smile lines worn into his face, an ambiguously evil/innocent-looking old man named Sam Comfort. The other man, the one with the .45, wasn't a man at all—he was a boy. At first Breen thought it was Billy Comfort. He thought both dead Comforts had come back from the grave after him. But it wasn't Billy; it was Terry. Thin-faced, fair-haired Terry. The sole surviving Comfort, Breen had thought.

Till now.

And the laugh, that ironic laugh at the thought of man bites dog, caught in Breen's throat like a chicken bone, and he felt naked. Naked as hell, more naked even than he was.

"No," old Sam said. "I ain't dead. But you are."

And the old man swung the shotgun, firing, noise and smoke and fire exploding out one barrel, and the sound was a sonic boom in the little room, rattling the boxes of liquor, breaking bottles, shaking everything.

Breen swallowed, wondering why he was alive.

Then he looked to his right, looked over to where old Sam had swung the shotgun.

Looked over in the thankfully shadowy corner of the back

room where the plump body of the barmaid had been tossed, flung, like a life-size inflatable doll with the air slowly seeping out of it. He looked at yellow hair and blood and the rest of what used to be a head with a pretty face on it, dripping down the side of the wall.

"Where's Nolan?" old man Comfort said.

2

"I know who you are," the man said, sitting down. He was an executive type, in his mid-forties, wearing a powder-blue pinstripe suit with matching vest and soft-yellow shirt and powder-blue tie, none of which had been ordered out of a Sears catalog. His hair was dark, untouched by gray (or retouched by something else) and had been cut—no, styled—by a barber who considered himself an artist. His eyes seemed the same color as his suit, but in the dim light it was hard to tell, exactly; maybe they were gray. A handsome man, in a cold, sterile, dull sort of way, like an aging male model or over-the-hill pretty-boy actor who would never make it in character roles.

Nolan said nothing. He just folded his hands and looked out across his knuckles at the man across the table.

They were in the Pier, a seafood restaurant on the banks of the Iowa River, in the cocktail lounge, a long, rectangular dark-paneled room with lots of black vinyl-covered furniture and some oil paintings of steamboats, ship captains, and Mark Twain at various stages of life. The main floor, above them, was a tribute to the ingenuity of Nolan's friend Wagner, who had bought the building left vacant when the Fraternal Order of Elks, Iowa City Lodge, moved to newer, larger digs out in the country; the big dining room, with several other, more intimate rooms off to either side, was given a twenty-thousand-leagues-under-the-sea atmosphere via black light and other otherworldly lighting effects that played tricks with Day-Glo wall murals. An oddly illuminated aquarium built into and running the length of one wall furthered the underwater feeling, while menus printed in fluorescent ink glowed the various seafood and steak selections to customers who had by now completely forgotten they were sitting in the old, mostly unremodeled Elks Lodge. The upper floor, a ballroom, was rented out occasionally but otherwise went unused, and the lower, which housed the cocktail lounge, was pretty much the same as it had been when the Elks were loose in it, except for the nautical oil paintings.

The two men had the lounge almost to themselves. It was a cold, snowy Wednesday night, and nobody was there who didn't have to be: just the help; Nolan, the Pier's new co-owner and manager; and this man in the powder-blue pinstripe suit, who'd come to see Nolan.

The man leaned across the table, smiling, his teeth so perfect and white, they were either capped or a miracle, and said, "I said I know you."

Nolan shrugged with his eyes.

"And you know who I am, too, don't you?"

Nolan nodded.

"Don't you wonder why I'm here?"

There was something in the man's voice—what it was, Nolan couldn't quite pin down…smugness maybe, maybe nervousness.

"Doesn't it…bother you, my being here?"

Both. It was both.

"No," Nolan said.

"No? Why not?"

"Because," Nolan said, leaning forward himself now, returning the smile, whispering, "when you leave here, a friend of mine is going to shoot you, toss you in the trunk of his car, and dump you in a ravine." And he leaned back and stopped smiling.

A tic got going at the left edge of the man's right eye, and they were gray eyes, not blue, Nolan decided.

"I…don't believe you."

Nolan shrugged again, this time with his shoulders. "Do what you want. All I know is I saw you come in twenty minutes ago. You sat down and started staring at me. I left the room, used the phone. My friend'll be outside now. And there's only the one exit, you know."

All of that was bullshit, but the man didn't know it. There had been no phone call. Nolan had left the room—to go up to his office and get a .38 snub out of a desk drawer. The gun was stuck in his belt, under his sport coat, but he of course had no intention of using the thing in a public place like this, even if it was a slow night. And the only friend he had in town who could conceivably help him was Jon, who was as unlikely an assassin as Nolan could think of. Even the bit about the exit was crap: there were three, as a matter of fact.

Not that Nolan wouldn't kill this man if he had to. And he was starting to think maybe that'd be the case.

Nolan was fifty years old and did not look it, particularly, though at times like this he certainly felt it. He was a big but not huge man, lean but deceptively muscular with a slight paunch one of the few visible signs of his middle age. His hair was dark, slightly shaggy, widow's peaked, graying at the temples; he had had the permanently dour countenance of a western gunfighter and the thick, slightly droopy mustache to go with it; at the same time he had high cheekbones and narrow eyes somehow suggestive of an American Indian. It was as if somewhere in his ancestry there'd been a Cochise and Doc Holliday both.

He was a professional thief, recently retired but with no pretense of having at last joined the "straight" world. He had been a thief too long to ever think of himself as anything else, and he'd be fooling himself if he tried. He had heard a supposedly true story about a guy named Levitz, who was a very smooth, very successful con man back in the thirties, but who had a complex about being Jewish. One day Levitz was walking down the street with another successful con artist of the era, a hunchback named Lange, and as they went by a synagogue, Levitz said, "Did you know I used to be a Jew?" And Lange said, "Did you know I used to be a hunchback?"

Nolan knew better than to try and con himself; he was a thief and had no pretensions otherwise. Besides, the money he had invested in the Pier was heist money mostly, and if you're going to build a new, socially acceptable life for yourself on that kind of money, you're wise never to forget where the foundation came from.

Because forgetting who you were—who you are—could be dangerous as hell.

Take this situation, for instance.

The man in the pinstripe suit, sitting across the table from Nolan, was the president of a bank: the First National Bank of Port City, Iowa, a town of twenty thousand just forty miles southeast of Iowa City. The man's name was George Rigley. A little over two years ago, the two men had sat across from each other in a similar manner. At George Rigley's desk. In George Rigley's bank.

Two years and a month or so ago, Nolan, his young friend Jon, and two others had robbed George Rigley's bank. Nolan, Jon, and a guy named Grossman had posed as examiners to gain after-hours admittance to the bank, and therefore hadn't had the luxury of wearing masks. And so it was possible, perhaps inevitable that bank president Rigley would recognize Nolan.

Nolan had considered the possibility, when he chose to live and work in Iowa City just two short years after that robbery, that a problem like George Rigley might crop up. He'd known it was possible for employees of that particular bank to wander

into the Pier now and then, and since Nolan had worked exten-
sively in the rural Midwest (where banks were relatively easy
pickings, oftentimes not even insured by the FDIC, meaning
no FBI), veterans of other Nolan robberies could have possibly
turned up as customers at the restaurant and lounge. But he'd
been counting on several factors to take care of any such problems—for one thing, the generally lousy memory of most people;
people often have trouble recognizing even a familiar face in
an unexpected context. And Nolan had been twenty pounds
lighter at the time of the robbery, and had been disguised for
the occasion: his hair and mustache had been powdered white,
and he'd worn tinted glasses. Later, he'd seen the drawings that
appeared in the papers, based on the descriptions of the witnesses, and hadn't recognized himself. So why should any of
the witnesses do any better two years later in Iowa City, in an
unexpected context?

It was a total fluke, of course, that Nolan had ended up in
Iowa City at all. Or a series of flukes, anyway. His connection to
Iowa City had been Planner, an old guy who used an antique
shop in town as a front for doing what his name implied: planning
jobs for guys the likes of Nolan. Planner had been a middleman,
a heist broker—an old-time heist man himself who hadn't liked
the tension and danger of the life but who didn't know any
other so continued dabbling in it into his semiretirement.
Planner would use his guise of eccentric old antique dealer to
travel around and scout up prospective targets, working out
detailed packages to sell to Nolan and a few others like him—
that is, a suggested method or methods for pulling the caper
off. He also served as a line of communication through whom
others in the heist trade could be contacted and with whose
help you could assemble a first-rate string.

Two years ago, needing money, the Family hot on his ass and

nobody in the trade wanting to share the heat with him, Nolan had turned to Planner for anything Planner could come up with for him. And Planner had given him the Port City job. Seemed that Planner's nephew, Jon, a kid of nineteen or twenty, was in with a couple of other lads, one of whom was a pretty young bitch who worked as a teller at the Port City bank, which these kids were planning to rob. Nolan decided that having an inside person at the bank was an advantage that might offset the lack of experience and the immaturity of the kids, and out of sheer desperation, he went ahead with the robbery.

And so had begun his relationship with Jon. Jon was a somewhat naive, basically shy kid who had dreams of drawing comic books for a living some day; he was a smart kid, a strong little bastard who lifted weights and all that and had been a state wrestling champ in his high school days. Jon's only (if over-riding) eccentricity was this thing of being a comic book nut: drawing the things, collecting them, talking about them almost constantly. Nolan didn't mind, figuring everybody had a right to a quirk or two, but in the beginning he certainly hadn't pictured the boy as someone he'd be entering a long-term partnership with.

But after the Port City bank job, when some Family people caught Nolan with his pants down, it had been Jon who'd hauled Nolan's ass out of the fire—and a bullet-riddled ass it had been, too. He'd taken Nolan to Planner's and stayed by him like a damn nurse for six or eight fucking months. Nolan was not the sentimental type, but Jon was no longer just a silly damn comic book freak to him; Jon was a silly damn comic book freak who had saved Nolan's life, and that was different.

A lot had happened since then. Planner had been killed, shot to death in the back room of the antique shop when some old "friends" of Nolan's had come calling. Nolan and Jon had evened the score as best as possible, but lost a pile of money in the process. In the meantime, Nolan's long-standing feud with the Chicago Family finally fizzled out when a new regime came into power; the new Family people even hired Nolan, and he ran a motel and restaurant complex for them for a while. But he soon got a bad taste in his mouth, working for people who were in his opinion just a bunch of pimps and pushers and killers come up in the world. So he'd quit, amicably, and had decided to take the offer made him by another of his old working cronies who was retired and living in Iowa City, a very close friend of Planner's named Wagner, who was having some health troubles and wanted Nolan to take over his restaurant business for him. Thanks to a heist he and Jon had pulled in Detroit a few months back, Nolan had had the necessary capital to buy in, and now here he was: settled down perhaps too close to the site of a fairly recent bank job, which was a risk, yes, but a risk he'd decided was worth taking.

Now, however, as he stared across the table at George Rigley, president of the First National Bank of Port City, he wasn't so sure.

And George Rigley didn't seem so sure of himself, either, at the moment. Nolan's blunt threat of death had undermined Rigley's confidence, shattered that slick, obnoxious superiority so many bankers project. For thirty seconds now, the man had just sat there, quietly shaking in his powder-blue pinstripe, the tic at the corner of one bluish-gray eye revealing that he was close to panic.

"You better have a drink, Rigley," Nolan said. "You look like you don't feel so good."

Rigley showed momentary surprise that Nolan remembered him by name, tried to cover it, then went on. "You don't scare me. I know you won't kill me or have me killed. Not right away.

You're not a stupid man. Don't you think I left word where I'd be? Don't you think someone knows where I am, and why?"

Well, Nolan certainly didn't know why.

But one thing was becoming clear: Rigley had not just stumbled onto Nolan. He hadn't just walked in, recognized Nolan, and come over on impulse to confront him. Evidently Rigley had spotted Nolan at the Pier some time earlier, last weekend maybe, when it was so crowded and Nolan wouldn't have been as likely to notice Rigley as tonight, a slow, snowy Wednesday.

No, not a chance meeting, but a planned confrontation, contrived for some special, specific reason. *But what?* Nolan wondered.

So he asked, "What do you want, Rigley?"

Rigley smiled his unreal smile. The tic at the edge of his eye stopped.

"I want you to rob my bank again," he said.

3

Two weeks ago, after the first real snowfall, Jon had gone out and bought a Christmas tree. An artificial one, a two-foot-high affair that was an aluminum tube with holes you stuck plastic piney branches in, but a Christmas tree. Then, when he got home, he got embarrassed thinking about how Nolan would react to any such deck-the-halls bullshit, and he tossed the thing, still packed away in its cardboard box, unassembled, into a closet and forgot about it.

But today it had snowed again, and it was beautiful snow. He had looked out the window, and the world was a damn Christmas card. It had snowed yesterday too, but that was slushy, messy stuff. Today was colder, the snow dry, like a fine white powder, and he had gone straight for his sketch pad and grabbed his winter coat and gotten in the car and driven out into a wooded area and began drawing. At dusk he headed back, with half a dozen detailed sketches under his arm (some in the styles of cartoonists whose winter scenes Jon admired—Milton Caniff, George Wunder, Stan Lynde) and stopped downtown at the Airliner to warm up over something alcoholic. By the time he got back to the antique shop and inside and upstairs in the living quarters that had been his uncle Planner's and were presently being shared by Nolan and himself, Jon was full of Christmas cheer, and soon he was hauling the artificial tree out of the closet and putting it together pine by plastic pine.

Jon was twenty-one, short but powerfully built, with a headful of curly brown hair and the sort of pleasant, boyish blue-eyed features that made girls want to cuddle him. Which was an asset, of course, but Jon himself didn't much like the way he looked, and didn't much care, either, his wardrobe running to sweatshirts with comics characters on the front and old worn-out jeans with patches on the ass.

He was a cartoonist, or anyway wanted to be. He'd loved comic books since he was a kid, and had been trying to write and draw them himself as long as he could remember. He'd kicked around from relative to relative and from school to school while his mother (a third-rate nightclub "chanteuse") was on the road, and fought the trauma of his fatherless, all but motherless childhood by escaping into the four-color, ten-cent fantasy world of the comics. It was a hobby that grew into a way of life, and would, hopefully, one day become a livelihood.

So far he was unpublished, but he was getting pretty good, so it shouldn't be long now. But drawing comics was a risky field to try to go into. Right now, with comic books suffering because of distribution problems, and underground comics having run out of steam after the goddamn Supreme Court's obscenity ruling, and newspaper comics being shrunk down to the size of postage stamps, he'd do better going into blacksmithing.

But what the hell—he loved the comics. He would stay with it.

He put the assembled tree on top of the television set. It looked naked. *Pretty girls*, Jon thought, still full of Christmas spirit, *look good naked; plastic trees do not.* He had neglected to buy any decorations or tinsel, but guessed he would get around to that tomorrow. Maybe some gifts under the tree would improve things.

"Yeah, gifts," he said out loud, turning on the television. (Some cop show was on—he couldn't tell which, as they all looked pretty much the same to him, especially the ones with helicopters flying around constantly.) He flopped onto the couch by the wall and watched without watching.

The artificial tree, barren of gifts, made him think how absurd it was of him to decorate the living quarters of a man like Nolan with the sentimental ornamentation of the season. It was equally absurd to think of buying gifts to put under the tree. What did you buy a tough guy for Christmas, anyway? Maybe wrap up a box of .38 slugs in a bright red bow and put it in his stocking mask?

Yes, it was a real problem, buying a bank robber a gift.

And then Jon remembered.

Hey, he thought. *Those days are over.*

It hit him, perhaps for the first time, and he had the strangest damn feeling: a mingling of glad and sad, loss and gain.

Nolan was retired.

Nolan wasn't a thief anymore. Nolan had put his long-barrel .38 Colt and shoulder holster away in mothballs, hadn't he? To help an old buddy run a restaurant. Retired.

Which meant Jon, too, was retired. From that particular precarious lifestyle, anyway. Heists and guns and bullets and blood were back in the paperbacks where they belonged, back in the movies and comic books, back on the tube, like that mindless cop show he wasn't paying attention to, and Jon was relieved. The game was over, and he was relieved.

And vaguely sorry.

But mostly relieved, shit, when he thought back on it, on two years of breaking the law and having people shooting at you and, Christ, sometimes shooting back. He shuddered, wondering how he'd ever let himself get mixed up with somebody like Nolan in the first place.

He liked Nolan. He admired him. But he did not worship the man, even if at one time he'd come close to doing so; in the very beginning, he'd seen Nolan as a living personification of the strong, silent heroes of popular mythology—the supermen of the comics, the gunfighters and private eyes of the movies. Nolan was like somebody who'd walked right out of Jon's fantasy world, and it had been exciting.

Now, however, Jon knew there was a fuck of a lot of difference between fantasy and fact; now he knew the reality of seeing people he cared about—Planner, for instance, and Shelly, a girl Jon'd made love to—die, brutally, cruelly, with hands cupping their own blood, as if they were trying to catch and hold onto the life that was gushing out of them and dripping through their fingers. Jon had known the terror of having the police after you, and he had known what it was like having people far worse than police after you, trying to kill you. And you trying to kill them back.

It wasn't that he'd grown moral all of a sudden. He still felt being a thief wasn't any worse than being a politician or a business executive, although he felt thieves were generally more honest. And insurance companies were dens of damn thieves, dealing with customers, trying to screw *them* like thieves, and who were at least partially dependent on the self-admitted thieves like Nolan to keep in business. No, all of the old rationalizations held up for him. *In a corrupt society*, his uncle Planner had once told him, *a thief at least has a chance to be an individual, to be honorably corrupt*. The idea of being a thief didn't bother Jon.

The idea of killing did. Jon valued human life. He had respect for it, did not believe in hurting people. He did not enjoy seeing people suffer, could hardly *bear* to see someone suffer.

On the heist in Detroit, two months ago, he had killed a man.

A crazy old man named Sam Comfort, who was pointing a shotgun at Nolan, getting ready to let loose that shotgun straight into Nolan's guts.

And Jon had shot Sam Comfort.

A man who was a double-crossing, probably psychopathic and wholly corrupt thief, in the worst sense of that word, who had betrayed his compatriots time and time again. Killed time and again. A man who, in the opinion of many, deserved to die anyway.

In this case, however, Jon couldn't make the rationalizations work for him. He hadn't had a decent night's sleep since Detroit.

And Detroit wasn't all. He would lie awake and think back to the earlier heist, the very first one, the Port City bank job, and realize that that time the same thing could have happened: guns could have started going off. He and Nolan had been holding guns on innocent people at that bank, innocent people who could have gotten in the way of guns going off and been killed.

It was hard enough living with the thought of killing a Sam Comfort. But the thought of even the possibility of causing the death of an innocent person, a "civilian," as Nolan would put it, was something Jon could not bear.

So he was glad the game was over. He would miss the positive side of it, the excitement, the heady rush brought on by the presence of danger, the satisfaction of working well under pressure, and of meeting Nolan's high professional standards; but as for the dark side, the blood and killing and all of that, good riddance.

The cop show on the tube seemed to be ending, a shootout in progress. People were dying in that sterile, bloodless way people die on television. He got up and switched the channel and the same thing was going on, but with slightly different faces. He turned it off, got his sketch pad, and began to doodle, finally roughing out a graphic story idea he'd had in the back of his head a while. He lost himself in the drawing, and the upsetting thoughts of death and violence left him.

Around nine he heard Nolan coming up the steps.

"How come back so early?" he asked Nolan as he came in, not looking up from the sketch pad.

"Here," Nolan said, and Jon looked up.

Nolan was tossing something at him.

"You're maybe going to need that," Nolan said.

Jon looked down at what he'd caught: a gun.

Nolan disappeared into the bedroom.

Jon stared at the snubnose .38 as if he couldn't remember what it was for. In a moment Nolan was coming out of the bedroom, getting into his shoulder holster.

"I had a visitor at the Pier tonight," Nolan was saying. "George Rigley."

"Uh, George *who*?"

"Rigley." He was loading slugs into the long-barrel .38 now. "President of the Port City bank."

"Port City...Jesus. Did he...?"

"Recognize me? Like a long-lost identical twin brother."

Jon didn't say anything. He was having trouble just thinking. Talking was out of the question.

"He wants us to rob the Port City bank again," Nolan said.

Jon felt his mouth drop open, but nothing came out.

"We got two choices, kid. The guy's evidently been doing some book-juggling, and wants us to rob his bank for him so he can cover, and we can do that. That's one choice. The other choice is obvious."

The other choice was to kill the bank president.

"Well, Jon," Nolan said, shoving the gun down snug in the underarm holster. "What's your preference? Choice A or B?"

"How...how about 'none of the above.' "

"That'd be my choice too...if it was a choice."

"Then...then I suppose we rob his fucking bank. Christ."

Nolan sat on the edge of the couch. Jon was sitting up now; it wasn't the kind of news you took lying down. Nolan said, "There are some things we have to do tonight. Kid? You listening?"

Jon let out the breath he'd drawn in and had been holding for forty seconds or so. "Yeah. I'm okay. Go ahead with what you were saying, Nolan. Shoot."

4

Rigley's cottage was little different from any of the others along the Cedar River. Like most of them, it looked more like a small house than a cottage: an unassuming white clapboard high on a bank that sloped down gently to the river.

Nolan shrugged out of his heavy leather coat as he came in, tossing it on a plaid upholstered couch. Rigley followed, got out of a gray, fur-collared coat, and hung it on the rack by the door; he hung Nolan's there too.

This front room—which apparently took up at least half the floor space of the cottage—had a comfortable masculine look to it. The walls were paneled in pine, and big pine-shuttered windows faced the river and flanked either side of a central fireplace, a massive affair of rust-color brick with a healthy blaze going in it. The furniture was lived-in looking, and there was no overhead lighting, just a standing lamp here and there. Rigley was an outdoorsman, evidently, or anyway fancied himself one; a mounted fish hung over the fireplace, and some pictures of ducks in flight flew above the couch. And down at the far end of the room, a small but overstocked bar was watched over by one of those big, lighted-up beer signs of an animated outdoor scene—a stream running through lush green woods. A masculine-looking room, all right, but a woman lived here. Nolan could see her in the neatness of the housekeeping; the dazzling polish of the hardwood floor, which was reflecting the glow of the fireplace like a huge mirror; the floral centerpiece of an otherwise rugged-looking picnic-type table. She was here now: Nolan could feel her presence. He could smell her.

But Rigley said nothing about a woman being here, or anyone else, for that matter.

Which didn't explain why the fire was going when they got there.

The conversation between Nolan and Rigley at the Pier had been a brief one. Rigley had wanted to continue the conversation elsewhere, out of the public eye, a sentiment Nolan couldn't have shared more. Rigley mentioned this cottage of his as a possible meeting place and Nolan accepted, but suggested that the two of them not be seen leaving the restaurant together. So they'd agreed to meet at ten in the parking lot of the Target store on the way out of town; Nolan would then follow Rigley to the cottage on the Cedar River, between Iowa City and Port City. Which had given Nolan time to stop at the antique shop and fill Jon in.

And now here he was with Rigley, at the cottage, with someone —some woman—listening on in another room.

Rigley was behind the bar, fixing himself something. "What can I build you, Mr. Logan?"

Logan was the name Nolan was using at the Pier.

"Nothing," Nolan said.

"Come on, now," Rigley said, with patronizing smile and tone to match. "I see no reason why we can't be sociable. We're going to be working together rather closely for the next few weeks, after all."

Nolan sighed. He plopped his ass down on the couch. The couch was close to the door. He unbuttoned his jacket and folded his arms to prevent the gun under his arm from showing. Between Rigley's phony pleasant attitude and knowing somebody was in the next room, Nolan felt pretty uncomfortable. Rigley hadn't turned on any lights yet, so there was just the light from the fire, which was short on illumination and long on creating a sinister, shadow-throwing atmosphere. Nolan said, "Make it a beer then."

Rigley brought Nolan a beer, pulled a straight-back chair from somewhere, and sat facing him. Looking down at him. *All he lacks*, Nolan thought, *is his goddamn desk*.

"Before we begin, I think I should explain something," Rigley said, sipping his drink, a Manhattan. "I have everything worked out. I know just how we can bring this off...simply, efficiently, safely and, most importantly, profitably. *Extremely* profitably. All you will have to do is follow my instructions explicitly, and everything will..."

Nolan stood.

He walked to the fireplace, leaned against it, made Rigley turn to look at him. Looking down on Rigley, he said, "Make all the suggestions you want. But no instructions."

"Mr. Logan, I..."

"You're a banker. You know everything there is to know about banks. Except one thing. How to rob them. That's my department."

"You don't understand—you see, I have everything worked out."

"You're the one who doesn't understand. Either I'm in charge, or I'm out."

Rigley thought that over for a moment, then shrugged his acceptance of Nolan's terms. "You're right. I came to you because you have expertise in this particular area of endeavor. I wanted a professional on the team...otherwise I could have just as well settled for some lowlife out of a riverfront dive. So I must agree. You *are* the one most qualified to make the decisions in our forthcoming venture." He made a toasting gesture, drained the remains of his Manhattan, and rose and fixed himself another.

But when he came back from the bar, he had more with him than a fresh drink: he was carrying a manila folder, which he handed to Nolan, saying, "I think you'll find this of interest."

Nolan emptied his beer in two long swigs, set the empty can on the hearth, took the folder. He was getting more and more irritated with Rigley's constant barrage of bullshit, and was wondering if the guy was a little drunk or was just naturally a pompous ass. With a bank president, it was hard to tell. He looked in the folder.

It contained photographs of Nolan and Jon, separately and together, taken at the Pier, outside the antique shop, and elsewhere around Iowa City. There was also the newspaper clipping that included the composite drawings of both Nolan and Jon (neither very good, but a resemblance could be seen, if you tried hard enough) and a Xerox copy of a signed statement by Rigley in which he stated his belief that "Logan" and Jon were two of the three men who had robbed the Port City bank two years ago.

"My lawyer has a duplicate folder," Rigley said. "Sealed, of course. He won't open it unless anything should happen to me, in which case…well, I'm sure you can guess where the contents of the folder would go."

Nolan said, "I don't like blackmailers."

"I don't mean it to be blackmail. This is simply a matter of business. If it was blackmail, I wouldn't be offering you money, would I? And there is a great deal of money to be made here for you and that young friend of yours. There were four of you involved when you took three quarters of a million dollars from my bank two years ago. This time, there would be only a three-way split, a third for me, a third each for you and your young friend. The purpose of the folder is one of leverage—to convince you to help me, join me in this undertaking. And to remind you that while I may, in the execution of said undertaking, choose to defer my position of leadership to you, I am *still*, in reality, in the overview, in charge."

Nolan folded the folder lengthwise several times and walked over to Rigley and swatted him in the face with it a few times.

"You," Nolan said, "are in charge of shit."

And he hit him a few more times with the folded folder.

"Stop it, stop it!" Nolan had stopped slapping him with the folder, but Rigley was cowering anyway, holding his hands in front of his face like a man trying to keep out the sun.

Nolan grabbed a handful of Rigley's expensive suit coat and lifted him off the couch and shook him a little. "Listen to me, asshole. You're in so far over your fucking head, you can't even tell you're drowning."

"Don't...don't hurt me."

"Don't hurt you?" He thrust him back against the couch, and Rigley bounced limply, like someone already dead. "I'm probably going to kill you, you stupid, smug son of a bitch! Can't you even see that?"

"You're not...going to kill me," Rigley said. It was assertion, question, and plea all at once, but mostly the latter; he had seen the gun in the holster swinging under Nolan's shoulder.

"That remains to be seen," Nolan said, pacing, deciding.

"You don't really think I'd be fool enough to bring you out here to a...remote spot like this without having...having someone to back me up, do you, Logan?"

"I think you're a fool—period."

"We're not alone, Logan. I'm warning you. Don't try anything. We're not alone; I can have you at my mercy at the drop of a hat."

Nolan laughed, and the laugh sounded harsh even in his own ears. "It's too bad you don't have a hat, then, Rigley. At your mercy, Jesus."

"Julie," Rigley called. "Julie, get in here, quick!"

Nolan shook his head and said, "Well, you're right about one thing, Rigley. We aren't alone. Come on in, Jon."

Jon came in through the doorway opposite the fireplace, with Rigley's partner in tow. He flicked on a standing lamp by the couch, where he deposited his pretty P.O.W., from whom he'd taken a double-barreled shotgun, which was cradled over his left arm, making the snubnose .38 in his hand look like a toy. Meanwhile, the girl was angrily removing the slash of white tape Jon had forced over her mouth a few minutes earlier.

"I hope you don't mind Jon coming in the back way, Rigley," Nolan said.

Rigley said nothing. He sat motionless, except for that facial tic that had started up again.

But the beautiful young woman in her mid to late twenties sitting next to Rigley didn't seem the least bit shaken. Pissed off, yes; shaken, no. She was tall, probably five-ten or more, with dark brown hair that curved around her face in a way that reminded Nolan of the way women wore their hair in the forties, the what was it?—pageboy. She had big eyes, huge damn eyes, as brown as her hair and as beautiful; all of her features were beautiful in an exaggerated way. Her mouth was overly large, but nicely so—a sensual mouth that seemed to Nolan designed for any number of erotic pastimes—and her nose was nearly too small and put together so perfectly, it seemed unlikely God could have done it without help. She was full-breasted, small-waisted, lavishly hipped. She wore a matching sweater and pants outfit the color of the rusty brick fireplace; the shadows from the fire were licking her, and he didn't blame them.

Nolan went over and took the shotgun from Jon, and it was in his arms as he looked at Rigley and said, "There are two alternatives for dealing with blackmailers. Go along with them. Or kill them. I can't see going along with you, Rigley. For one thing, I don't think I can stomach your pompous fucking bank president attitude. And I don't think my temper will last long around stupid goddamn stunts like that folder full of threats you shoved under my nose, or having your busty girlfriend cover me with a shotgun from the next room while we talk. I just cannot see getting involved in a heist with irrational, incompetent amateurs the likes of you two. And so I'm left with that other, unpleasant alternative."

Rigley was pale and looked almost dazed, but the girl, Julie, said, "He's bluffing, honey. Don't pay any attention to him."

Nolan went on, still talking over the twin barrels of the shotgun. "I'm willing to offer you a third alternative, Rigley. I'm willing to let this end right here. Quietly. Without violence. I'll forget about you, your embezzling, your pipe-dream robbery. And you do likewise where I'm concerned."

Rigley seemed to be thinking it over, when the girl said, "If they were going to kill us, honey, they would have by now."

Smart girl. The brains of the outfit. And the balls too, most likely.

But she was still talking. To Nolan now. "Are you going to shoot that thing or not? Or were you planning to talk us to death?"

And for a moment Nolan was ready to kill them both and screw the consequences. He felt his hand tighten around the shotgun stock and was a hair away from it, and it must have showed, because he saw Jon cringe.

He broke open the shotgun and spilled the shells onto the floor. "You're right," he told the girl. "I'm not going to kill anybody." He tossed the empty shotgun on her lap, hard. "Tonight."

He put the .38 away, sat in the hard-back chair facing the couch. "Okay, then, Rigley," Nolan said. "What did you have in mind?"

5

It was still snowing, but the roads were clear; the wind was keeping them that way. Jon sat and stared out at the snow swirling in the beams of the headlights and let himself be hypnotized, not wanting to think.

Then he realized Nolan was saying something.

"Uh, what, Nolan? I wasn't listening."

"I just said are you okay, kid?"

"Yeah. I'm fine."

"What did you think of what Rigley had to say?"

"His plan, you mean? It's all right. Couple rough spots, maybe. How come you didn't question any part of it? I know you weren't satisfied with it completely."

Nolan yawned, sat up in the driver's seat, leaned over the wheel. "I guess I figured I put him through enough strain for one night. He isn't the strongest guy I ever saw. So I figured ease off for now, let things ride. We'll wait till we get together Saturday with them, when he brings that stuff I asked for: timetable of employee activity, photos of the interior and exterior of the bank, the floor plan, and so on. I don't remember the place all that clear."

I do, Jon thought. He remembered it all, every sweaty second. To Nolan, the Port City bank job had been just another heist, to Jon it had been the first and, he'd thought at the time, only one he'd ever be involved in.

"Little did I know," Jon mumbled.

"What?"

"Nothing."

"You know," Nolan said after a while, "I think I had Rigley pretty well bluffed out. Rigley I think I could've handled without much trouble. But that bitch. Shit. I wouldn't want to play poker with her."

Jon managed a smile and said, "Not even strip poker?"

"And freeze my bare ass off in this snow? No thanks. But I admit she's something to look at. Looking at her, I begin to understand how a straight the likes of Rigley could get mixed up in something like this. Better men than our bank president have sold their souls for a lot less woman, believe me."

"Men like you, you mean, Nolan?"

"Well, I'm out of the question," Nolan said, smiling a little. "I lost my soul at a carnival when I was twelve years old, to considerably less beautiful a Mata Hari than Rigley's. How about you, kid? She get a rise out of you? Bet you copped a nice feel wrestling with her back at that cottage."

"Yeah, well, the shotgun she had kind of took the fun out of it."

"Would you rather been out front getting your ass bored off by Rigley?"

"I don't know—he doesn't seem like such a bad guy to me. Victim of circumstances, looks to me."

"Victim of circumstances, my ass. We're the damn victims, and he's the blackmailing little son of a bitch who's screwing us in the ear with his goddamn circumstances."

"Come on, Nolan. You know who's screwing us in the ear, and it isn't Rigley."

Nolan yawned again, then said, "Yeah, you're right. It's the bitch doing it. Christ, you'd think getting screwed by her would be more fun."

They drove in silence for a while. Soon the trailer courts on the left-hand side of the highway signaled Iowa City's closeness, and as they came into town, the clear highway gave way to snow-packed, icy city streets. Then they were turning down the quiet residential lane at the end of which was the antique shop. It was a street of double-story homes with modest, well-tended lawns and lots of trees—a beautiful, shade-bathed street in summer, equally beautiful in winter, with the bare branches of the trees catching handfuls of snow and holding them, occasional white strokes of an artist's brush in a scene predominantly gray. But right now only the gray seemed apparent to Jon: skeletal, dead branches on skeletal, dead trees, the houses themselves dark and cheerless. Energy conservation was leading to less brightly lit Christmas seasons than those of the recent past: the bright colored lights were at the moment unlit, the nativity scenes on lawns and Santas climbing in chimneys were minus spotlights, and only for a few hours each evening would the seasonal glow be switched on at all. The world still looked like a Christmas card to Jon, but a gloomy one, sent by an atheist.

Nolan pulled the Buick into one of the spaces alongside the antique shop, and they got out. The shop was a two-story clapboard building that looked more a part of the residential area it bordered than the business district it began, with a Shell station next door and various chain restaurants (like the Dairy Queen across from the Shell) nearby. Jon had kept the shop closed since his uncle's death, and had no intention of continuing in the antique business. There was a guy—a friend of Planner's—set to come next month and make a bid on all the antiques and junk in the place, and after that Jon was considering turning it into a candle shop, to be run by Karen Hastings, his on-again-off-again girlfriend (off-again at the moment, though he felt he could patch things up, if he decided he wanted to) and running a mail-order business himself in old comic books and related items. Actually, things were beginning to settle into place in Jon's life: he had invested his money in the Pier with Nolan, and it was a good investment that should keep both of them solvent for untold years to come; and he had inherited the antique shop and its contents, which would provide more cash and a place to live and do business out of; and he had Karen, if he got around to patching up their relationship; and his artwork was getting better all the time and getting close to where he really thought he might actually be able to make a living drawing comic books. And a fresh, new year was coming up in a matter of days.

And now this.

Another robbery.

He and Nolan went in. Nolan went upstairs, Jon to the room in back on the first floor, where he slept and kept his studio. It had been a storeroom when his uncle Planner turned it over to him, a dusty, dirty oversized closet that Jon had converted into a shrine to comic art, plastering the gray wood walls with colorful homemade posters of Dick Tracy, Batman, Tarzan, Flash Gordon, and half a dozen other comic heroes, drawn by Jon unerringly in the style of their original artists. A few splashes of bright color in the form of throw rugs transformed the cement floor into something livable; a few pieces of furniture—the genuinely antique bed and chest of drawers given him by Planner —turned storeroom into bedroom. A drawing easel and a file cabinet containing his rarest comic artifacts, and boxes of comic books lining the walls made the room a cartoonist's studio. He had consciously decorated and organized the room so that it would be a cheerful, constant visual reminder of who he was.

There was also a poster of perennial movie bad guy and sometime spaghetti western hero Lee Van Cleef, wearing his black mustache and dark gunfighter's outfit, fondling the six-gun on his hip, looking a hell of a lot like Nolan. The six-gun, and the .357 Magnum Dick Tracy was brandishing, and Flash Gordon's ray gun—these and other implements of the fantasy violence he'd so enjoyed for so many years—irritated and disturbed him tonight, and he thought, *What a bunch of bullshit*, and left the room.

He went upstairs. The lights were off, but he knew his way around. Nolan was already sacked out. Snoring. Jon stretched out on the couch. He just didn't want those fucking fantasy faces staring at him, even in the dark; he couldn't sleep in that room tonight. He didn't know why exactly, he just couldn't.

But he didn't have trouble getting to sleep. It should have been a sleepless night, the way his state of mind was, but he was just too goddamn tired to be an insomniac, after his afternoon of running through the woods with a sketch pad up his butt, and an evening that included riding/hiding on the floor in the back seat of Nolan's car and sneaking in back of that cottage and wrestling a shotgun away from that damn amazon, and shit... too tired to do anything now but sleep...

And dream.

He dreamed he was on a heist. Not the Port City bank heist, past or future. Nolan wasn't in the dream, either. And it wasn't a bank at all. It was a museum. He was trying to steal a diamond. It was like some movie he'd seen once. He was in a museum, trying to steal a diamond, and he had people helping him, people he'd gone to junior high and high school with, people he hadn't seen in years. One was a kid with greasy black hair and a bad complexion, who'd shared a joint with Jon in the john at a high school dance and Jon had gotten nauseous and afraid of being caught. And now here this kid was, years later, helping him steal a diamond from a museum. And there was a girl, that sluttish girl Jon had taken behind the bleachers at a football game in junior high and gotten his hands in her pants, and a week later, when some skin started peeling off his fingers, he'd wondered if he could have caught some awful disease off her or something, she was here too, with the greasy-haired kid, and they were stealing this diamond. And then cops. Cops came rushing in. The museum was dark at first, just a big pool of black with a circle of light on the display case where the diamond was. But now cops were rushing in, and it was a huge white room, full of light. There weren't any walls in sight, just blinding white light and cops in blue with guns, rushing at them. He knew some of the cops: one of them was the art professor he'd argued with at the U of I before dropping out—the professor who had told him comics were junk and to whom Jon had said, *Who are you to say, with your crappy fucking abstract pretentious art.* And another cop was a guy his mother had lived with for a while, an ex-army sergeant who'd hated Jon and got drunk one night and tried to beat Jon up and Jon had cleaned his clock—he was there, a cop, shooting. And old Sam Comfort, the man Jon had killed. He was a cop too. Shooting. And the sluttish girl and the greasy-haired kid, they turned into other people all of a sudden, they turned into Shelly and Grossman, the two friends of Jon's who'd been in on the Port City heist, who had died in the bloodbath aftermath of that heist, and who were dying again, as the cops, the prof and the ex-army sergeant and Sam Comfort were shooting .357 Magnums at them while Jon tried to run but his legs were rubber and there were no exits anywhere, just smooth white walls, and Shelly and Grossman were dying again, spurting blood in slow motion like the movies, Grossman screaming Jon's name, Shelly flopping onto the display case with her blonde hair streaked with blood…

"Kid."

"Uh, what, uh ... ?"

"Hey. It's okay."

"Nolan?"

"You were dreaming."

"Dreaming?"

"Yeah, dreaming, and making a hell of racket at it. Like to wake the dead."

He sat up. It was daylight. His mouth tasted foul. "What the hell time is it, anyway?"

"About ten o'clock."

"That's impossible, I just fell asleep here a…"

"Yeah, you just fell asleep. Nine hours ago."

"Shit," he said, rubbing his eyes, "I don't feel like I slept at all. I'm tired as hell."

"You wore yourself out dreaming and making noise."

"Goddamn nightmare."

"I didn't figure it was a wet dream."

"Not the one I remember, anyway. I was dreaming all night, I think, but I only remember that last one I was having."

"Yeah, well, I never dream."

"Everybody dreams, Nolan. You just don't remember yours."

"I don't dream. You want breakfast? I'm fixing myself some."

"What, eggs?"

"Yeah."

"I'll have a couple, over easy."

"You'll have them scrambled."

"Scrambled's fine. And bacon."

"Sausage."

"Sausage. Just what I wanted anyway."

They sat in the kitchen and ate.

"Kid."

"Yeah, Nolan?"

"This is really bothering you, isn't it."

"What?"

"The idea of hitting that bank again."

"No. I'm okay. Really."

"I don't like it any better than you do."

"Yeah, sure, I know that, Nolan. Forget it. It'll be a snap."

"Look. I think maybe we better call a man in."

"The way Rigley has it mapped out, just the two of us is plenty."

"No, I think an extra man would be better."

"What for?"

"Somebody ought to stay behind and keep an eye on the bitch. I don't trust her."

That was bullshit, and bullshitting wasn't Nolan's style. Jon didn't know how to react. "Me, you mean? I should stay behind and watch her?"

"Yeah. We'll call in somebody else to help on the job itself."

"You don't…don't think I'm up to it, Nolan?"

"You're up to it. You done fine every time so far, and we been through some rough weather the last couple years."

"What, then?"

"Nothing. I just don't trust the bitch, is all."

"It'll mean less money."

"We'll pay the guy a flat rate. Anyway, I don't care about the money so much. The money is fine, sure. A person can always use more money. But I'm more interested in protecting our interests here in Iowa City, seeing to it the job goes smooth so we can come back home and go on with our happy retirement."

"Whatever you think is best, Nolan." Jon was ambivalent toward Nolan's suggestion—relieved to be off the line of fire, hurt that Nolan might not feel him up to the pressure.

"So who you got in mind, Nolan?"

"Well, I pretty well kept a lid on my retirement. Lots of people in the trade think I'm dead, think the Chicago boys got me. And it's nice being dead, if you know what I mean. Nobody to come 'round tempting me with prospective heists—except for an occasional bank president, of course—and nobody to come 'round looking for a handout. Besides, I don't have that many friends left. Most of the people I worked with in recent years are punks, present company excepted, who I'd just as soon stay dead to. Most of the good people are dead. It's that kind of business. So anyway, I'll call in Breen, since he knows I'm here already and is a good enough man and can probably use the money."

Jon nodded. "Breen would be fine. Unnecessary, but fine."

After breakfast they went out in the front room, and Nolan stopped a moment and looked at the Christmas tree on top of the television set but said nothing. Then he sat on the couch and used the phone on the coffee table.

Jon wasn't paying attention to the conversation at first, but it didn't take long for it to become apparent something was wrong on Breen's end. When Nolan hung up, Jon asked him what the deal was.

"Breen's dead," Nolan said. "Somebody blew him apart with a shotgun last night."

6

Nolan had never been to Breen's house before, but he didn't have trouble finding it. Indianapolis was an easy town to get around in, for all its size, a town whose streets crisscrossed like a big checkerboard. And anyway, he'd been to Breen's bar a number of times, and the house was in the same neighborhood.

He parked the Buick in the driveway, behind a battered green Mustang he recognized as Breen's. There were no other cars in the drive, though there was room; none were parked along the curb in front, either. Which surprised Nolan. Breen's funeral had been in the morning, and this was fairly early afternoon, so he'd expected a bunch of cars belonging to friends and relatives who'd be making sympathetic shoulders available to the bereaved widow. But then, it would be like Mary Breen to tell everybody to get the hell out. She always was a private person, who at a time like this wouldn't be about to put up with the hypocritical condolences of, say, her brother Fred, who had never really gotten along with Breen anyway and probably at this very moment was entertaining visions of taking over the bar for himself, or her mother, a cafe waitress at fifty-four, who felt her daughter had married below her station.

The street was quietly middle class, not unlike the one in Iowa City that the antique shop was on. The house was a brown brick two story, a shade smaller than most in the neighborhood, but then, only Breen and Mary had lived there, so it had been plenty big, Nolan supposed. There was snow on the ground in spots, and the sky was overcast, and he guessed it had been a good enough day for a funeral: a somber day but not a depressing one, really.

There were two sets of four cement steps up a tiny terraced lawn, and another set of four steps to the door, which had a plastic Christmas wreath on it. Nolan knocked.

She answered right away.

She looked good. She also looked sad, of course, but he didn't think she'd been crying, or anyway not much.

"Nolan," she said with soft surprise. "I didn't expect you to come."

He had said he would try to, on the phone yesterday, but evidently she had figured he was just saying that.

"It's cold out here," Nolan said. "I didn't come all the way from Iowa City to stand on a stoop and freeze my ass off in Indianapolis. Invite me in already."

She grinned and shook her head. "You're something. Come on in."

He did, got out of the coat, and Mary took it and went somewhere with it. He was in a small vestibule. The stairs to the second floor were in front of him, a study to the left, the living room to the right. It was Breen's house, all right; a gambler's house. Nothing but the essentials: some serviceable, warehouse sale furniture; bare hardwood floors, not even a throw rug; a console TV that looked ten years old at least and was probably black-and-white; bare walls. That was the living room, if you called that living. The study was pretty good size but was also mostly empty, just a desk with chair and a single filing cabinet. It was actually a bigger room than the living room, and Nolan thought he knew why: Breen must have done the bar's bookkeeping out there so that he could call it his office, which would rack out to a sizable tax deduction.

Mary came back from wherever she put the coat and said, "Let's go out in the kitchen."

She fixed him coffee out there. It was a bright room, white

trimmed in red, with all the necessary appliances and some unnecessary ones too. Mary was not the type of woman who would let Breen extend his gambler's stinginess where she was concerned, not without a hell of a fight, anyway.

She was a good-looking woman. She looked like what Marilyn Monroe would have if the movie studios hadn't fixed her nose and bleached her brown hair and told her not to smile with her gums showing. She was Marilyn Monroe at forty-one, a house-wife Marilyn, getting a little pudgy.

She sat at the kitchen table with Nolan. She was wearing a dark green turtleneck sweater and dark green pants. Her eyes were light green, not red at all.

Nolan looked into the light green eyes and said, "Isn't it time you cried?"

She looked into her coffee. She smiled. Her gums showed. It was a nice smile anyway. Fuck the movie studios.

"I'll get around to it," she said.

"Tell me about the funeral," he said.

"Do you really want to hear about the funeral?"

"No."

"Why did you come?"

"I thought you might want somebody to talk to who knew the score."

She laughed. Not much of a laugh, but a laugh. "Nobody at the funeral knew what he was, you know. Except for Fred, who knows vaguely. But nobody else. It was mostly his regular customers from the bar. None of you people. Not that I expected any of you. I know it's a thing you people have, not poking into each other's private lives. It's a sensible thing, seeing each other only when you're working. It's a cold business. Necessarily cold, I guess."

"I came."

"You did come, Nolan. Damn it if you didn't. But you didn't come to the funeral. Why?"

"I don't go to funerals."

"Neither did he. Till today. Tell me something, Nolan. Do you ever think of me?"

He sipped his coffee. "Every winter. When it first snows. I think of you then."

She smiled again, faintly this time, and said, "The back seat of a car. Like a couple teenagers."

"Well, we were younger."

"Yeah, but not that young. Snowing to beat hell, and we're out in the country, God knows where, in the damn car parked with the engine going and the heater going, and I'm in that fuzzy coat and you're dropping your drawers. Christ. Maybe we were that young at that."

"You got some more coffee for me?"

"Sure."

She poured coffee, sat back down, and said, "I don't blame you for skipping the funeral, Nolan. I don't blame any of those other people who worked with him, either, for not coming. I mean, how the hell are they supposed to know he's even dead, right? You people don't keep in such close touch, I mean. If you hadn't happened to call, even you wouldn't be here, right? So his bar customers are there. Nobody else, except for his first fucking wife, the bitch who sucked him dry for alimony and child fucking support—she has the balls to be there. With his two kids, who that bitch has already ruined. Jesus."

"Hey. Take it easy. Who the hell did you think would be there?"

She slammed her fist on the table, and the coffee cups jumped. "Where were those fucking bookies? They're there when it's time for Breen to pay up. They're there with a hot tip for the sucker. They're there extending credit at shylock rates.

But when Breen's planted in the fucking ground, oh, no. They aren't there then, even though they fucking put him there!"

So that was why she hadn't cried: she was too angry. She was too pissed off about her husband's death to mourn him yet.

"Is that what happened?" Nolan asked. "Do you think it was somebody he owed money to who killed him?"

"Well, the cops say it's robbery. He probably had, what, fifty bucks in the till, and the cops say his head was blown off for that. Can you buy that, Nolan? Fifty bucks got his head blown off? Not me, no, I don't buy it, I don't buy it at all."

"Mary, people been killed for a lot less."

"I know, but people like my husband? A guy like him, a professional thief who always dealt in the thousands of dollars, getting wasted by some cheap punk for a few bucks? I mean, it's too cute, too...you know, ironic, too...it's bullshit, is what it is."

"Maybe. Wasn't there someone with him when he was killed?"

Her jaws clenched. She rubbed her cheek, as if she was sanding wood. "Yeah there was someone with him. There was a bitch with him. But what about this morning, at his funeral, Nolan, where were they then, his bitches, his young goddamn cunts? Where were they? They'd lay him, yeah, but not to rest. Shit..."

"Mary."

"Will you tell me something? Will you tell me something, Nolan? Am I some ugly old woman? Am I a wife you cheat around on?"

"Settle down. You're not old, and you're not ugly. But Breen did cheat around on you. You know that. I know it. I also know seven years ago, before you and Breen were married, when you and Breen were just going together, when you were just a barmaid of his yourself, that one time you and I went for a ride when it was snowing out."

Her mouth quivered a little, and she said, "Yeah, well, I

knew then. I knew that he loved me, in his way, that he wanted
to marry me, but that he was getting in other girls' pants every
chance he could get and I had to strike back somehow. Not that
I told him, or wanted him to find out, Christ no. But after that I
could live with it better somehow, live with his running around
on me. And what the hell, I liked you, Nolan. But you were
hopeless. You were a goddamn wall no woman could hope to
get behind and make something at all permanent with you.
Maybe now there'd be a chance, but then? No way. And so we
went for a ride in the country that time, and it was snowing,
and it was something special to me. I never cheated on him
again, did you know that? And when he cheated on me, when I
knew he was or thought he was, I'd remember that time, hold it
close to me like some precious goddamn stone, and...shit I'm
going sentimental on you, Nolan. Can a tough guy like you take
it? Jesus."

"Mary. Do you think it could be the barmaid?"

"Do I what?"

"The killing. Could it have been somebody after the barmaid. A jealous husband. Jealous boyfriend."

"Maybe. Maybe. I hadn't thought of that but maybe. Or one
of his other bitches, jealous of the new one. Are you saying you
agree with me, Nolan? That you think something's strange
about his death?"

"Yeah, I agree. Or sort of agree. Coincidences bother me. I
know they're possible. I been caught up in them before. But
I never believe in a coincidence till I look down its throat and
up its ass. *Then* I believe in it. Not until. So. Could you give
me a list of the people Breen was involved with, with his
gambling?"

"Easily. We didn't have any secrets where his gambling was
concerned. Hell, I helped him handicap. I never caught the

bug, but I was around the gambling scene too long not to be at least semi-involved."

"Good. What about his girls?"

"In that case he was a little secretive. Mostly the girls working in the bar, I guess. They would stay on as help till they tired of him, or vice versa, but usually vice. He was not the best lay in the world, you know."

Nolan smiled. "That's not the way he used to see it."

"Well, he wasn't really in a position to know, if you know what I mean. Hey, Nolan, what are you going to do? Play detective? Find the killer? I didn't know you read Mickey Spillane."

"You want me to level with you, don't you, Mary?"

"Of course I want you to level. Did you come clear from Iowa to bullshit me?"

He spread his hands. "Personally, I don't give a damn who killed your husband. Matter of fact, he ran out on me one time. Justifiably, but I just mention it by way of showing I don't owe him any posthumous favors. However. In this business, when somebody you worked with is killed, in circumstances that are even remotely suspicious, it doesn't pay to ignore the matter. Your husband worked with me on a lot of jobs. Something out of one of those past jobs might have crawled out of the woodwork and killed him. Which affects me, obviously. So I can't feel comfortable till I find out who was responsible for your husband's killing. Plus, I admit I got some feelings for you. I figure maybe you would feel better if you knew what was really behind his death."

"Do you ever think about it, Nolan?"

"About what?"

"Dying. Death."

"No."

"Why not?"

"When you think about it, you get paranoid. Then you're slow when you should be fast. Punchy when you should be alert."

"Is that what happened to my husband?"

"Maybe. Sometimes you can't avoid it. Sometimes you get hit by a truck even when you look both ways. That's the way it is. Life. A gamble."

She smiled, rather bitterly, he thought. "Well, my man never was much of a gambler."

"I'm sorry about Breen. I really am. He was a good man."

"Even if he did run out on you once?"

"Even then. I'd have done the same in his place."

"That's what it's about, isn't it? Survival."

"You could put it that way."

"Nolan. Tell me."

"What?"

"Why did he do it?"

"Heisting, you mean? You know why. To support the gambling."

"Not the heisting. The women. Why…why wasn't I enough?"

"Why did he gamble? Why can some men quit smoking and others puff away, even after they've seen the X-rays? I don't know. I don't understand people. I can barely tolerate them, let alone understand them."

She sighed. "More coffee?"

"No."

"I loved him, Nolan."

"Yeah. Well, you must have. To put up with his gambling and his women both. And not every woman can stand being married to somebody in my business."

"I thought you were out of the business."

"You're never out."

"I guess not. Listen, there's…there's something I want to talk to you about."

"Okay."

"I want to talk upstairs. There's something of his I want to give you."

"Okay."

She led him upstairs.

Into a darkened room.

The shade was drawn, but some of the light from outside was seeping in; overcast day that it was, the seepage didn't amount to much. But he could see the bed, the double bed, and he could see Mary, disrobing.

She stood and held her arms out to him.

She stood naked and said, without saying it, *Am I so ugly? Wouldn't I be enough for most men?*

She would have been plenty, for just about anybody. Sure, her thighs were a little fleshy, and there was a plumpness around her tummy, and she had an appendix scar. And her breasts didn't look quite as firm as they once had. But big breasts never do, and they were nice and big, pink nipples against ivory flesh. He walked over and put a hand on one of the breasts, felt the nipple go erect. He put his other hand between her legs. He put his mouth over hers.

There was carpet up here. Downstairs, bare floors. But up here, on Mary's insistence, no doubt, was plush carpeting, tufted fuzzy white carpeting, and they did it on the floor, and when she came, she cried finally, and they crawled up on the bed and rested.

Outside, it snowed.

7

She walked him out to the car. They had rested for several hours, and then she fixed him something to eat—nothing fancy, just a sandwich—and it was early evening all of a sudden, and he was saying he had to get back. Something doing in Iowa City tomorrow, he said, and she got his coat for him.

She'd been surprised how good he looked. She hadn't seen him for several years, since the last time he'd stopped at the bar to talk to her husband about some job. She'd heard from her husband of Nolan's troubles, that he'd been shot damn near to death several times the last couple of years, and she'd expected that to show on him. No. Some gray hair at the temples, but Nolan stayed the same. Handsome, in that narrow-eyed, mustached, slightly evil way of his. His body remained lithe, muscular; scarred but beautiful. He'd felt so beautiful in her....

"You'll be back then?" she said, leaning against the car, by the window. He was behind the wheel; the engine was going. The snow had let up.

"I'm going to poke into your husband's killing a little, yes," he said. "But it's not the movies. No revenge, Mary. I don't believe in that. I'm doing it to protect my own ass."

She smiled. "And my ass has nothing to do with it."

"Well. Maybe just a little. Take care of that ass, okay, till I get back and can take over?"

"Sure. And watch your own while you're at it. Next week, did you say?"

"Probably. I'll probably give you a call."

And he was gone.

She went back into the house, into the kitchen, and drank the last of the pot of coffee she'd made.

She wondered if Nolan would really find her husband's murderer, and if he did and took care of whoever it was, would she feel any better about it?

Now she felt very little. Anger, there was anger. Some sorrow. But more than anything there was confusion. Her husband had been blown to hell by a shotgun. In the company of one of his barmaid bitches. Naked, the two of them.

She wondered if there was any significance to the bitch's body being in the back room, while her husband had been in the outer bar. To open the cash register, she supposed; it would have been locked after closing, and he would have had to reopen it for the thieves. She wondered if she should have mentioned any of that to Nolan. And that one other strange thing: the bottle her husband had had in his hand. He'd evidently grabbed for that bottle off the shelf just as he'd died, or as he'd realized he was about to die. What kind of crazy reflex action was that? To grab a bottle of Southern Comfort off the shelf?

8

Friday, while Nolan drove into Indianapolis to see Breen's wife, Jon drove to Cedar Rapids in his Chevy II to buy a pair of hunting jackets. He didn't know why he was buying the jackets, exactly, just that Nolan had told him to.

He was also supposed to stop at a place called Blosser's Costume Shop and Theatrical Supply to pick up a package for Nolan.

And of course it was like Nolan to give Jon a task or two to carry out without explaining the task or two's significance. Jon was used to it. But he still questioned Nolan about such seemingly absurd assignments, getting nothing in particular back from the man for his trouble.

"Hunting jackets?" he'd asked. "What for?"

"One for you," Nolan said. "One for me."

"Okay, one for me, one for you, sure. But for what purpose, Nolan? I mean, hunting jackets? And why go all the hell the way to Cedar Rapids to get them?"

"Just do it. Yours is not to reason why."

"I don't believe you sometimes, Nolan."

"And buy one of them at one store, and the other at another."

"Why?"

"Because I want the jackets bought at separate stores."

"Jesus. Okay. All right. I'll do it. But what's the costume thing about? Will you tell me that?"

"Ask for the manager. Blosser, the manager–owner. He's a friend of mine. He knows about me. You can talk freely. He has a package for me. Oh, he may have you try something on. In fact, maybe you ought to insist on trying one of them on."

"One of what on?"

"One of what's in the package."

"What *is* in the package?"

"Let me do the thinking."

"Wait a minute, let me see if I got this straight. *I* buy the hunting jackets and pick up the packages, *you* do the thinking. Is that the way it goes?"

"That's it exactly."

"Well, I just hadn't had it explained to me properly before. Once it's explained to me, then I understand. But would you tell me one thing?"

"What?"

"Why do I still bother asking you questions?"

"Kid, that's one question I wish I could answer for you."

And so he had driven to Cedar Rapids, had bought one hunting jacket (a green plaid) in his own size, at a sporting goods store downtown, and another (a red plaid) in Nolan's size, at a sporting goods store in an outlying shopping center, paying cash in both instances, as Nolan had also instructed.

He realized the hunting jackets had something to do with the robbery. That was self-evident. What galled him was that he couldn't figure out what, and he knew Nolan wouldn't tell him till the last moment.

The costume shop was on the way out of town, in a rather run-down section that was commercial along the main strip that ran through the area, but back behind which was a neighborhood that could be called lower middle class if you were in a charitable mood. It was a one-story, faded brick building sandwiched between a bait shop and a used book store that was, damn it, closed. Jon peeked in the windows of the old book store and saw thousands of used paperbacks in ceiling-high bookcases, and what looked like some old comic books and for sure some Big Little Books in locked showcases similar to those in Planner's shop. He ran across such shops every now and then, and they were invariably closed. He sighed, shrugged, and went on into the costume shop.

The interior was spare but not seedy, with a counter and a waiting room area, similar to a laundry. An attractive if hard-looking woman of thirty or so was behind the counter, with coal-black hair, a beauty mark to the left of a red-painted mouth, and braless bouncing breasts under a satinlike yellow blouse. She looked as though she was preparing to audition for a local production of *Carmen*.

"Hi, honey," she said casually, and Jon looked around to make sure she was talking to him.

She was, so he said hi himself, and did his best to return her suggestive smile. Maybe the woman did look sort of cheap and whorish, but she was also sexy-looking, in a second-rate men's magazine way.

"What can I do you for?" she said. She was chewing gum. Not blatantly, though—not a cow chewing cud—but playing with it in her mouth, playing with it with her tongue.

"Uh, I'd like to see Mr. Blosser."

"Not here."

"Oh. You expect him soon?"

"Nope. Won't be back today."

"Well, uh, I was supposed to pick up a package for a friend of his. A Mr. Nolan?"

"Oh, sure. Your name must be Jon."

"Yeah, that's right."

"I'm Connie. The boss's daughter, in case you was wondering."

"Oh. Yeah, well, I'm pleased to meet you, Connie."

"I'm sure. How is Nolan these days?"

"Fine. Fine. I didn't know you knew Nolan."

She grinned. She really was a good-looking woman, cheap or hard or not. "I know him. You ask him if I know him or not." She laughed and her breasts jiggled.

Jon swallowed. "Okay, I'll tell him you said hello."

She reached under the counter and flopped two large white string-tied suit-type boxes up in front of her. "Here. This one is yours. It's a small. You better try it on." She motioned him behind the counter, and he followed her through a narrow hallway to some dressing cubicles in the rear of the store. She handed him the box marked "Small" and left, pulling the cubicle's curtain shut on him.

He opened the box.

There was something red in it.

Red and partly white. Trimmed in white.

The red was a cheap but plush-looking velvetlike material; the white was fluffy stuff—cotton, he guessed. There were also red gloves of the same material, trimmed in the same white fluff.

It looked like a Santa Claus costume.

He took it out of the box.

It *was* a Santa Claus costume.

He put it back in the box and went back out front, quickly, leaving the costume behind.

"That was quick," the woman said. "Fit okay, does it?"

"No. I mean, I don't know…I didn't try it on."

"How come?"

"Well, there has to be some mistake."

"Oh?"

"Yes, it's a…would you come with me a minute?"

He took her back to the dressing cubicle and showed her.

"Yeah," she said. "A Santa Claus costume. So?"

"This is what is *supposed* to be in this box?"

"Sure."

"What's in the other box?"

"Another Santa Claus costume. That's a total of two. One small, the other's large."

"And that's what Nolan wanted me to pick up for him?"

"Shit, yes. Didn't he tell you?"

"I'm afraid he doesn't tell me much of anything."

"Yeah, that's Nolan, all right Listen…you need any help getting into that, honey, just give Connie a call, you hear?" She winked and chewed her gum seductively and left him there with a hard on and a Santa Claus suit.

It fit fine. He looked at himself in the cubicle's shadowy mirror, and damned if the world's shortest, most clean-shaven Santa Claus wasn't staring him in the face. He asked Connie about the lack of a beard, after getting back into his street clothes.

"Oh, the beards are in the other box, with the large suit," she said. "The caps are in there too."

"Caps?"

"Caps. You better try yours on." She opened the other suit box and got out a floppy red cap with white ball on the end. "The beards are adjustable, around the ears, but the caps could be trouble…there, see? You got too much hair for a small. I'll go back and get a medium."

She did, and insisted that Jon try that one on too, and he did, and she tweaked his cheek and said, "Gonna bring me anything for Christmas, Santa?"

He grinned, trying to keep the red from crawling up his neck. "We'll see," he said.

"I wonder what the heck Nolan wants with Santa Claus suits," she said, shaking her head. "Somehow he don't seem the Santa type. Unless he's gonna empty stockings instead of fill 'em."

Jon nodded his agreement and watched her put the cap back in the box and tie some string around it.

"Don't forget to tell Nolan I said hi," she said. "And maybe I'll see you when you bring the suits back after Christmas, huh, honey?"

It took him almost an hour to get back to Iowa City. The overcast day had everybody cautious and using their headlights, and he got caught behind some old ladies going forty-five. So did a lot of other cars; the traffic was heavy, and passing was difficult—no, impossible—and he followed the old girls to the Interstate, after which he was back to Iowa City in short order. He parked the Chevy II behind the antique shop and went in the side door, which was unlocked.

That wasn't right; surely he'd locked the door when he left. Yes, he *remembered* locking it.

Too early for Nolan to be back from Indianapolis. Wasn't it?

He shut the door. Softly. Silently.

Listened.

Heard nothing.

Quietly he moved behind the long, saloon-style counter behind which his uncle had sat day after day puffing his foul-smelling cigars. He set his packages on the counter. In a drawer, below the cash register, was one of his uncle's .32 automatics. Jon got it out. Softly. Silently.

He explored the downstairs. Nothing in the main room, with its antiques and showcases and counter and all. Nothing in his own room, except half the comic books in the world.

But what about the other back room? The one that had included Planner's workshop area, as well as where many very valuable antiques were crated away for future sale, and where the big old safe was....

The safe's door was open.

Otherwise, the room was as empty as the rest of the downstairs.

But someone had been in here, opened the safe and, of course, found nothing in it. There hadn't been anything of value kept in the safe since Nolan and Jon's money had been stolen from it months before, the time Planner himself was killed defending that money. Killed in this very room. Jon had, in fact, scrubbed his uncle's blood from the floorboards of this room....

He felt a chill, and for a moment was very scared, and then it passed. Whoever it was had been here and gone. He walked out into the other room and put the gun back in its drawer.

He was halfway up the stairs, his arms full of the packages with the hunting jackets and Santa Claus suits, when he heard the noise.

Talking.

Someone was talking up there on the second floor. And it sure as hell wasn't Nolan.

And the talking was coming this way. Toward the stairs. They were going to come down the stairs!

He couldn't be soft or silent about it now. He had no choice but to clomp down the stairs and head toward that drawer with the gun in it, but they were closer to him than he had imagined, on his damn heels before he was even out of the stairwell. And the packages were flying and he was face down on the floor, one of the men on his back and the other standing in front of him. Jon couldn't see anything of whoever it was except shoes. Black shoes and white socks. The shoes were old-fashioned, lacing halfway up the ankle. Clodhoppers, shoes a farmer might work in; the socks were loose and dirty.

That's all Jon saw of the two men, as he later deduced the number of his assailants to be: the shoes and socks of one of them, and nothing of the other, because the other was on Jon's back, holding him down.

Nobody said a word; certainly not Jon, whose lips and teeth were mashed into the wooden floor.

And then one of the black shoes flew at Jon's temple, and Jon went away for a while.

He woke up on the couch upstairs.

There was coldness on the side of his head.

"Oh…fuck…" he heard himself saying. He sat up.

The coldness, an ice pack, slid off the side of his head.

Nolan handed Jon a cold beer. Jon grabbed at it, guzzling at the can like the Frankenstein monster taking his first drink.

"Aren't you even going to ask me how my day in Indianapolis went?" Nolan said.

Jon just looked at Nolan. Then laughed. "Hey. You got me an ice pack. For my kicked-in head. You're some kind of nurse, Nolan. Didn't know you had it in you."

"If you want a doctor, I can get Ainsworth over here. That's a hell of a lump you got. Concussion maybe."

"No doctor. I'm okay."

"You mean you think you're okay."

"I don't think anything. I think all my think got kicked all over the floor downstairs."

"Somebody was into the safe."

"Yeah, I know."

"I think they were looking around upstairs, too."

"Nothing valuable taken?"

"Nothing valuable to take. Except some of the antiques, which they didn't touch. And a couple thousand in the wall safe, which they didn't find. So you got here before they left, and they kicked you in the head? See who it was?"

"I know exactly who kicked me in the head. We can have the cops put out an APB, my description is so exact."

"Who, then?"

"A black farmer shoe with a dirty white sock and a foot in it."

"Terrific. Another beer?"

"No. This one'll do me. I'll just lay back down here. What the hell time is it?"

"Oh, around eleven I guess."

"When did you get back?"

"Not long ago. I hauled you upstairs and got you an ice pack and you woke up."

"I'm not sure about that last part. Jesus. Now I know what they mean when they say ain't that a kick in the head."

"Listen. Breen was murdered."

"Yeah, I know. That's why you went to Indianapolis."

"I mean Breen was murdered, and then you were kicked in the head and our place was gone through. Nothing's gone, but it was gone through, all right."

"You think there's a connection? Between Breen and today?"

"I don't know. What do you think?"

"Me? You're asking me, Nolan? For an opinion? Christ, I'm not ready for that. You better just kick me in the head. That I can handle. That I've had experience with."

"This heist. Maybe we should scratch it."

"Yeah, sure, only we aren't calling the shots. Rigley is. Or Rigley's girlfriend is."

"Maybe Rigley and company'll change their mind when I explain something funny's going on."

"*Is* something funny going on?"

"I don't know."

"So what are you going to do?"

"I think I better try to talk Rigley out of it. The back of my neck is starting to tingle on this thing, and I think we better get out, if we can."

"And if we can't?"

"Go ahead with it, I guess. I think we better forget about bringing in another man. That okay with you? Breen would've been perfect, but he's dead, and with what I got in mind for the heist, there really isn't the time to recruit anybody else. Or the need either. We can get by, just the two of us. Don't you think?"

Jon rubbed the lump over his temple. "Maybe I will have another beer." He got up and went after the beer, then came back and said, "*Santa Claus* suits?"

9

She got back to the cottage at five-thirty. She was bushed. Fridays at the beauty shop were always busy, but today had really been a bitch; she'd worked all morning without a break and straight through lunch and fought hunger pangs throughout the long and hectic afternoon. And now, home finally, she was so tired, she wasn't even hungry anymore. Take a bath and get rid of the smell of hair spray and customer (and her own) perspiration and just flop in bed. She unlocked the door, stepped inside, and George was there.

Sitting at the table with glass of booze and accompanying bottle in front of him.

Terrific.

"Hi, baby," he said. A little sheepishly. A little drunkenly. Sitting in his shirtsleeves, his coat and vest and tie tossed on the couch the way a kid tosses off his jacket after coming in from school. George was a handsome man, in that slick executive way of his, but when he got the least bit drunk, his eyes started drooping, and he began getting a rather stupid look to him. She hated him when he looked stupid like that, which was, unfortunately, a way he'd been looking more and more lately.

She closed the door, slipped out of her cloth coat, hung it on the rack. She was still wearing her white beautician's uniform. After nine solid hours of doing her best to make other women's hair look presentable, her own was matted from sweat and generally a mess. She didn't smell good. Or feel good. And George was here.

Terrific.

She walked over to the table and stood over him as he sat fiddling with his half-drained glass of bourbon. She looked down scoldingly and said, "I thought we agreed not to get together. Until tomorrow, when we meet with your robber friends."

"Well, baby, I…"

"I thought we agreed you'd spend some time with your wife."

"Baby, you know I can't stand being around her when she's drinking. You don't know what it's like being around somebody who's drinking all the time."

"Don't I?"

He looked down into his bourbon, then hung his head. "I… guess I deserve that, don't I? I have been drinking a lot myself lately, haven't I?"

She thought, *why don't you shape the hell up, you self-pitying son of a bitch?*

She said, "It's okay, honey. You've been under terrible pressure. I understand."

And as she said that, she patted his head, twisting some of his slightly curly dark brown hair in her fingers playfully, affectionately.

He touched her arm. "Sit down, baby. I'll get you a glass, if you'll just sit down and have a drink with me, and we can talk."

She didn't sit down. Instead she plucked the bottle off the table and put it behind the bar on a shelf with all the rest of the bottles and came back and kissed his neck, nuzzlingly, and then took him by the elbow, saying, "Now, come on. Be a good boy and shoo. Go home. I want you out of here."

And he looked at her with tearful eyes, still slightly stupid eyes, but compelling, too, in their way. "Julie. I need you. Let me be with you."

Goddammit, he was almost *whimpering*. Seeing him act like

this made her want to slap him silly, in a way, and in another, want to hold him.

She did neither.

She went and got his coat, vest, tie, and topcoat and put them on the table in front of him and said, "Go home, George. I'll see you tomorrow."

"I need you tonight."

"Tonight I need for myself, George. I need some time to rest, some time to get myself together for what's coming up. Please."

"Julie...surely you understand how I feel, how I'm...I'm shaking inside, Julie. How I'm scared out of my mind thinking about...about what we're going to do and...how I need you. To hold me."

Shaking inside, he said. And outside, too. He was a wreck, a nervous damn wreck, and she had to do something.

She sighed.

"All right," she said. "Go on into the bedroom."

"Baby...it's not that....We can just talk....I just need to be with you right now, I don't...."

"Go on in the bedroom and wait for me. I have to take a bath. I have to relax a minute. I'll be in in a while. Now scoot."

She drew a hot bath. So hot her skin turned lobster red as soon as she dipped into it. She liked a hot bath. She liked to burn away the dirt, burn away the thoughts. Just settle into a steaming-hot tub. Hot bubble bath—millions of bubbles; she liked the smell of the soap, the bubble bath smell, the slickness and smell of the perfumy bath oil. It was a peaceful experience, the way sleep was supposed to be.

She luxuriated in the tub, sliding her hands over her oil-sleek body, the globes of her full breasts bobbing above the surface of the bubbly water, nipples erect. And she stroked them, soaped them, her breasts, nipples, pussy, thick soapy-silky triangle of hair, sliding hands over firm, muscular oil-slippery thighs. She leaned back and enjoyed herself.

She honestly got more pleasure, more sexual, sensual pleasure out of a good hot bath than the act of sex. Fucking had never been much more to her than a way of pleasing and controlling a man. And she'd gotten even less pleasure from her experimental couple of flings with other women.

But this *was* pleasurable. Soaking and soaping herself. Indulging that fine body of hers. And it *was* a fine body; she knew it was. She didn't really blame men (or anyone) for wanting her.

Conceit? No, not really—at least she didn't think so. She had an ability, she felt, to assess herself in a detached, realistic manner. She saw her body, for example, as a tool, even a weapon. Nice tits, nice ass, but like all tools (weapons), meaningless without the brains to put them to use.

Take her high school years, for instance. She'd blossomed rather late, well into her teens, and consequently had that muted contempt for her admirers that all former wallflowers feel. She used her good looks to be popular, to date the cutest guys from the wealthiest families, to be a cheerleader and homecoming queen candidate and generally overcome a somewhat poverty-stricken background. (Her father had worked for the railroad and earned a decent wage, but not decent enough to properly feed, house and clothe six kids, a wife, and mother-in-law. As the oldest, Julie had all but raised her two sisters and three brothers, as her mother had had enough to do just to cook, keep house, and look after her own ailing mother.) The highlight of her climb out of the lower-middle-class muck came shortly after graduation, when she won the home-town beauty pageant that could have led to Atlantic

City and beyond, if it hadn't come out about her and the one judge.

They let her keep her scholarship money (held in trust for use in educational pursuits only), and she eventually used it, to go to beauty school, but first she got knocked up by one of the few non-wealthy guys she'd ever gone out with, a sandy-haired football hero who she figured would probably go on to make a fortune playing pro ball someday. She began to think she'd figured wrong when he flunked out of school the first year, trying to study, play football, hold a job, and be a husband/father simultaneously. He got drafted. Sent to Vietnam.

She divorced him while he was still overseas. It was a gamble, because he still might come back and be a pro ball player and get rich, but then again he might also get his leg blown off over there, so she'd dumped him, left her kid (a girl) with her mother, who had the time to look after a kid now that most of her own were grown and gone and with Grandma dead and gone, and enrolled in beauty school.

That was where she had latched onto Claire. Claire was a rich man's daughter and hadn't been smart enough to make it in a real college or university and had ended up at the beauty school in Iowa City. Nobody at the school liked Claire because she was stupid and spoiled and a closet lez. But Julie liked Claire. Or anyway Julie liked Claire's money, and soon they were roommates; she even gave Claire a free feel now and then. And when they got their diplomas and passed their state boards (the fix *had* to be in for Claire to pass, the stupid bitch) Claire's rich old man had given her the beauty shop in West Liberty (which was a small town midway between Iowa City and Port City) as a graduation present. And Claire had invited Julie along.

And Julie had gone, figuring it would do till something better came her way.

Like a George Rigley.

She'd known it would only be a matter of time before a George Rigley entered her life. A wealthy, my-wife-doesn't-understand-me type who wanted some nice, young, sympathetic snatch. And she was eager to fill that role...until the time came when she could take over the wife's role, and step into the plush, easy life hard cash could bring.

But it had taken her longer than she'd thought: her small-town location limited her prospects, and the two men who preceded Rigley as her benefactors (an attorney from Iowa City and a doctor in West Liberty) had not proven the long-term meal ticket she'd hoped.

Then, finally, three years ago last summer, she met him. She'd been on the prowl, sitting at the bar in that new place in Iowa City, the Pier, wearing as little as possible—baby-blue flimsy halter and short shorts. George Rigley, sitting a stool or two away, asked her if he could buy her a drink; she'd said he could, and it went on from there. He was at first as smooth and superficial as he no doubt was when he was sitting behind his desk at his bank. But later, after they'd taken a table off in a properly dark and secluded corner, he'd blurted out, "Listen, I'm nervous as hell. I mean, I'm new at this, and you'll have to forgive me if it shows."

She'd given him a coy smile and said, "New at what? Forgive you if what shows?"

"What I'm saying is it's been a long time since I've tried to make conversation with a pretty girl."

"Don't you mean it's been a long time since you tried to make a pretty girl, period?"

And he'd grinned. An honest and shy sort of grin that had been her first peek behind his executive mask. Her first peek at the insecure child lurking behind his plastic, practiced pose. And a child needs a mother. And a mother can manipulate a child into doing most anything, if a mother is ballsy enough....

So she had listened patiently to the story of Rigley and his wife, and of his recently dissolved affair with a friend's wife (though she guessed there'd been several of those over the years) and of the unhappiness he was experiencing as he sank deeper into middle age, most of it because of a marriage that had been a good one once but now was stagnant, without even the usual children to hold it together. It wasn't a new story, or even a very interesting one, but she wasn't looking for a new and interesting story—just one with money in it.

And money had come her way during her three years plus as George's secret little girlfriend. He provided the cottage (which was, of course, more a house than cottage), and though on paper she paid him rent it was more the other way around. She continued to work with Claire at the beauty shop in nearby West Liberty but only to keep appearances up, only until she could step completely into the wife's role and trade in the cottage, nice as it was, for a hundred-and-fifty-thousand-dollar home the likes of the one the present Mrs. Rigley was using to do her drinking in.

Julie would have it all, *if* George held up through the strain of the days ahead.

Well, she thought, rinsing her hair under the cold rush of water from the tub's faucet, *I'll just have to see to it he does.*

Because she was not about to spend her life a damn kitchen slave like her mother, or as a lousy shitty working girl slaving her ass off over fat old ladies and their thin gray hair, no goddamn way in hell. She'd have a life worth the living or not at all. A life with money in it. A life that would be one long, luxurious bath.

She stepped out of the tub, then stroked her body dry with a crushed-cotton towel and wrapped another towel, turbanlike, around her damp hair.

The bedroom was dark.

She slipped under the sheets.

She touched the side of his face and said, "Do it to me, honey."

And let him.

And afterward she cradled him in her arms, patted him, soothed him. He was trembling. The sex hadn't taken care of his trembling.

"It'll be over soon, honey," she said. "We'll be together and there'll be no sneaking around and no worries. Just you and me and all that money."

"Is that…that all I am to you? Money?"

There was no bitterness in his voice; more like fear.

"How can you even think that?"

"Would you…nothing."

"Would I what?"

"Would you want me, even if I didn't have the money?"

"You *don't* have the money, George."

"I'm going to. We're going to. But would you? Love me? Without money?"

Would you love me without my tits, you silly ass?

"Of course I would," she said.

George Rigley's home was two miles outside the city limits, on a bluff overlooking the winding blacktop road that a mile later connected with the highway to Iowa City. Rigley's was one of a handful of homes on the three-mile stretch of blacktop, which was a thickly wooded, exclusive area whose beauty was matched only by its real estate value. A gravel drive ascended the bluff to the sprawling wood and brick ranch-style home, with its private tennis court, swimming pool, and separate garage the size of an average house.

Space and privacy. All the space and privacy you could ever want. The nearest neighbor a quarter mile away. Enough rooms to sleep a small army: three bedrooms, a den, a game room, huge living room, kitchen, dining room, TV room, assorted bathrooms. What sane person could want more?

And that was the problem. What sane person could want *this* much? Certainly not Rigley himself: he preferred the cozy, rustic (rustic compared to this, anyway) cottage. No. It took somebody crazy to want a secluded expanse of loneliness like this. Somebody crazy like Cora. His wife.

What else would you call it besides crazy, to want all this space when there was just the two of them. They had no children—hadn't been able to—and the bloated house was designed mainly to satisfy Cora's need for entertaining (but partially, he'd have to admit, to fulfill his own need for status), and if it wasn't a cocktail or dinner party going on, it was relatives. Relatives meant a lot to Cora. He'd hate to think how many weeks out of an average year they shared with visiting relatives of hers. Rut then, he was in no position to complain, considering what Cora's family had meant to his career.

Of course it'd been different, these last few years, with her parents dead (killed in a light plane crash, with Cora's only sister). And with her beloved cousins and uncles and aunts snubbing Cora since her parents had snubbed them in their will. The flow of relatives had subsided somewhat.

But the flow of liquor hadn't.

That flow had increased.

His wife had always been a drinker, but never a drunk really, not till the death of her parents and sister. She was not a loud drunk. Never a conspicuous drunk at all. Socially, her drunkenness didn't cause any harm; at a party she just flirted with the men and flattered the women, in a playful sort of way that just seemed to make everyone like her all the more—everyone except Rigley himself, of course. And her drunkenness at home just meant she was asleep most of the time. On the couch in the TV room, usually. Sometimes in bed. He had to have a woman in to do the cleaning for her, but they could afford it. And he'd often come home and find no dinner ready, but they (or he, if she was especially tight) would go out to eat; they could afford that too. And if friends called, Cora would come around, shake off her drowsy drunkenness, and be her charming, if a bit blurry, self. She wasn't an annoying drunk to be around at all.

Unless you were married to her.

He was standing in his living room, Manhattan in hand, listening to his vice-president at the bank, Shep Jackson, rattle on about local politics. Jackson was a younger version of Rigley: smooth, dark-haired, tan, handsome, and handsomely dressed in a gray tailored suit. Rigley hated him for it. Jackson was the man the board had hand-picked to replace Rigley, and both men knew it and pretended they didn't.

And Rigley wasn't really listening to Jackson, either. He was pretending about that too.

What he really was doing was watching his wife circulate through the small crowd (eight couples who all had season tickets for the Broadway Series at the University of Iowa's Hancher Hall in Iowa City; it was their ritual to gather at the Rigleys' for a cocktail party in the late afternoon and then drive, two couples to a car, to the play and have a late dinner out afterwards), and he marveled at how good she looked, for as much as she drank.

Her face, especially, looked good, but maybe that was just the face lift. The smooth skin enhanced the beauty of her large brown eyes and full mouth and small, sculpted nose. She looked something like Julie, as a matter of fact, except in Cora's case the hair was honey yellow and thickly, if stylishly sprayed. Or he should say it the other way around, shouldn't he—Julie looked like Cora. He'd picked Julie out because she looked like Cora had when he'd fallen in love with his wife-to-be over twenty-five years before.

They had gone to high school together. A small, small town in northeastern Iowa. Her father was in the banking business. He was principal stockholder of three banks in various small farming communities in that area, and was a landowner, too; he had three or four farms (he was always selling and buying farms like somebody adding hotels in Monopoly) and lived in the biggest house in the county. Rigley's father was a schoolteacher. So was his mother. Between the two of them, his parents brought in a good living, and Rigley never wanted for anything; he was definitely a boy born on the "right side of the tracks," a cliché that rang true in their small town. Anyone born on the *wrong* side would be considered a social climber if he tried to date Cora Pierce.

But that's just what he'd been, secretly—a social climber. He knew no family fortune awaited him. He knew the limited benefits of schoolteaching were not for him. And he knew Cora Pierce had had her eye on him since the seventh grade, and so in high school he'd latched onto her and never let go.

They went to the same college (Iowa State) and were married after their sophomore year. Cora dropped out at that point and got a job in a bank there in Ames, with her father's help. Rigley resisted any of his father-in-law's efforts to pay his way through school, however, knowing that (a) his own parents had saved enough to put him, their only child, through four years of college, and (b) he would want to call on old man Pierce for bigger and better things in the future, after establishing himself in the family eyes as "his own man" and a pillar of integrity.

And old man Pierce had come through. He'd paid Rigley's way through graduate school in the East (Wharton) and got him his first job, as installment loan officer in a big downtown Chicago bank. And then a vice-presidency at Port City, and finally the presidency, when he'd barely turned forty. Everything had turned out as he'd hoped.

Except maybe the marriage itself.

In the beginning, he had loved Cora. Or anyway he had convinced himself he did. It wasn't hard to convince yourself you loved the wealthiest and most beautiful girl in the county. And Cora was all of that. She'd been homecoming queen and Representative Senior Girl back in high school. (He'd been Representative Senior Boy and most likely to succeed.) She was also valedictorian, whereas he was barely in the top ten percent of their small class. And to this day she was, in her way, the smarter of the two of them. The brains of the family, and the boss too, never letting him forget where the money came from. Never letting him forget that Daddy had pulled the strings to put George where he was today.

Still, Cora wasn't the loud-mouth, obnoxious woman most bossy women are. She was dominant, yes, but quietly so. Not a bitch, not even a nag; just a decision-maker. And he didn't mind being dominated at home; after all, he was dominant at work, wasn't he? He didn't mind being second in Cora's heart to Daddy (no, make that third—her mother came second), and he didn't mind the way she planned his life for him: parties, vacations and all. He was too busy at work, making the bank go, to have to worry about anything else in his life; let Cora handle it.

Cora was easy to put up with, as long as the sex was good. And it was good for a long time.

Until they found out, definitely, that they could have no children.

Until she had her "female trouble" and the possibility of having a child (which had always been slim, because of his near-sterility, but still had been at least a possibility) became nonexistent. After her "female trouble" (Cora never could bring herself to say "hysterectomy," just as she always said "poop" instead of "shit," never having outgrown her goddamned sheltered small-town conservative Iowa upbringing; thank God *his* parents had been liberals), sex gradually became something that happened only on special occasions, and then wasn't particularly special for either one of them. Separate bedrooms came about for the stated reason that Rigley liked to read at night and Cora wanted the lights off, and the marriage became as sexually dead as their reproductive possibilities.

Even so, the marriage still seemed okay, superficially. Cora seemed comfortable with him. She liked the security of their life, and now that her parents were gone, she seemed desperately inclined to cling to what remained, which was Rigley and their stagnant marriage together. She surely must have realized just how desperate a dead end it was they were both heading down, and that probably helped explain the drunkenness.

But the possibility of divorce had never occurred to Cora, as far as Rigley knew. And he was glad. Divorce meant disaster to Rigley. He doggedly continued being nice to her. Complimenting the way she looked. Ignoring her drinking, as much as possible. Kissing her cheek goodbye in the morning and hello coming home at night. And never, ever arguing with her.

Maybe theirs had always been a superficial marriage. Maybe even before these sexually barren last five years, they had had an empty marriage. Who could tell? Rigley figured he certainly wasn't the only guy who, with a wife who shared his marital apathy, went through the paces of marriage, putting in time like somebody who keeps at a job he hates in hopes of eventual retirement. He wasn't the only guy who enjoyed brief, relatively meaningless affairs with the wives of friends. Surely a marriage like this one wasn't anything out of the ordinary these days.

In fact, the only thing he imagined was out of the ordinary where their marriage was concerned was the lack of arguments.

They almost never argued.

Because Rigley felt he couldn't risk arguing with Cora.

Divorce was something he did not want to even *think* about.

Not with a wife who was worth well over half a million dollars.

Rigley excused himself with Jackson and walked over to the serving table and nibbled at some chip and dip and made himself a Manhattan.

"You should be playing bartender, honey," Cora said, coming up behind him.

He turned and looked at her. Her large brown eyes were droopy with drink, but they were still attractive. Her lips were perfectly formed, lovely. The facial skin was smooth, and her low-cut hostess gown gave hints of a body that was still something to see as she lolled around that pool outside all through the summer. Too bad she screwed like a faggot shakes hands.

"I'm sorry, baby," he said, touching her cheek with Manhattan in hand. "Jackson cornered me and started babbling about the local elections."

She turned and smiled at Jackson, who was well out of earshot, and said, "He's such a poop. Why the board hired him is beyond me. If Daddy were alive…"

"If Daddy were alive, he'd be proud to see how pretty his baby looks this evening."

"Thank you, dear. Hey…what's the matter? Are you still acting sick? You're not going to get out of going to this play just by playing sick."

"I'm not playing sick. I've felt lousy all day—you know that." He had told her earlier that he thought he was getting the flu.

"Now listen to me," she said, smiling much as she had to Jackson and speaking in the same only-you-can-hear-me-George undertone. "You are not going to spoil tonight for me. You are going to the damn play and that is that."

And she smiled some more and patted his cheek and threaded her way through the room, talking momentarily with everyone.

At seven people began filing into the den, where they'd left their coats. There was an eight o'clock curtain at Hancher and a forty-five-minute drive, not counting the madhouse of the Hancher parking lot, and the cocktail party was over.

And finally only the Harrisons, the couple the Rigleys were riding with, their oldest and dearest friends in Port City, remained.

Ray Harrison was a lanky bald man who looked like Ray Milland and sounded like Ernest Borgnine; his wife was a vapid, pretty little aging blonde lady who didn't speak often enough to sound like anyone. Rigley gathered the Harrisons and Cora by the door, everyone having climbed in their coats but him, and said, "I'm going to have to cop out on you tonight, I'm afraid."

Cora said, "George," the way a razor slices across a wrist.

"Baby," he said, "I'm just not up to it. And I'm not going to let myself ruin the night for you by going along and complaining constantly. You go on with the Harrisons. I insist. You'll have a fine time without me. I'll just be a party-pooper tonight, and you know it."

"Well," Cora said, softening slightly, but still with an edge, "I'm not *about* to stay home. I'm not going to miss this play. It's supposed to be one of Neil Simon's best."

Ray Harrison said, "I just don't understand why we should have to drive all the way to Iowa City for a little culture." He obviously would have liked to stay home himself, but was being bullied into it by his publicly silent but apparently privately vocal wife. He made a plea to Rigley. "This restaurant we're going to try ought to be worth the trip, George. The Pier. Ever tried it before?"

"Uh, no," Rigley stuttered. "Never have."

"Say," Ray said, "you do look sorta sick at that."

And then Cora finally gave in, as there wasn't that much time to waste arguing, with an eight o'clock curtain to make. And, too, she'd buckled under the element of surprise, as she always did when they argued. They fought so seldom that when Rigley *did* stand up for his rights, he almost invariably won just on the sheer novelty of it. He'd been counting on that.

He was alone in the house now, with the aftermath of the cocktail party: the discarded glasses and napkins and half-eaten sandwiches and the general disgusting mess well-to-do people leave behind them after such affairs. He wandered aimlessly through the rambling house, sipping his Manhattan, thinking about his wife, his life, his situation. He ended up in Cora's bedroom. Their bedroom, before he started sleeping across the hall. Blue wallpaper with open-beam wooden ceiling. Cream-color satiny spread on the queen-size bed. Nightstand by the bed. Their wedding picture was on it. He went to the nightstand and opened its single drawer. Amidst the jewelry boxes was the gun. The .32.

He didn't touch it He just looked at it, pearl-handled silver .32 automatic there with the jewelry in the drawer, and thought about his wife.

And suddenly he *was* sick.

Sick with fear and self-hatred and God knows what other wretched emotions, and the emotional sickness brought with it physical sickness as well, and he rushed to his wife's private bath and heaved into the stool, heaved out all the cocktail-party booze and chip-dip and crust-trimmed sandwiches, heaved till there was nothing left to heave and then heaved some more.

When he was finished, he went across the hall and got out of the suit and took a shower and got into some comfortable, casual clothes. It was Saturday night. He had a meeting to go to.

Bank business, of a sort.

11

Nolan rode. Jon drove. It was Jon's car, the Chevy II. Thursday night they'd taken the Buick, Nolan's car or, rather, the car Nolan had been left to use by his business partner, Wagner, who was currently enjoying the Florida warmth while Nolan and Jon froze their asses off in Iowa. Nolan felt it unwise to have one certain car seen several times in the area of the Rigley cottage within these few days, even though the cottage was pretty well isolated and there wasn't really much chance of anybody seeing either car. When he explained all that to Jon, the boy said, rather skeptically, "Well, I guess it doesn't hurt being careful."

And Nolan said, "It's not that being careful doesn't hurt, kid. It's that being sloppy can kill you." Jon hadn't seemed so skeptical after that.

"Is that the turn up there?" Jon asked.

"Is it?" Nolan said.

It was, but he wasn't about to tell Jon. He'd spent all day with Jon, driving the gravel and blacktop back roads of the area, familiarizing himself and the kid as well with all the possible routes between the cottage and Iowa City and the cottage and Port City. And he had it all down, himself. But Jon would be doing the driving, so it was Jon who had to know where he was.

"It's the turn," Jon said. "I recognize that farmhouse over there."

"Well, then. Turn."

Jon turned. He said, "I'm only having trouble because it's dark. It won't be dark the day of the heist, you know."

"If you can find your way around these roads in the dark," Nolan said, "daytime won't be any problem."

Jon thought about that, seemed to get the point, yawned and said, "Anyway, they keep this blacktop nice and clear. Not like some of those others we were on today."

It hadn't snowed since Thursday, but it had stayed cold, and the ground was snow-covered.

"Some rich bastard farmer owns most of this," Nolan said, gesturing to the side of the road that was cornfield; trees lining the river were on the other side. "County keeps the roads around here clear for him and a couple others like him."

"Yeah, well the Iowa City streets are still packed with ice and snow."

"Maybe if you bought a couple hundred acres of farmland in downtown Iowa City, that'd change. Hey, slow down."

Jon did, but said, "What for? Rigley's cottage isn't for a half-mile or so. And anyway, I'm only doing forty-five in the first place."

"Stop a second. I want to get a look at that cottage there. Rigley's closest neighbor. See anything?"

It was a small, paint-peeling clapboard cottage, crowded by trees, close to the river, on stilts—nothing lavish, nothing at all like Rigley's. No cars were around. No lights on inside.

"Nothing," Jon said.

"Rigley says the people who own it don't use it much. Trying to sell it. He says they don't use it at all this time of year."

"Looks like he's right."

"Looks like."

They drove on.

The little bluff Rigley's cottage sat on was the only clear spot along a good three-quarters of a mile of thickly clustered trees —long, tall, skinny things growing close to and even in the water like weeds gotten out of hand. Ugly damn trees. Especially in their wintertime gray and skeletal state, though Nolan figured they probably weren't any beauties even in the green of summer. The close-to-a-mile stretch of land Rigley's cottage was in the midst of was damn near swamplike, and accounted for the isolation of the cottage in an area otherwise heavily populated with cottages and cabins. The bluff, an island clearing in the sea of tree-littered and marshy land, provided safety from flooding, which made possible the houselike luxury of the cottage. Isolated as it was, it seemed acceptable to Nolan as a meeting place; even suitable, perhaps, as a place to gather after the heist to split up the take.

A gravel drive cut through overhanging trees to the cottage, which wasn't visible from the blacktop, and as he pulled onto the drive, Jon said, "You think these hunting jackets are really necessary?"

They were wearing the hunting jackets Jon had gone to Cedar Rapids to pick up.

"Yes," Nolan said. He had already explained that as hunters they wouldn't raise undue suspicion in the wooded river area.

"So who's going to see us with all these trees and everything?"

"People in cottages across the river, maybe. Anybody else who happens to be driving along that blacktop back there."

"But it's dark out. It's the darkest damn night I ever saw, Nolan. The river's right over there, and I can't even see it."

Nolan was getting a little bored with Jon's questions and complaints and said, very deliberately, "It won't be dark the day of the heist, you know."

"Oh. Yeah. So we'll be wearing the jackets then, too."

"Yes."

"I didn't know that."

"Now you do."

"That doesn't explain the Santa Claus suits."

"No, it doesn't."

Jon sighed and said nothing. He pulled the Chevy II in beside Rigley's Eldorado and parked it. They got out. The cottage was dark.

"Listen, kid, I want you to do something for me in there."

"Sure. What?"

"Don't be a smart-ass."

"Don't be a smart-ass? What do you mean?"

"I mean don't be a smart-ass in there. Be nice to them."

"*Nice* to them! After all that shithead and his bitch did to us, you say be…"

"Nice to them. I'm going to be nice to them. I'm not going to like it, but I'm going to do it. So are you."

"Why?"

"Think about it. If you can't figure it out, I'll tell you later. Now let's go in."

He went up four wooden steps and knocked.

The girl, Julie, answered right away. She looked good. Pink fuzzy sweater caressing her abundant boobs, pink plaid slacks hugging the accommodatingly wide hips. She was one fine piece of ass, Nolan had to admit, even if she was kind of heavily made-up, especially around those huge brown eyes of hers, as if they needed any emphasizing.

She didn't ask them in; she just held open the door and stepped aside. A cold, businesslike bitch, her attitude contrasting with the almost blatant sexual come-on of her makeup and wardrobe. All of which, she seemed to be making clear, was exclusively for Rigley. Nobody else was to get any ideas.

Which normally would have been fine with Nolan. He didn't believe in getting sexually involved with somebody else's woman, at least not on a heist, he didn't. But he didn't like the bitch's icy attitude. He wanted to break through that. He wanted to build both her and Rigley's confidence in him.

And that wouldn't be any simple task. As he stepped inside, Nolan could feel waves of uneasiness shimmering in the room like heat over asphalt. He got out of his hunting jacket. Jon was doing the same. The girl made no move to hang them up. No hostess-playing for her. Nolan handed his coat to Jon to hang up.

The fire was going. The animated outdoor-scene beer sign was also going. There were no other lights on in the room. All the shutters were shut, as if the overcast, black night out there was high noon or something. Rigley was behind the bar, mixing up a pitcher of Manhattans. He was casually attired, for Rigley anyway: yellow and gray pattern turtleneck sweater and (Nolan saw as Rigley came around the bar to greet them) gray slacks that looked as if they'd never been worn before—in fact, they hardly looked as if they were being worn now.

Pitcher of Manhattans in one hand, Rigley extended the other, giving Nolan a smile as white and perfect as it was insincere. Rigley's executive cool was even phonier tonight than usual: the tiny ice cubes inside the pitcher were clinking around, keeping time with the banker's trembling hand, and yes, the tic at the edge of his right eye was going again. Nolan had the urge to take the man by the shoulders and shake him and say, "Settle down, damn it!" But it passed.

Rigley lifted the pitcher as if making a toast, and said, "Can I pour you one, Logan?"

"That'd be fine," Nolan said. "Jon'll have one too."

"I don't think I want…" Jon began, then caught Nolan's look and said, "That'd be…nice. Thank you."

The girl was looking at Jon's T-shirt, which had some under-

ground comic character on it (a guy with a pointed head and
five o'clock shadow in a clown suit, labeled "Zippy the Pinhead")
and she seemed almost on the verge of a smile. And suddenly
she was speaking. Saying to Jon, "I like it. Your shirt. It's really
cute."

"Yeah, well, thanks," Jon said.

"I wouldn't mind having one myself."

"Well," Jon said, looking at her breasts with a cheerfully
awestruck expression, "I'm not sure if they come in your size."

And the girl smiled. Even showed some teeth. She was
proud of those big boobs of hers, and Jon had said just the
thing to win her over. A more obvious off-color sort of remark
might have soured her, especially had it come from Nolan; but
Jon's boyish, almost naive manner put it over perfectly. Nolan
nodded his approval at the lad, who then proceeded to nearly
undo the good he'd just done by blurting, "Couldn't somebody
turn on some lights? I'm going fuckin' blind in here."

Rigley looked puzzled for half a second, then embarrassed,
as evidently he was the one who'd thought dimming the lights
would provide the appropriate atmosphere for crime and con-
spiracy.

Nolan looked at Jon and Jon looked away, and Nolan said to
the girl, "Maybe if you could turn on that light behind the bar,
there," and the girl did.

The awkward moment passed, and Rigley went back to what
he was doing, which was distributing Manhattans to each of the
four seats at the table.

Nolan told everybody to have a seat.

He waited for everybody to get settled and was about to
begin when Rigley got up quickly, saying, "Oh, I almost forgot,"
and brought back a manila folder, identical to the one he'd
shown Nolan Thursday night. The one chock-full of blackmail

material. And there was almost another awkward moment, as Nolan felt himself getting mad all over again.

This time, thankfully, the folder contained material of a more agreeable nature: the photographs of the interior and exterior of the bank that Nolan had requested of Rigley, as well as a listing of employees and a timetable of their work activities, plus a floor plan prepared for the occasion by Rigley, which indicated where each person worked and where each alarm button was located, and a wealth of other pertinent information. Rigley had done a good job, and Nolan told him so.

"And I have to admit," Nolan continued, "your basic plan for the robbery is a good one. Some refinements would be necessary, of course, and I'd need to go over these photographs and plans and such you brought me first, but otherwise I see no reason why your scenario wouldn't be followed very close. Almost to the letter."

All of that was true—it was a good plan—but the point of all the compliments was to put Rigley at ease. And it did. Rigley's tic, his overall nervousness, seemed to have disappeared. He was smiling, sipping his Manhattan.

"However," Nolan said, "I'm afraid all of your work maybe was for nothing."

"What do you mean?" Rigley said, brows knitted.

The girl was silent, but her expression asked the same question.

"Now, I don't want anyone to misunderstand my motives," Nolan said, "but I think it would be best all around, for all concerned, if we called it off."

"What?" Rigley said. Almost shouted. "Call it off? Call off the robbery? Why, for Christ's sake?"

Nolan shrugged. "The only way I can explain it is by saying I've reached fifty years of age and never spent a day of it in jail, even though for the better part of the last twenty I was robbing banks like yours, Rigley. And do you know how I managed that? Managed to stay alive and not behind bars? By being careful. By having certain rules. By demanding certain conditions... *ideal* conditions...for any heist I was part of."

"What in hell could be more ideal than this?" Rigley demanded. "What in hell more could you ask in a bank robbery than the help of the president of the bank? I mean, I've heard of inside tracks, but this is ridiculous."

"You're right," Nolan said, nodding. "But I'm not talking about the job itself."

The girl, who had the painfully skeptical expression of a doctor listening to a patient explain how he caught clap off a toilet seat, leaned forward and said, "Then just what *are* you talking about?"

And Nolan told them about the break-in Friday. He told them of two men (neither of whom Jon got a look at) who came in, rummaged through the entire antique shop, including opening a safe, apparently but not necessarily looking for money, and were interrupted by Jon, whom they promptly conked on the head before getting the hell out.

Before Rigley and the girl could begin expressing their obvious disbelief, Jon leaned forward, parted his hair, and showed them the bump. Then he sat back and said, "And that ain't special effects, boys and girls. I'm too much of a coward to let myself be conked on the head just to back up a phony story."

"All right," the girl said, taking over (as Rigley seemed too confused at the moment to actually talk), "suppose it's true. What exactly does any of that have to do with anything? Two people break into your shop and try to rob you. So what?"

"First let me tell you about something else," Nolan said. "Something that happened to a friend of mine. A guy who set up a robbery Jon and I were on not long ago, and who worked with me on a lot of things over the years. Real pro. Thursday night he was murdered. For the contents of a cash register, amounting to maybe fifty bucks. He ran a bar, you see, and after closing, somebody came in and blew my friend's head all over the wall."

Nolan paused for dramatic effect, but the girl was not impressed. She said, "I still see no relationship to what we're doing here."

"Maybe there isn't any relationship. I'd go so far as to say there probably isn't. But I don't like coincidences. A thief, a friend of mine, is killed for nickels and dimes. Call it cute, or ironic, or anything you want. Only the next day, two guys break into where I live, and Jon interrupts them before much damage is done, but anyway they're apparently trying to rob us. Again, ironic, cute, robber gets robbed. Big laugh. But suppose something's going on. Some old friends or enemies of mine are in the neighborhood with something in mind."

"Isn't that rather far-fetched?" Rigley said, finally regaining his faculty of speech.

"Isn't it rather far-fetched that within twenty-four hours, a few hundred miles apart, two professional thieves who did a lot of work together are the object of two robberies themselves? One of them killed, head blown off by a shotgun like the one you were waving around the other night, sweetheart."

"Wait one fucking minute, now," the girl said. "You aren't accusing us of having anything to do with…"

"I didn't say that. Thursday night, we were together, so the shotgun thing is a true coincidence. I grant you that. But from my point of view, why not? Why couldn't you have hired some people to dig up further blackmail material on Jon and me? That would at least explain the break-in at our place."

"I think it's all a bunch of bullshit," the girl said.

"We had *nothing* to do with it," Rigley said. "Any of it."

"Okay. So who did?"

"You're making mountains out of molehills," Rigley said. "You're desperate to find an excuse to get out of this situation, and so are trying to scare us out, confuse and frighten us into letting you off the hook."

Nolan smiled. A friendly smile. It hurt him to do it; he hated Rigley and the bitch, and being civil to them would give him an ulcer if he had to keep it up much longer. But he smiled. He said, "I'm not trying to get off any hook. It's a good heist. It really is. It'll be easy, fast money for Jon and me. We've done it before, so why not again? But don't you see the reason the two of us are around to rob your bank a second time is that we're careful, we only work under certain conditions, and that it's foolish to pull a heist when there's possibly something going on that could fuck up that heist? Don't you see that?"

"No."

"No."

"Okay. I tell you what. We'll postpone it. Postpone it a month. Give me time to see what's going on, if anything. That's all I ask."

"No!" Rigley shouted. He slammed his hands on the table, and everybody's drinks spilled, the pitcher, everything. "No! No, goddammit, you're just *playing* with us, I'm *not* postponing *anything*, no!"

And Rigley got up and ran behind the bar and got a bottle off the shelf and shakily poured himself a shot and downed it and then another and…

The girl, quietly, leaned over and touched Nolan's hand. Her touch was warm, and for the first time she extended a trace of sexual promise to Nolan. She said, "Please. Understand.

This is hard for George. He's been a respectable member of the establishment for too many years for this to be easy for him. Do you have any idea how long it took him to gather the courage to approach you at that restaurant? He's been watching you for months. Planning this, building himself up, gearing himself to be capable of an act that he is barely capable of even now. Asking him to postpone the robbery would be suicidal not only for George, but for all the rest of us, for *any* of us involved with the robbery. George is an intelligent and capable man in his chosen profession, just as you are in yours. But where crime is concerned, George is an amateur. We *have* to go ahead with the robbery, and as soon as possible."

Nolan nodded. "All right. Go settle him down and bring him back here. And get a cloth and clean off this damn table, will you?"

She went to Rigley, and Jon said, "That's why you wanted me to be nice, isn't it?"

"Yeah," Nolan said. "It's bad enough working with amateurs, let alone *uptight* amateurs. If we're going through with this, our asses depend on George Rigley coming through for us. So we got to make sure he's comfortable, got to have him confident in us, got to put him at ease."

"What about the girl? She's an amateur too, isn't she?"

"Her? An amateur? Kid, she could give us lessons."

And then the girl was wiping off the table and Rigley was settling down in the chair, nervous but better.

"There's one thing I have to ask," Nolan said, "before we go any further."

"What is it?" the girl said.

"It's you," he told her. Then he turned to Rigley and said, "Your robbery plan includes her. Her role is pretty minor, but she does have a role, or she wouldn't be here right now, would she? Yet you aren't asking for a share for her. Three-way split, you say. Why? I'd say she deserves half a share at least."

"I...I can't believe what you're saying," Rigley said. "You're complaining because you'll be getting *more* money than you have coming to you? Nobody in his right mind would make a complaint like that."

"Nobody in his right mind would give money away," Nolan said. "Especially not a bank president. Why are you?"

The girl said, "May I explain? It was meant primarily as an incentive for you. To assure you this arrangement is based not on coercion, but more a business proposition. And George only needs a relatively small amount...around one hundred thousand...to cover what he, uh..."

"Embezzled," Rigley said. "That's the word—embezzled. You see, I'm losing my job, Logan. My embezzlement would never have been found out, as long as I was president. But I'm losing my job, and as soon as a new man gets in my chair, my handiwork will be discovered. All I want is to replace what I took—and lost, on the stock market—so that I can leave the bank with my reputation intact. In fact, I already have another position lined up: president of a bank in a little town in New Mexico, and Julie will be going with me."

The girl cut in, saying, "But that's getting into areas that are of no concern to you, isn't it? Does it answer your question?"

"It does," Nolan said. He thought for a moment, then said, "All right. Why don't you people have something to drink, whip up a fresh pitcher of booze if you like, Rigley, and everybody relax. Go sit in front of the fire or something I want to study this folder of material for a while and see how it fits in with what I have in mind."

The girl touched Nolan's hand again. "How soon do you think we can get on with it? The robbery, I mean."

"Soon. Sooner than any of you, including Jon, will like, I think."

Rigley said, "How...how soon do you mean?"

"Well, tonight's Saturday. You need some time to absorb what I'll be laying out for you tonight, and also some time to hopefully get some rest, though I doubt any of you'll get much of that. Anyway, Monday morning."

"Which Monday morning?" the girl asked, eyes wide.

"Monday morning," Nolan said. "You know. The day after tomorrow."

12

The first night Terry Comfort spent in prison, he was raped in the shower by a short, muscular, middle-aged bald black man. Terry was serving a year for statutory rape. He didn't think of what the black man did to him as poetic justice. He didn't know anything about poetic justice. He just knew he'd been screwed, a couple of ways.

He was tall, slender, in his mid-twenties; his thin sliver of a face was pale from months inside, and his sandy-color hair was shorter than he would have liked, but it wasn't bad, considering he'd only been out a few days. They let them wear their hair longer inside these days, and things were generally better in there than Terry had heard from his father and others who'd been in. The food wasn't bad; the work wasn't hard; there was TV, and magazines and movies. But they still raped you. Especially if you were skinny and fair-haired and had the light blue eyes and delicate nose and full mouth Terry did.

He got to where he could stand it. Not like it, but stand it. He let the bald black man lay claim to him, since it worked out better for Terry that way; the black man wasn't queer, really, just naturally horny, and once a week was enough for him, and once a week Terry could stand. At first, he swore the day would come when he'd kill the black man; but then he came to almost like the poor old bastard, who'd been in since he was Terry's age, having been sent up for killing his wife. Who could blame the guy for that? He'd found his wife in bed with some other nigger and killed them both. Anyone would have done the same. Unwritten law. Of course, it had probably gone hard for

him in court because of his using a hatchet to do it and dis-
posing of the pieces down various sewer gutters, but then, a
guy will do things that are a little weird when he gets taken
advantage of.

Most of the people inside were like the black man and didn't
deserve to be there. Terry himself, for instance, sent up for
statutory rape—what a bullshit charge! Who ever heard of a
girl thirteen having tits thirty-eight? She'd said yes, hadn't she?
And went down on him and got to teaching him things he'd
never even thought were possible, and then started talking that
marry-me shit. Jesus Christ, one wham-bam and the little whore's
talking marriage, and he's telling her to fuck herself for a change,
and the next day the law comes around.

After all the robberies he and the old man and brother Billy
had pulled together the last six or seven years, with people getting hurt and sometimes killed along the way, for Terry to get
nailed for humping a thirteen-year-old, well, it was pathetic. It
was more than pathetic; it was downright embarrassing.

But he was out now, sentence shortened for good behavior,
and he was ready to get back to the business of making some
money with his old man. And to find some more nice young
pussy ripe for plucking. He had lost time to make up for on
both accounts.

Right now was Saturday night, or more like Sunday morning,
going on two o'clock Sunday morning. He was in an attic, a
dusty, cramped attic you couldn't stand up in without banging
your head against rafters. He was on his stomach. Next to him
was his father. Old Sam Comfort.

Sam Comfort was in his early sixties, had short, unruly white
hair, needed a shave, and had the same deceptively kindly features as his son, only Sam's eyes were a smoke-gray color and
his face was wider, with jowls. He was shorter than his son—a

little. And he was as skinny as his son, though until fairly recently he'd sported a considerable pot belly. He'd been sick.

They had been in the cramped attic for a long time. Since early evening, when it first got dark. The attic was above the second-floor living quarters over an antique shop in Iowa City. The antique shop was where the two men who had killed Sam Comfort's other son, Billy, were living. They would not be living for long, however, if old Sam had his way.

That was probably what the old man was thinking about right now, Terry thought, studying those smoky eyes that were hard to read anyway but impossible to scrutinize in the darkness of the attic, which was relieved only by the slight filtering-in of street light through the attic's single, small window. Still, Terry could pretty well tell what his father was thinking, most of the time. But he could never be sure. You could live with Sam Comfort your whole life and never be able to predict for sure what he'd do next.

And the old man—who had always seemed eccentric, even to his sons—hadn't been right in the head since Billy died.

Anyway, that was what Lou had told Terry, Lou being the Detroit pawnbroker who fenced what the Comforts stole. Lou was short, chubby, mustached, and dependable. He was the one who had found Terry's father the night Billy was killed. The one who had come out to the house to talk to Sam Comfort and found the aftermath of a shooting and robbery and managed to get the old man to a doctor and into a private hospital that specialized in publicity-shy (and police-shy) patients.

It seemed a guy named Nolan, and some other, younger guy that hung around with him, had come to the Comfort homestead one night a few months back and tossed in some smoke grenades and made it look like the place was on fire; old Sam had of course grabbed his strongbox of cash—the old man didn't believe in banks, having spent a good portion of his life span emptying them—and Nolan and this lad were waiting outside to relieve him of it. But brother Billy had caught on to the ruse, and was in the process of doing something about it when Nolan shot Billy in the chest, killing him, and Nolan's young pal shot old Sam in the chest too, but higher, not fatally.

Only it had looked fatal to Nolan and the kid, who exchanged some bits of conversation (the kid calling Nolan by name) that the semiconscious Sam had heard before blacking out completely. Since the pair had worn stocking masks, this slip was a big help; but the really big help was Lou, who had come along a few minutes later and found the badly bleeding Sam Comfort, left to die by Nolan and company. And he would have died, too. Like Billy had died.

Terry and Billy hadn't been close. Terry was three years older, and Billy had always been the favored one, the baby, and so had stayed kind of immature. Like, for instance, Billy was into dope—not just smoking it, either, but cocaine, speed, everything but heroin, Terry guessed. Billy had also been into that crazy music that went with the dope thing, instead of country-western, like any sensible person. The brothers hadn't gotten along, and Terry was sorry his brother was dead, but he was probably more upset about that two hundred thousand bucks of theirs Nolan had stolen.

Terry's father didn't share that sentiment. Old Sam, for once in his life, didn't seem to give a damn about money. He wanted to kill Nolan, and kill Nolan's kid friend, too. And that was all. That was all the still-weakened Sam Comfort had on his mind. Kill Nolan. Kill the kid. Kill them both.

Terry had spent the better part of the few days he'd been out trying to reason with his old man. "Killing 'em's fine, Pop, I'm for that," he'd say. "But what about the damn money? We gonna just kill the peckerheads and let some damn bank keep our two hundred thousand? That's all the money we got in the world, Pop."

And old Sam would say, in a voice soft with traces of the Georgia accent he'd never lost, though he'd only lived there as a child, "We still got the farm. We can work it, if we have to. Don't give a shit about the goddamn money. We're going to kill those bastards. Kill 'em slow."

Work the farm? That was crazy. They'd never worked the farm in their lives. Besides, they just owned a few acres and leased them out to a neighboring farmer and used the farmhouse as their home base. The old man just wasn't thinking.

Anyway, he wasn't thinking where the money was concerned. Where revenge was concerned, he was doing fine. Old Sam had figured out that a guy named Breen, who owned a bar in Indianapolis, had been in on the job with Nolan. Not on the scene, probably, but fingered the job. Breen had been working with Billy and the old man, filling in for Terry while he was inside. Sam and Billy double-crossed Breen at a rented farmhouse just outside of Iowa City, Breen's usefulness having run its course since Terry was getting out soon; but Breen had gotten away, shot-up, but alive. Evidently Breen had gotten to his friend Nolan for help and then told him about how the Comforts had all this money, and given him an inside-and-out description of the Comfort place (where Breen had been several times) and generally helped set the heist in motion. Sam's deductions were based on Breen and Nolan having worked together a lot of times, and on the fact that Breen, who'd been in debt up to his ass with gamblers and had thrown in with the Comforts to take care of those snowballing debts, was back in Indianapolis, in his bar, with no apparent money problems.

So Terry and his old man had gone to the Indianapolis bar

and found Breen humping some plump blonde bitch, who old Sam had shotgunned to make the point of how serious he was. Then he found out from Breen where Nolan was and shotgunned Breen, too.

And of course it had turned out Nolan was in Iowa City, and the old man had cussed himself for not figuring it. It only made sense that Breen, shot up and in Iowa City, would run to Planner's antique shop, Planner being the old guy who had planned most of the jobs Breen and Nolan had pulled together.

That night, the night they'd double-crossed Breen and let the bleeding man get away from them, the old man and Billy Comfort had gone to the antique shop. The old man had thought of Planner immediately, but when he went there, to the shop, nobody was around except some damn kid about Billy's age. Planner's nephew, the kid said he was, and didn't seem to know anything about the darker side of his uncle's activities. Sam had chalked that one up as a blind alley, and it wasn't till he held a shotgun in Breen's face and heard about Nolan being in Iowa City that the old man linked the kid at the antique shop with the kid who'd been with Nolan that night at the farm, when the air was full of smoke and blood.

Yesterday, when no one was there, Terry and his father broke into the antique shop, to wait for Nolan and the kid and kill them. At least that was the elder Comfort's concern. Terry convinced him they should make some attempt, anyway, at finding out if any of the money was in the antique shop. Old Sam said that was nonsense. Breen had told them Nolan was running a fancy restaurant/nightclub place, and all the money was probably sunk in that. But Terry had insisted there might be some money in the shop somewhere, as it wasn't like a thief to keep all his money in a bank, and so they got into the safe, but there was nothing in it; they looked upstairs for a wall safe and couldn't find one. Terry did find a little notebook, in a drawer in what was apparently Nolan's room, with a rough sketch of what seemed to be the floor plan of a bank, and a list of "projected expenses" that included the entries "costumes, $100," "jackets, approx. $60," "van rental, $1,000," and other equally confusing items. Terry showed the book to his father and said, "I think they're planning something," and his father said bullshit, the man's retired, and Terry said, "A retired thief? Don't kid me, Pop."

He'd gone on to try to convince his father that if Nolan was getting a heist together, it'd be wise for Terry and his father to wait it out, wait till the heist was over and take the proceeds off Nolan's hands before killing him. But revenge was still foremost in the old man's mind, and he rejected the notion.

And then the kid had come home, and they knocked him out before he'd seen either of their faces, which was a lucky break. But then Sam wanted to kill the kid then and there, which was stupid, and Terry told his father so.

"You want to kill this kid and sit here waiting with a corpse God knows how long before Nolan shows up? How do we know Nolan is even in town? We got to deal with these two both at the same time, Pop, or else you kill one, and the other finds out and knows something's up and comes looking for us instead of the other way around. Come on. We'll leave now and they'll just think somebody came in off the street and tried to rob them."

So they left, and waited and watched for Nolan to come back to the shop. Across the street was an old school, which was evidently set to be torn down, but no work was going on, maybe because of the cold, snowy weather; at any rate, it was empty, no one around to stop them from going in and finding a first-floor window to look out of and watch the antique shop across the way. Both father and son pulled up desks designed for grade school children and sat, their skinny frames fitting easily enough.

It wasn't till late in the evening, around ten, that Nolan came back, and by that time Terry's father had fallen asleep, and Terry didn't wake him. Terry wanted to stall his father long enough to find out whether or not a heist was in the offing, and he let his father spend the night in the cold, empty grade school in a third-grader's desk. In the morning, when old Sam was waking up (and almost immediately began cursing his son for falling asleep on the job), Nolan and the short curly-haired kid drove out from around back of the antique shop, from the garage, in an old and somewhat battered Chevy II. And the Comforts went scrambling out of their third-grade desks, out of the condemned school and into their car, parked in an alley behind and, keeping a discreet distance, followed the Chevy II out of town. Soon the Chevy II disappeared off onto a back country road, and following them became impossible.

They drove back to Iowa City, to their deserted school and the desks by the window. The old man was trembling with near rage, and Terry, who'd been hit by his father on more than one occasion, was afraid a family fight was about to begin. But as weak as the old man was, Terry doubted that would amount to much.

"Pop, don't you see?" Terry said. "There is a heist coming up. They're preparing for it. Driving the back roads, figuring out getaway routes. Don't you see it?"

But the old man didn't see.

And so they again broke into the antique shop. To wait. For Nolan and the kid to come back together. Sam Comfort was going to settle his score as bloodily as it had begun. And God only knew what the old man would do, what gruesome goddamn

lengths he'd go to to avenge the killing of his favorite son. It
was like that black guy Terry had known in prison, who'd come
in on his wife humping somebody else—people do things that
are a little weird when they get taken advantage of.

They had found this attic. The apartmentlike upper floor
had a low ceiling, and they could jump down into the kitchen
easily from the attic perch. It was the old man's idea, and for a
change Terry liked it: Nolan was just too competent to deal
with flat out; better to let him come home and think everything's cool, tuck himself in bed for a nice night's sleep, and
then boom. Nolan was not the type of guy you could allow any
slack. You had to have him cold, and even then better watch
yourself.

They waited up there. Flat on their bellies. The lidlike door
that opened above the kitchen cracked open a shade, so they
could hear Nolan and the lad coming in—hear what they were
doing, keep track of them, wait for just the right moment to
spring the trap. Furthermore, the attic had a second hatchway
over the garage, so if a hasty retreat was necessary, no problem.
It was ideal.

It was also stuffy and cramped and hell to spend four or five
minutes in, let alone hours. Terry was to the point of giving up
on his idea of waiting for Nolan to pull off a heist before killing
him; to forget about the money and just get on with it, just let
his old man get his revenge rocks off. After all, Terry'd only
been out a few days. He was horny. He wanted to be the one
who did the screwing for a change, and he didn't want any
damn boy, either. He wanted to get drunk, and he thought he
might smoke a little shit, too, a little tokin' of respect for his
late doper brother. Christ, after all those months inside, was
this any way to spend his time? Flat on his belly in an attic that
had less room to move in than his cell?

Noise downstairs.

Old Sam gripped Terry's forearm.

Terry patted his father's hand soothingly.

Between them was the shotgun.

"I'm sorry, Nolan." Young voice. The lad. Nolan's buddy.

"It's okay. You almost killed us, but it's okay."

"That's never happened to me before. Falling asleep at the wheel, I mean, Jesus."

"Maybe it's a good sign."

"How do you figure?"

"Shows you're relaxed, if nothing else. I doubt Rigley and the girl get that much sleep between now and Monday. No, I take that back—the girl'll sleep fine. She'll sleep better than any of us."

"Listen, Nolan, I'm tired, and I know you are too. I mean, you slept all the way back yourself."

"Except when you almost ran into the semi. That woke me up."

"Yeah, except then. Anyway, I wonder if you'd mind going over a few things with me. I feel like there's a few things you're going to want me to know that Rigley doesn't have to. After all, all he has to do is stand there."

"Couldn't it wait till morning?"

"I'll sleep better if we go over it now."

"I didn't notice you having any trouble sleeping when you were behind the wheel."

"I'm wide awake now."

"Okay. I tell you what. I'll take it from the top, and you stop me any time you got a question."

After Nolan had gone over the heist in detail with the kid, the Comforts allowed time for everybody downstairs to go to sleep, then sneaked out through the garage.

13

Most of the downtown Port City buildings were brick and had a decaying look to them. The bank, on the corner, was an exception. It was white stone, two stories of nicely chiseled Grecian architecture dominated by three pillars carved out of its face. Above the pillars the word BANK was cut in the stone and the date 1870; the bank's electric sign, nearby, didn't date back that far. The sign was attached to the corner of the building and hovered out over the sidewalk; it said FIRST NATIONAL BANK OF PORT CITY above a field of black, on which white dots grouped to form the time and then regrouped to form the temperature. Right now the sign said the time was 1:27. The time was 7:26. And the sign said the temperature was 98 degrees. The temperature was 20 degrees. The sign was broken.

Jon was nervous. Yesterday, Sunday, had been busy, and he hadn't had time to be nervous; he'd been moving all the time, almost all night, too. But now he was sitting, and he felt himself trembling, like an alcoholic who needed that first drink.

He felt a hand on his shoulder and almost jumped.

"Easy," Nolan said. "Easy."

Nolan's hand. A reassuring hand. Jon looked at Nolan, who smiled from behind his white whiskers and said softly, "Ho ho ho."

"Yeah?" Jon said. "And I hear your wife puts out for the elves. Stick *that* up your chimney."

And they looked at each other in their Santa Claus suits and laughed, a little, and Jon was less nervous. A little.

Rigley was behind Nolan, crouching. The man didn't seem

at all nervous, but somehow he didn't seem calm, either. He hadn't said a word since they'd stopped by his house to pick him up a few minutes before.

They were in a red panel truck that was parked in front of the Salvation Army store just down the block from and on the same side of the one-way street as the bank. On the sides and rear of the panel truck it said "TOYS FOR TIKES, Davenport, Iowa" in white letters. Toys for Tikes was an organization of area businessmen whose panel trucks (identical to this one) were a common Christmas-season sight in these parts. The trucks went around to various businesses that served as drop points for the broken and/or discarded toys that Toys for Tikes collected, refurbished, and distributed to needy children. Sometimes, close to Christmas, when there were more deliveries than pickups to be made, the drivers dressed as Santa Claus.

Today was December 24.

The bank was on the corner of Second Street and Iowa Avenue. The panel truck was parked on Second Street. Traffic was less than heavy, more than sparse; at any rate, the Toys for Tikes van attracted no undue attention. The morning was clear, crisp-cold; no overcast sky today; no threat of snow.

At 7:28 a man who looked remarkably like a younger version of Rigley rounded the corner from Iowa Avenue on foot, having left his car in the riverfront parking lot a block down and across the four wide lanes of Mississippi Drive. The man's name was Shep Jackson. He was a vice-president at the bank; technically, his job was that of auditor. He wore an expensive-looking gray topcoat with a black fur collar. He had short dark hair and a tanned complexion. As he walked, he looked at himself in the reflecting glass of the modern double doors between the first and second pillars and the big curtained window between the second and third. He stopped at the employees' entrance, the furthermost door, which opened onto a vestibule that joined the stairway to bookkeeping and the side door to the bank lobby. Keys were needed to open both doors, but the outer one he left unlocked, while the lobby door he locked behind him.

The vault's time lock was set for 7:30, at which time Jackson would dial the combination, whirl the wheel, and open the vault.

Inside the vault was a shiny silver wall of drawers the cast and gloss of newly minted coins, separately locked drawers that held the trays of money for the teller cages, drafts, trust vouchers, money orders, securities, and so on. There was a small inner safe, built into the lower half of the shiny silver wall. The bulk of the bank's money was in the interior safe. Just under $400,000, Rigley said.

The second safe, the one inside the vault, had its own time lock. At 7:45, Jackson would have four minutes to dial a combination and open the safe. From 7:30 to 7:45, Jackson would busy himself with the menial task of turning off the night alarms and emptying the small night depository vault up front, which would contain twenty-five or so locked, separate bags of coin and cash and checks left by merchants for overnight safekeeping. These he would carry to a teller's window and leave. That would give him five or six minutes to sit at his desk, relax, have a smoke, and wait for the time lock on the vault's interior safe to go off.

Jon looked at his Dick Tracy watch. "Seven thirty-eight, Nolan," he said. "Better get going, don't you think?"

"Another minute," Nolan said.

They waited.

Nolan hadn't told Jon the reasons for going with December 24, Christmas Eve morning, but Jon could figure them out for himself. The bank ran a skeleton crew on December 24; barely half the regular personnel would be on hand. Furthermore, if all went as planned, it would all be over before any (or at least many) of the bank employees had even showed up, the exception being Shep Jackson, who had to be there early to open the vault. Most people resent having to work on a holiday, even on a near holiday like December 24, so it was unlikely anyone would show up early today, and possible most of them would come dragging in five or ten minutes late. Also, the bank vault was overflowing at this busy shopping time of year; the Friday before the weekend was probably one of the biggest days of the season for local merchants. And, of course, there were the Santa Claus suits, which were to keep anybody from getting a look at Nolan and Jon's true appearance, to keep anybody from realizing the Port City bank was being robbed by the same people again. Jon hadn't been surprised when Nolan said the robbery would be Monday, because if it was any later than Monday, using the Santa Claus suits would be crazy. Although, sitting here in his false whiskers and red padded suit, Jon felt pretty crazy as it was.

"Okay," Nolan said. "Let's go."

Nolan opened the rear doors of the van as Jon pulled up alongside the bank; Rigley got out first and Nolan, in his Santa Claus suit, followed. They went in the employees' entrance. Through the glass door Jon saw Rigley working the key in the side lobby door. When Nolan and Rigley were both inside, Jon turned right on Iowa and drove past the bank and into the bank's customer-only parking lot.

The lot was behind the bank and bordered by the alley, across from which were big empty buildings, a hotel, warehouses, reclaimed for urban renewal. Jon parked in the far corner of the lot, by the rear door to the bank, a metal door at the top of half a flight of metal steps. Nolan would be coming out that door in ten minutes. It would have been a nice way to go in, but it could only be opened from inside; somebody inside had to look through the peephole and unbolt the door and let you in. So Nolan and Rigley had gone through the front.

The lot was recessed, the bank having a neighboring building that extended clear to the alley's edge, meaning the lot was open to view only on the Iowa Avenue side. Directly across from the lot was another, public parking lot, presently empty. But down the street half a block was a cafe. A police car was parked outside the cafe.

Jon slumped behind the wheel of the van, sweating in his Santa Claus whiskers and suit despite the cold, wondering what prison was like.

14

Nolan had a laundry bag in one hand and a .38 in the other. The laundry bag was empty. The gun wasn't. He stood silently beside Rigley in front of Shep Jackson's desk, at the rear of the bank, near the vault. The bank was silent, too, and dark, only the lights in the rear having been turned on as yet.

Jackson was wearing a money-green sportcoat and pale green slacks, the latter approximating the shade his complexion had turned to a moment before. He had the same sickly handsome look as Rigley, only younger, of course, like someone who had stepped out of an Arrow shirt advertisement. He'd been sitting at his desk, feet propped up, smoking a cigarette, reading yesterday's *Wall Street Journal*. He had stood as the bank president and Santa Claus approached; he had smiled, a smile at first amused, then puzzled, and finally not a smile at all, because Santa Claus had a gun.

Three minutes remained before the time lock on the inner vault safe would go off.

"Shep," Rigley said, emotionlessly, "there is a man at my house holding a gun to my wife's head. There's a man with a gun outside, waiting. And, of course, there's this man. They want the money in the vault. They came to my house this morning and brought me here; one of them stayed behind to hold my wife hostage. I will be leaving with them. I'm a hostage, too."

"Oh, my God," Jackson said, touching his cheek.

"Take it easy, Shep," Rigley said. "I've been robbed before. The bank has. My experience is that if we follow instructions, no harm'll come to anyone. They want the money, and that's all. But if we don't follow their instructions, my wife will be killed, and quite possibly so will I."

Nolan was pleased with Rigley's words, but not with his performance. There was a mechanical quality to it, a coldness, like a bad actor reading off cue cards. Fortunately, Jackson seemed too unnerved to notice.

"At eight-thirty, Shep, you'll open and conduct business as usual. This man is going to take all of the money in the vault safe, but will leave the tellers' money alone. So you should be able to carry on as if all was normal. Sometime around mid-morning, they intend to release my wife and me, they say, and you'll be contacted. *I* will contact you. And at that time you can call the authorities. But until then any effort to do otherwise, I have been assured, will result in my wife's death and my own. So please keep everyone away from the alarms. Now. I think the time lock should be open and you can give this man what he's after."

Jackson nodded nervously and said, "Uh, people will be coming pretty soon, George. How should we…I…handle that?"

"I'm going up to stand by the front door now, to explain the situation to anyone who might come in early. This will be over, though, before very many, if anyone, shows up. So it's going to be up to you to gather everyone in the back conference room and explain what is happening."

Jackson nodded again and walked gingerly toward the vault. He walked inside the vault and crouched to open the safe, then turned to Nolan and said, "All right, it's open." And Nolan held out the laundry bag to him, making him come for it, not entering the vault itself where Jackson would have him in a confined area that might lend itself to idiotic heroism.

It took less than three minutes to empty the safe, to make the laundry bag bulge with the packets of money.

Jackson pulled the bag by its neck, out of the vault, and turned it over to Nolan. Nolan slung it over his shoulder, Santa-style.

Rigley, who was standing up front, by the side lobby door, saw that Nolan and Jackson were done, and rejoined them. He had a blank look on his face. It disturbed Nolan somehow that Rigley had taken this in such easy stride, that Rigley's tic under the corner of his right eye hadn't been here today.

Nolan motioned with his gun for Jackson to lead them through the back room that led to the bolted back door. The room was lined with filing cabinets and had a Xerox machine and a counter for a coffee pot and a table; a coin-wrapping machine and a couple of other machines Nolan didn't recognize were grouped around the massive metal back door, which was bolted three times. Bag over his shoulder, gun trained on Jackson, Nolan peered out the magnifying peephole in the door and saw Jon sitting behind the wheel of the red van. No one else was in the parking lot. The alley was empty too.

Nolan motioned to Jackson to unbolt the door.

Jackson did.

Rigley said, "If you haven't heard from me by eleven, you can call the police." Rigley turned his blank face to Nolan and asked, "Is that right?"

Nolan nodded.

Jackson said, "If I haven't heard anything by eleven, call the police. Otherwise business as usual."

Rigley nodded and said, "Don't let me down, Shep. It's not just me, it's…"

And here was the damnedest thing: Rigley's voice cracked, as if there was some genuine emotion going on behind that blank mask.

"…It's Cora's life too."

And Rigley turned to the massive door and opened it.

Jackson, who seemed pretty calm by now, said to Nolan,

"You...you don't say much, do you? You're not your everyday Santa Claus, are you?"

Nolan tapped Jackson's shoulder with the gun, in a not unfriendly way, and said, "It's better to give than receive," and went out.

They'd been inside seven minutes.

15

Rigley, feeling as though he were moving through a strange but amazingly real-seeming dream, crawled inside the Toys for Tikes van. The laundry bag of money was tossed in after him. The doors, slammed shut. It was dark inside the van; Rigley sat and looked at the rear doors and saw nothing but darkness. His back was to the kid, Jon, who was getting the engine going, and he heard the door slam as Nolan (who Rigley knew as Logan) got in on the rider's side. And then the van was moving. Backing out, into the alley.

Nolan said, "Cops over at the cafe, like Rigley said they'd be."

They ate breakfast there every morning.

Jon said, "You can see their backs if you look through the window there. Sitting at the counter, see? Never even looked over here once."

"Well let's not wait till they do. Go."

And they were driving down the alley, and Rigley bounced in the darkness, wondering if dying was like this, darkness and an empty feeling—as if you were starving to death but felt no hunger. Next to Rigley, the bag of money bounced too.

At the end of the alley, on the right, was a filling station, behind which was a self-service car wash, four stalls, two of which you could enter from the alley. Rigley felt the van swing into one of the stalls, and the van wasn't yet fully stopped when Nolan was out and pulling down the garage-type door on the stall.

It was a totally private cubicle. Though the filling station adjacent was open, there were no attendants at the car wash—strictly self-serve. It was simply a garagelike stall you drove into, a gray cement cubicle where you deposited fifty cents for five minutes' use of a long-nosed gun affair attached to a hose, which shot a steaming-hot spray of soap and water; to switch from soapy water to rinse, you just squeezed the trigger again.

The van doors opened.

Nolan was still in the Santa Claus suit, but the whiskers were in his hand now. He said to Rigley, "Shake it."

Rigley got out.

Nolan joined Jon inside the van, where they began getting out of the Santa Claus suits, under which they wore street clothes. Rigley pushed the doors shut, but not all the way, leaving them slightly ajar so Nolan and Jon could move if they had to. Rigley got out two quarters.

He deposited the coins in the slot and squeezed the trigger on the long-barreled rifle, which immediately spurted hot, soapy water onto the van.

The red van began turning white. The "TOYS FOR TIKES" lettering dissolved. The red color streamed away, melting off the van under the blast of the water rifle, finally being swallowed noisily by the drain beneath the vehicle. It was an easy job. Only the roof was hard.

It seemed absurd to be standing here, hosing down the van, down the block from the bank they had just robbed—*his* bank. And as the air turned cloudy with steam in the cubicle, Rigley felt more and more that this was a dream, that none of it was happening.

He squeezed the trigger on the water rifle and began the rinse. Red gurgled down the drain, leaving whiteness behind.

This morning, forty-five minutes before Nolan and Jon had come by to pick him up, he had gone into his wife's room. She was sleeping. Her hair was in curlers; her face was pale, her mouth open. She was snoring, quietly. She did not look pretty. But she didn't look ugly. She was just Cora, sleeping, snoring, in curlers, in a cream-color nightgown with the covers down around her waist and the plumpness of her bosom reminding him of better times. There was an empty bottle of Scotch on her dresser to remind him of the current state of their marriage.

Julie had been there. With him. Standing behind him. In the bedroom.

She had never been in his house before.

She and Cora had never met.

But now she stood in the bedroom, behind him, Cora snoring quietly in bed a few feet away, and Julie whispered, "Go on. Do it. Now. Here. Take it."

And he had taken the shotgun from her.

It was heavy. He had never noticed it as being so heavy before. He had gone hunting with it plenty of times. It never seemed heavy to him then.

He raised the shotgun.

He squeezed his eyes shut, felt the wetness dangling between his lids.

He opened his eyes and turned to look at Julie, who was nodding, and back to Cora, who was sleeping, and their images blurred together; they were one person, one beautiful woman he had loved and let dominate him. And he squeezed the trigger.

He squeezed the trigger and squeezed shut his eyes and dropped the gun to the floor and ran blindly out of the room and dropped to his knees in the hallway, sobbing, wanting to scream but the scream getting caught in his chest, as if a webbing in his chest had caught the scream and was holding it there, letting only a rasping, wheezing cough-sound come out of him. And he got to the bathroom in the far part of the house, the one off his study, and hung his head over the stool, but he didn't vomit. He hadn't eaten anything for two days; there was nothing there. He just held onto the side of the stool and cried and cried and cried and Julie was patting his shoulder, saying, "There, there."

Later, moments, minutes—a lifetime later—he looked up at Julie. He was still clinging to the cold porcelain of the stool. His ears rang from the sound of an explosion he hadn't really heard. He said, "I'm sorry, baby…I'm…I'm sorry…sorry…"

"She never felt a thing," Julie said.

"I…don't know if I can go any…further with this."

She kneeled beside him. She kissed his cheek. She dried his eyes and cheeks with Kleenex.

"We're going to have to get going, honey," she said. "You're going to have to pull yourself together. Jon and Logan'll be here soon."

"How…how can I wait in the house here with…her?"

"Wait outside. Go outside and wait for them. Cold air will do you good."

"I…I hate this."

"The worst is over."

"Is…it? What about the others?"

"My responsibility. Just lead them to me."

"Like a…like a…Judas sheep."

"They're nothing but thieves, George. Killers and thieves."

"That…that Jon is just a kid. A boy."

"The two of them are criminals, George. They'd do the same to us, if they had to."

"They…they haven't. They could have, and they haven't."

"Why should they, honey? They're in this for the money."

"We forced them."

"No. They're in this for the money. That's the truth. Now get hold of yourself. You all right?"

"All...right. I'm all right."

"Can you compose yourself? At the bank?"

"I'll be all right."

"All right. I'll go get your coat. Stay put."

She left the bathroom.

He got to his feet.

And walked through the study.

Walked down the hall.

Looked into the bedroom.

At the blue wallpaper. The open-beam wood ceiling. The nightstand with their wedding picture on top. The nightstand drawer was pulled out, to reveal the .32 amidst the jewelry boxes. Julie had thought to open the drawer. The nightmare didn't touch her, did it? She was cool, efficient, even in crisis. The girl had a good head on her shoulders.

Which was more than could be said for Cora.

He shuddered.

And looked away.

Then he looked back, and emotion had drained out of him somehow.

Cora wasn't there. Not really. There was this headless thing in the queen-size bed, a dressmaker's dummy in a red-spattered cream-color nightgown. And some strange, surrealistic stain of colors—red again was dominant—splashed on the blue-papered wall behind the bed. An abstract painting. Not Cora.

"Don't," Julie said.

She was standing behind him again, as she had earlier. She had the shotgun again. She'd be taking it with her. It was part of the plan. To kill Cora and, later, Nolan and Jon, with the same shotgun.

"Don't look at her," Julie said.

"Look at who?" he said.

"George. Get out of this room, George."

"It doesn't bother me." His voice sounded remote to him, as though he was speaking down a well and his voice was mingling with its echo. "That's not her."

"Come on. Get into your coat and wait outside. They'll be here soon."

"Wait with me."

"George! Snap out of it!" She grabbed his arm and pulled him out into the hall. "Snap out of it. I'll be here. Inside. But those two can't see me, George. I'm not supposed to be here! George? We've gone over this a thousand times, George. Goddammit!"

"I'll wait outside."

She sighed. And smiled. A tight-lipped little smile. "I'll help you with your coat. Here. Now. They should be along in fifteen minutes or so. Stand out there and relax."

Julie would wait till Nolan and Jon had picked Rigley up in the van, and then she would leave, out the back way, and walk on foot to where she had left her car.

Rigley went outside and stood in the chill air. The cold felt good. He wished it were even colder. He wished it would freeze him.

The gun was empty. Some more rinse was needed. He deposited two more quarters, then squeezed the trigger on the water rifle. Red gurgled down the drain, leaving whiteness behind.

Nolan and Jon were getting out of the back of the van. Both wore the hunting jackets. Nolan wore tan trousers and a dark blue woolen turtleneck sweater. Jon wore the T-shirt with the cartoon figure of a pinheaded man on it, and blue jeans. Nolan had a green garbage bag; inside the bag were the Santa Claus suits.

"You about done?" Nolan asked Rigley. Nolan was tying a knot in the neck of the big plastic bag.

"Yes," Rigley said.

The van was white now. It had been painted with a water-base paint, and stencils had been placed on the sides while it was being painted so that the "TOYS FOR TIKES" lettering had been formed from the natural white beneath.

Nolan opened the garage-type door and peeked out into the alley.

"All clear," he said.

He put the green garbage bag with the costumes in it next to some similar bags set out for trash pickup by the filling station management.

Rigley got back in the back of the van. Nolan shut the doors on him. Darkness swallowed him up again.

Then they were moving. Out of the car wash, out of town. To Rigley's cottage. Where Julie and the shotgun waited.

16

She unfolded the plastic sheet. It had come off a roll and had been folded up like a huge tablecloth. She'd bought it months ago, at a paint store, with today's purpose in mind. She began spreading the sheet across the floor, and when she was done, it covered nearly half the room—from the doorway, past the couch, on to the edge of the fireplace. She smoothed it, as though making a bed. Then she moved to the other side of the room and sat at the picnic-style table over near the bar. The windows in the cottage were shuttered, and none of the lights were turned on; there was nothing to catch the plastic surface and reflect. They wouldn't notice the sheet of plastic when they came in, not until they'd stepped on it, heard it crinkle under-foot, and they wouldn't begin to have time to realize that the plastic was there to catch the bloody mess they'd make, dying. Because they'd be dead already. The moment they stepped in the door.

She got herself a drink.

Her hand was steady, or as steady as could be expected, anyway. She would admit to butterflies in her stomach, but she wasn't what you'd call nervous, not really; not any worse than waiting to go on stage in one of those beauty pageants she'd been in years before. Anyway, the Scotch and soda felt good going down. Warm, despite the ice. It settled her, calmed her.

She glanced at her watch: 7:55. The robbery itself should be over by now. They'd be getting in the van soon (if they weren't already) and driving down the alley and into the car wash. They could be here in fifteen minutes. Twenty, at most. At the very most.

The hairy part was she liked them. The young one, especially. Jon. George was right: Jon really was just a boy, a decent kid who'd somehow gotten mixed up with the older guy, the man she knew as Logan. If she could have thought of a way to spare the boy, she would have. And she'd take no pleasure in killing Nolan, either. She felt a sort of kinship with the man, though she didn't really understand why. She felt she had something in common with him, that they were somehow alike.

But she wasn't about to let any soft feelings about those two make it hard for her; killing them was an unpleasant but necessary part of what she and George set out to do. So it would be done.

And it would sure as hell be easier than this morning, she thought, sipping her Scotch, shaking her head.

She hadn't planned to be there with George, in the beginning. Ideally, George should have been able to carry out that end of it himself. But the more she'd thought about it, the more she knew he wouldn't be up to it without her beside him, supporting him, putting the gun in his hands. All but pulling the damn trigger for him.

It had been a risk, her being there. She'd made sure no one had any chance of seeing her go in or out of the place, but it was still a risk. Though after seeing how George had handled it, she was goddamn glad she'd been there. Oh, he'd managed to do it, managed to shoot the bitch, all right, but he'd gotten flaky as hell afterwards. Off his fucking nut. Thank God she'd been there to soothe him, to get him on his feet for the rest of the ordeal.

She looked at her watch again: not long now. Ten minutes and they could be here.

She finished her drink, got up from the table, and went into the bedroom.

The shotgun lay on the bed.

Twin barrels. Twin triggers. Sleek, black gun with walnut stock.

She'd practiced with it, in the wooded area around the cottage. Nothing elaborate; aim at a tree and hit it, that's all she needed to be able to do. It'd be close range. Just so she had the feel of the gun—was used to its kick. She'd have to fire twice, after all, and had to be ready to reload and shoot again, if something should go wrong.

In a few minutes, it would all be over—all but the final few grisly steps. She and George would transfer the bodies to the van; George would return to Port City to play bereaved widower; and she, after nightfall, would drive the van and its gory cargo and leave it along the side of a nearby (but not too nearby) back road. The shotgun would be thrown in the river. The authorities would be looking for the nonexistent third member of the robbery team, the man who had "held Cora Rigley hostage" while Nolan and Jon looted the bank, the man who killed Cora Rigley when she tried to take a gun from her jewelry drawer and defend herself, the man who then double-crossed and killed his two partners and disappeared with all that money.

It gave her a sense of satisfaction to have fooled a pro like Nolan. The crucial thing had been to make him accept the idea of Cora Rigley as hostage. George had insisted to Nolan it was necessary; he'd said that a bank president who is the victim of two bank robberies within so short a span of time is going to look somewhat silly and incompetent no matter what, but at least with his wife in jeopardy, some sympathy would be aroused. Besides, it would keep everyone at the bank from contacting the police right away. Nolan, of course, had balked at involving George's wife, but George had explained she wouldn't be involved at all—that Cora was a drunk who slept till noon; that he would cut their phone wires the morning of the robbery; that their second car was in the shop, leaving Cora stranded there at home.

"What about later," Nolan had wanted to know, "when your wife is questioned about being a hostage and knows nothing about it?"

George had explained, "I'll say you people grabbed me outside the house and that I never actually saw one of the thieves with my wife."

And, finally, Nolan had agreed the wife-as-hostage angle was worth including.

And it certainly was.

She smiled, sat on the bed, and cradled the shotgun in her lap, thinking about what life would be like as a millionaire's wife.

When she walked out with the shotgun into the other room, she was totally unprepared for the door to open and the two figures in hunting jackets to enter. It was too early. She hadn't heard the van approach. They couldn't be here yet.

But they were.

She fired the shotgun.

One barrel at a time.

And the two men in hunting jackets, the older man and the young one, too, caught the full blast and lifted off the floor and flopped bloodily back down again on the crinkly plastic shroud.

17

Jon was glad it was almost over. Flat, snow-covered farmland glided by as he drove the van along at a leisurely forty-five, the blacktop road not devoid of traffic, but damn near. Nolan sat next to Jon, looking almost bored; he hadn't said a word since leaving Port City out this back door of a blacktop. Jon's hands were sweaty on the wheel. The gun in his belt was a lump nudging his belly like something not fully digested. Like a reminder of what might have happened at the bank, had anything gone wrong. Of the ugly kind of things that can happen when a robbery goes haywire.

Like that time, a few months ago, at the Comfort farm. A simple job. Simple and potentially less dangerous than today's. And yet it had turned into a nightmare of guns going off and people dying. People getting killed.

One of them by him.

He felt the gun in his belt under the jacket, pressing into his gut, and thought, *Thank God I'm not going to have to use this fucking thing.*

"No shooting," Nolan had told him last night. "This job's not worth the risk. We got money. We aren't desperate. So if we get caught—well, okay, we make bail, get our asses out of the country. But if we start shooting, somebody might get killed, and they don't offer bail when somebody's killed."

"No shooting," Jon had nodded, relieved. "That means we'll be getting rid of the guns right after the robbery, then, right? At the car wash, when we hose down the van and dump those Santa suits?"

"No."

"No?"

"We'll hang on to the guns a while after that."

"I thought you said no shooting."

"Unless somebody shoots at us first."

"You don't mean cops…?"

"Christ no! Don't *ever* shoot at a cop. Jesus!"

"Then what the hell are you talking about, Nolan?"

"I'm not talking about cops, that's for goddamn sure."

"Well, who else is there…? Oh. I see what you mean. You… you really think that's a possibility?"

"Rigley and his bitch crossing us? Yes. If it was just Rigley, I'd say no. But it isn't just Rigley. So stay alert."

Jon's mental replay of the conversation of the night before ended as he pulled onto the blacktop off of which was Rigley's cottage. When they passed the run-down shack-on-stilts that was Rigley's closest neighbor, Nolan said to stop a moment: there was a car, a Buick Electra, parked next to the shack. Then he said go on. Jon did.

Jon was swinging the van down the tree-sheltered drive to the cottage when they heard the sound. "What the hell was that?"

"Gunfire," Nolan said, getting the .38 out of his belt.

"Gunfire?"

"Shotgun."

Jon brought the van to a halt alongside the yellow Mustang that belonged to the girl.

"Watch that fucker Rigley," Nolan said. He hopped out of the van.

Jon did the same. He wiped the sweat off his hand, took the .38 from out of his belt and went around to the back of the van and let a white-faced Rigley out.

"What's going on?" the banker said.

"You tell me," Jon said, and motioned at him with the .38.

Nolan had already disappeared inside the cottage, and Jon's teeth were clamped together in tense anticipation of further sounds from within the cottage.

He grabbed Rigley by the elbow and prodded him with the gun and pushed him forward, toward the cottage. The scary part was Rigley made no protest; a little indignation from the man would have gone a long way toward easing Jon's fears.

The door was open, but Jon couldn't see in. The cottage was set up too high for that; you'd have to climb the wooden steps to see what was going on in there.

He stood outside in the cold air for a few long moments, digging the gun barrel into Rigley's back, wishing to hell something would happen and at the same time that it wouldn't.

"Come on in, kid," Nolan's voice said from inside. "There's an old friend of yours here."

Jon shoved Rigley toward the door, up the steps. Inside.

And Jon couldn't believe what he saw.

Nolan said, "Shut the door, kid. Rigley, sit down."

Jon shut the door.

Rigley sat down on the couch.

On the floor lay two men. Both of them wearing hunting jackets similar to Nolan and Jon's. Both of them dead. They were face up, arms asprawl. A shotgun lay between them. So did a common pool of blood. Jon knew it was gunfire he'd heard, but the wounds looked like something else: it looked as though each of the two men had been stabbed repeatedly in the chest with an icepick. Their faces were twisted in surprise and, perhaps, disappointment.

One of them was Sam Comfort.

"The other one's his son Terry," Nolan said, in answer to the question on Jon's face.

Across the room, the girl, Julie, was sitting at the picnic table by the bar. She was wearing a red sweater and red slacks; the clothes clung to her lush figure. A shotgun was in her lap.

"But…how?" Jon said, pointing at Sam Comfort's body.

"Who knows?" Nolan said. "You didn't kill him after all, that night couple months back. That much is sure. And he's dead for sure, too, this time."

Jon still couldn't believe it, but managed to say, "What… what are…what were they doing…here?"

"It's obvious they're the ones who killed Breen," Nolan said. "And that Comfort and his boy were the ones who broke into the shop the other day, too. They came on a mission of revenge and got wind of this robbery somehow, and decided to wait till we'd pulled it off so they could have the money and their fun both. Our friends the Comforts being here explains a lot of things."

"They sure do," Jon nodded, beginning to snap out of it but feeling as though he'd been struck a hard blow in the stomach.

And Nolan looked pointedly toward the girl and said, "But other things remain a mystery."

"They came in and I shot them," she said. Coldly. Calmly.

"No kidding," Nolan said.

"You said it yourself…they were after the money. They thought they'd come in here and take care of me and wait for you. They didn't expect me to have a gun."

Nolan smiled. Almost pleasantly. "Neither did we."

"You knew I had a shotgun here. You expected me to be ready in case something went wrong, didn't you?"

"Let's just say I'm less surprised than the Comforts."

"I have no idea what you mean by that."

"I mean you were waiting for us. For Jon and me. The Comforts came in in hunting jackets, and in this nice, dim room you thought it was us and emptied your shotgun."

"That's silly."

"Oh? Then explain one thing to me, and I'll be happy. We'll

split the money and go our separate ways. Explain the sheet of plastic."

Jon hadn't even noticed it, he'd been so dazed, but there it was: a plastic sheet, smoothed across the front half of the room. He wondered what in hell it could be for.

And then he knew.

He looked at the two Comforts oozing blood from their identical clusters of icepick-like chest wounds, a puddle gathering between them on the plastic sheet, and all of a sudden Jon felt sick and he knew.

Nolan turned to Rigley and said, "Tell me something, George. How's the wife?"

Jon had almost forgotten about Rigley. The man had been sitting on the couch, hands draped loose in his lap, looking less alive than the Comforts. But as Nolan spoke, something happened in the man's face. Not much, just a tic, under the right eye. But a sign of life.

"I'm just guessing, of course," Nolan said. "But she wouldn't happen to be dead, would she?"

Jon had no idea what Nolan was talking about, but evidently Rigley did. The banker was staring into nothing, the tic jumping under his eye like a hand waving goodbye.

Across the room, Julie was smiling. Her smile was white in the darkness, a Cheshire cat smile. She was smiling at Nolan, who was pointing his .38 at her head.

Even when Nolan thumbed back the hammer, her smile didn't fade.

"Nolan...?" Jon said.

And Nolan looked at Jon. And sighed. He stuck the gun in his belt and said, "Come on, kid. Let's get out of here."

Jon swallowed and said, "That's a good idea," and put his own .38 away.

Nolan turned to go.

The girl swung the shotgun up from her lap.

Shit! She must've switched shotguns before Nolan came in, switched the one she emptied into the Comforts for the gun the Comforts brought with them. And while those thoughts ran through his head, Jon shouted, "Nolan!" and dove for him, knocked him out of the way as the blast of the gun cut the couch in half and chewed up the wall behind.

And she still had a barrel left.

"No!"

Rigley.

He'd been sitting on the couch before the shotgun cut it in half, and he was on his feet now.

Which was more than could be said for Jon and Nolan, who were on their backs, like the Comforts, looking up into the infinite darkness of the shotgun muzzle, their own guns tucked snugly in their belts. The only thing keeping them from getting blown immediately away was Rigley, who had moved between them and the girl, saying, "No! No more killing!"

And took the other barrel in the chest.

A bunch of Rigley went flying over Jon's head and splashed onto the wall, and the rest of Rigley, the bloody bulk of him, tumbled onto them, on top of them. But Nolan pushed the corpse aside and made a dive for the girl, whose shotgun was empty now. She swung the big gun at Nolan, and the heavy metal of those twin barrels caught him across the side of the head, and he went down, hard, at her feet.

Jon had lost his gun somewhere in the scramble, but he got himself out from under the dead weight of Rigley and got the girl by the arm before she was out the door. But she still had that damn shotgun, and empty or not, she was making a weapon of it. She caught Jon in the belly with the stock of the gun, and as he doubled over, she caught him again with it, on the back of the neck. He went down, not unconscious exactly, but conscious of nothing but pain.

It lasted maybe a minute, but he thought it was longer, thought it was an hour. He opened his eyes and looked into Sam Comfort's ghostly pale countenance from a distance of a few inches. He gagged, reeled backwards, and got groggily to his feet. Nolan was over in the middle of the room, on his side, still out. Rigley was over by the bar, where the shotgun blast had blown him. The stench of gunpowder and shit filled in the room. As Nolan had explained to him once, "When people die, they sometimes shit their pants. Wouldn't you, kid?"

He saw his .38 on the floor, over by the half-couch.

And he heard something outside.

A car starting!

He realized at once that his time perception had been screwed up and that the girl was probably still outside. He went over and scooped up his .38 and ran to the doorway.

She was in her yellow Mustang. The sack of money was in back; he could see it there, behind her, a back-seat driver looking over her shoulder.

He wrapped both hands around the stock of the .38 as Nolan had taught him and aimed and had her pretty face in his sights; all that was left was to squeeze the trigger and blow that pretty face away, in an explosion of windshield glass and flesh and teeth and bone and blood....

She saw him.

She got an animal look in her eyes—a cornered, crazed animal look—and there was no doubt in his mind that had the .38 been in her hand, he'd be dead by now. But she was unarmed and couldn't do a damn thing.

Except hit the accelerator and back out of there, in a hailstorm of gravel.

He jumped the steps, ran after her, firing, and fired at her tires; might have hit one. He ran into the cloud of her gravel dust and fired again, but she was gone.

He lowered the gun and put it back in his belt.

"Don't just stand there trying to figure out whether to feel ashamed or proud," Nolan said.

He was in the doorway, standing in the doorway at the top of the steps. He came down, slowly, rubbing the side of his head where the girl had struck him with the shotgun barrel.

"I'm sorry, Nolan."

"Sorry you didn't shoot the bitch? So am I. Get your ass in that van and let's get after her. I think you got her tire. She won't be going far."

18

Coming down the hill they could see the length of the several-mile-long straightaway beyond the Cedar River Bridge. There was no sign of the yellow Mustang.

"Shit," Nolan said.

"Maybe she turned back toward Port City," Jon said.

"With that fat sack of money sitting in back? Not likely."

The van rolled across the bridge, and they followed the highway as it curved and straightened out again.

Still no sign.

"Maybe I didn't hit her tire after all," Jon said.

Nolan said nothing.

The West Liberty city limits were up ahead. The girl worked there, had friends there. If she was anywhere, Nolan thought, that was where she'd be.

The speed limit dropped to forty-five, and Jon complied as the van took the crest of a slight hill and followed the highway as it snaked into West Liberty.

"Maybe she took the Nichols turnoff," Jon said. "Maybe she turned off on a side road. Maybe she stopped at a farmhouse."

"Maybe that's her up there."

The Mustang was parked on the shoulder of the road, inside the city limits, but just barely—a meat locker was on one side of the highway, a junkyard on the other; ahead were some mobile homes and lower-middle-class houses shuffled together as if a tornado had hit and nobody had bothered to put things back in order.

Also parked on the shoulder of the road, pulled in in front of the Mustang at an angle, was a two-year-old blue Ford.

On the side of the Ford, on the door, were big white letters: "WEST LIBERTY SHERIFF'S DEPT." Nolan doubted those white letters would disappear if the car were pulled into a car wash.

In the back seat of the Ford was the girl Julie. She was looking at the junkyard and either didn't see Nolan and Jon go by, or pretended not to.

Also in the back seat was the sack of money.

In the front seat was a man of thirty-one or so who had a pudgy face highlighted by a weak chin, close-set eyes, and five o'clock shadow. There was nothing impressive about the man except the badge on his cream-color uniform and the smaller, matching badge on his cream-color western-style hat.

What had happened was obvious: the small-town sheriff had stopped the girl because she was speeding in a car with a flat tire, hardly the safest and most inconspicuous activity a person in the girl's position might have done, and had stumbled onto something more than just your average case of reckless driving.

"Jesus," Jon said. "What do we do, Nolan?"

If it had been out on the highway, Nolan might have chanced it. He might have stopped the van, put the sheriff to sleep, and gotten the money back. But this was in town. By now the sheriff could have radioed for a deputy or the state highway patrol or the Port City sheriff or police department. And there were homes nearby, and people standing out in front of them and out in front of the meat locker too. And there were some guys working in the junkyard, besides.

The van rumbled across the railroad tracks, and Nolan glanced in the rearview mirror and saw that the sheriff's car had pulled in behind them. Just beyond the tracks was an intersection with a flashing red light. The West Liberty business district, such as it was, was to the left; Iowa City was straight ahead. The sheriff's car drew alongside the van, in the turning lane. The pudgy-faced sheriff was looking ahead, watching for an opening in the traffic, which was brisk for as small as the town was. Julie was in back. So was the sack of money. She looked over at Nolan and Jon, shrugged, and looked away.

"Nolan?" Jon said again. Almost whispering. "What are we going to do?"

"Go straight," Nolan said.

BOOK TWO

Scratch Fever

One

1

Jon, on stage, sweating, singing, mouth against the wire mesh ball of the microphone, hands on the black keys of the keyboard, looked out across the underlit, crowded dance floor, smoke drifting like fog, and saw somebody who was supposed to be dead.

He blinked the sweat away and looked again.

She was gone.

But he *had* seen her. Recognized her. He shouldn't have been able to—her hair was different, still long, brushing her shoulders, but streaked blonde now, heavily so—and she wore tinted glasses with dark frames. He'd never seen her in glasses before, but she had the kind of face that a change of hair and the addition of glasses made no less distinctive.

It was mostly her mouth, he supposed: full lips that wore a faint, permanent pout, like Elke Sommer, but cruel, somehow. Smug. A feature that attracted and repelled, promised and threatened. As did that shape of hers—big boobs, tiny waist, wide hips, perfect ass. She was a sexual exaggeration, a Vargas girl come to life. She was Julie.

Julie, in white skirt and jacket and black cardigan, looking like a businesswoman, coldly chic, talking to Bob, the club manager, a six-four former farmer who was sitting with her over at the bar, stage right, handing her a drink.

Only that had been before Jon blinked.

Now Bob was sitting next to an empty stool, looking toward the back of the room, the drink in his hand extended toward nobody.

Shit, Jon thought; she saw *me*, too, recognized me. He felt a chill, despite the heat of the stage lights, the row of alternating red/blue/yellow spots strung on a pole above him, the system the band carried with them.

No. She wouldn't have recognized him; she wouldn't expect to see him playing on stage with a rock band. She wouldn't know him with his hair cut off. He was just another musician, short, muscular, curly haired; there were hundreds of people who looked like him.

Yeah. Sure.

The song was over, he suddenly realized ("Pump It Up," by Elvis Costello), and he should be introducing the next one, but he couldn't remember what it was. He glanced over at the list of songs taped to the monitor speaker next to his portable organ (an old Vox Super Continental double keyboard), but the salty sweat in his eyes kept him from being able to focus on it.

The rest of the band, Les, Roc, Mick, Toni, stood and looked at him, waiting, and there was one of those two- or three-second pauses that most audiences don't notice but seem an eternity to the people on stage, and then his eyes focused and he saw on the typed song list "Accidents Never Happen" just below "Pump It Up."

"We'd like to do one by Blondie," he heard himself saying, his voice echoing across the hall, *"featuring Toni. She isn't blonde, but she's more fun."*

Toni did a little Debbie Harry salute/smile at the audience, and the faces out there smiled back at her, accompanied by a few laughs, and they went into the song.

The band—which was called the Nodes—did a lot of Blondie material, because Toni did resemble Blondie's Debbie Harry just a little, though her hair was brunette (but then again so was Debbie Harry's, really), and she had a similar busty little figure and could mimic Ms. Harry's voice to perfection, as well as half a dozen other women's, from Ronnie Spector to Pat Benatar to

Lene Lovich, which was no small feat. Toni was the most popular member of the band, and Jon didn't mind. But Les, Roc,
and Mick did, and that was probably the major reason this was
the band's last gig.

After seven very successful months—they'd been playing
the Wisconsin/Iowa/Illinois club circuit and pulling down $1500
a week, which for a band without a hit record was good money
—the Nodes were going their separate ways. Or at least Les,
Roc, and Mick were going one way, staying together as a trio,
while Jon and Toni went another, to a tryout in St. Paul, next
week, with a new band. Girl singers and keyboard players were
always in demand.

Besides, there was a split in musical tastes among the band.
Jon and Toni both liked new wave rock, like the Elvis Costello
and Blondie numbers that dominated the song list; but the rest
of the band (who had been together for years under various
names, among them Eargasm, Fried Smoke and Deep Pink)
were into heavy-metal rock, and it was at their insistence that
material like Aerosmith and Ted Nugent stayed on the list, much
to Jon and Toni's distaste.

The club they were playing was called the Barn, and it was in
the country, between two cornfields, ten miles outside Burlington,
Iowa. Part of it actually was a barn, or had been before it was
turned into a restaurant, with the rough wood and red and white
checkered tablecloths and barbecued ribs you'd expect of a
restaurant that used to be a barn. A huge tin shed had been
erected next to the restaurant and in this, still in a rustic manner,
an Old Town setting had been created, with fake storefronts
lining either side of a big dance floor. Between storefronts and
dance floor were more tables with red and white checked cloths,
and there was a bar on either side, plus another in back, in the
area that connected the restaurant and the club.

The audience here was a young one, teens to late twenties, with enough people in their thirties to make it a difficult mix for a band to please. The drinking age was twenty-one, but fake I.D.s were more common than real ones in clubs like this one. The manager, Bob Hale, insisted that the bands he booked in play "nostalgia," which meant fifties and sixties rock, and the Nodes carried plenty of songs in that area. And the band dressed like a British sixties group: sportcoats and skinny ties and short hair. Even Toni had a Beatle haircut and wore a skinny tie with her white shirt—of course, the white shirt and tie were all Toni wore, that and pantyhose, the shirt hitting her mid-thigh, like a mini-skirt, which was Jon's idea of "nostalgia."

Jon knew that to exist as a band in the Midwest it was necessary to cater to slightly crazed club owners, like Bob, who wanted bands that could appeal to everybody. The Nodes' tongue-in-cheek clean-cut look helped accomplish that, and the songs by the Stones, Kinks and Beatles, plus sixties camp like "96 Tears," "Dirty Water," and "Woolly Bully," pleased the patrons in their thirties as well as the eighteen-year-olds.

At the end of "Accidents Never Happen," tall, skinny lead guitarist Roc went into "Cat Scratch Fever." Several male voices, out in the smoky crowd, yelped and hooted. It was a popular song. It was also Jon and Toni's cue to step offstage for a break; neither her vocals nor his keyboards were required on that opus, and besides, they hated it.

There was a little room off to stage right, behind one of the fake storefronts, where he and Toni went to wait out the song.

He could hear Roc's toneless voice echoing out there: *"Make her pussy purr...."*

"Why do they like that shit?" Jon asked.

Toni was sitting on one of the hard black flight cases a guitar amp was carried in; her short, nice legs were crossed as she unscrewed the cap of a bottle of Cutty Sark.

"You mean Les and Roc and Mick," she asked, "or the crowd?"

"Both."

"Beats the fuck out of me," she said, and took a swig of the whiskey; her little-girl face lit up as it rolled down her throat "Then again, this is Iowa," she added.

Out in the other room, Roc's guitar whined; people whooped.

"If Iowa sucks so bad," he said, "why'd you leave New Jersey?"

It was a question he'd asked many times these past months.

The answer he got he'd heard before: "I thought maybe I'd stand out in a cornfield."

He usually laughed at that, but this time he didn't. He was thinking about the woman he'd seen—in the white skirt and black sweater. He was thinking about Julie.

"Something on your mind, Jonny?"

"I don't know. Maybe."

"Cat scratch fever…"

"I thought you looked like something threw you on stage there for a second—couple songs ago. Something to that?"

"Maybe."

She smiled; she *really* looked like Debbie Harry when she smiled. "Bet you spotted somebody in the crowd. An old girl-friend. Am I right, Jonny?"

"Not exactly."

"Well, these are your old stomping grounds, aren't they?"

"Cat scratch fever…Cat scratch fever…"

"Not really. I'm eighty or a hundred miles from home."

Home was Iowa City. Or it used to be, before he and Toni had met in a music store; she'd been playing with Dagwood, a group that did *nothing* but Blondie material, formed by the ex-members of Smooch, a band that had imitated Kiss in full makeup and regalia till the Kiss fad faded. It was driving Toni nuts, as they had insisted she dye her hair blonde, with a brunette patch in back, so she'd become a Debbie Harry clone. And even though she knew it was her fate, right now at least, to sing a lot of Blondie songs, enough was enough. Jon had grabbed her, had somehow got together with Les, Roc, and Mick, and had turned Deep Pink into the Nodes and hit the road.

"We got a week to kill," Toni was saying, "before the tryout in St. Paul. We going to visit your pal? What's his name?"

"Nolan, you mean."

"Yeah. Nolan. I'd like to meet that guy. We going to stay with him in Iowa City this week, or what?"

"He doesn't live there anymore. He moved."

"Oh, yeah? What about that place of yours, that antique shop your uncle left you?"

"I leased it to an old girlfriend of mine. She sells water beds."

"Oh, yeah, I remember her. The thirty-year-old hippie."

"All hippies are thirty years old now. Anyway, Karen's all right. She's got a kid I hate, but she's all right."

Roc's guitar screeched out there; guys in the audience hollered.

"Christ, his guitar playing bores me," Toni said, making a face, swigging some more whiskey. She drank a lot, but Jon never saw it take any noticeable effect.

"I did see somebody out there, you know," Jon said.

"Oh? If it's a girlfriend, I'd be jealous, if you and me were still an item."

"Two weekends ago we were an item. Kind of."

"Yeah, well, we're still friends, Jonny. If you don't have anything lined up, and I don't have anything lined up, we can still be an item anytime you feel like, far as I'm concerned. But you and I both know there's nothing serious in it for us."

He smiled. "You got nice tits, Toni. I'm real serious when it comes to your tits."

She uncrossed her legs, smiled at him. Gestured at him with the bottle of Cutty Sark. "C'mere, handsome."

He went to her. Gave her a little kiss. She draped her arms around his neck; the whiskey bottle was against his back.

"Want to be an item tonight?" she asked. "Want to be an item all next week? I got nothing better to do. How about you?"

"I got nothing planned."

"Unless it has to do with that old girlfriend you spotted."

He moved away from her.

"Hey," Toni said. "Something *is* wrong. What?"

Roc's guitar was screaming at the audience; the audience was screaming back.

"Nothing. I don't know. You know what I told you about? About me and Nolan, I mean."

"You told me a lot about you and Nolan."

"I shouldn't have."

"Well, you did."

"Well, I shouldn't have. You know what I'm talking about."

"I think I do. The robberies."

"The robberies and what went with it."

She screwed the cap back on the whiskey bottle, then hopped down off the amplifier flight case. "The guns and stuff," she said.

Jon laughed. "Yeah. The guns and stuff. Right. Well, I saw somebody from one of the things Nolan and I were into. One of the robberies."

"Somebody you robbed, you mean? Somebody who could recognize you?"

"Somebody that could recognize me, all right. Not somebody we robbed. Not hardly."

"*Scratch fever…Cat scratch…*"

"Somebody that was in it with you," she said.

"Right."

"So?"

"So it was somebody that was supposed to have died in a car crash, a year ago."

"Jesus. What's *that* mean?"

"It means…I don't know what it means."

"Maybe your friend would. Nolan."

"Maybe."

"You thinking about calling him?"

"Yeah. I am."

"You better do it on the break. Those assholes are almost finished 'making pussies purr.' "

Out in the other room, on stage, the trio was doing its big finish, which amounted to lots of sliding up and down on the bass neck for Les, some horrible high squealing lead up on the neck of the Gibson Explorer for Roc, and a frantic series of trips around the drum kit for Mick.

"Let me have a sip of that," Jon said, nodding at her whiskey bottle.

"You never touch this shit," Toni said, unscrewing the cap again.

"I know," Jon said, taking the bottle, swigging it. "But Nolan does."

Soon they were back on stage doing a song called "Die Young, Stay Pretty."

2

It was that kid, it was that goddamn kid!

Dammit!

What the hell was *he* doing here, playing in a rock band, for Christ's sake? His curly hair was shorter, but otherwise he hadn't changed; it was him, all right. Standing behind a portable organ, singing some unintelligible lyrics into a microphone, his voice booming out of the PA system.

The ironic thing was that it was this band—the Nodes—that had brought her here. She had heard the group was breaking up after this engagement, which meant they wouldn't have anything booked for the following week, which meant hopefully she could convince them to stay together long enough to play Tuesday through Saturday at her club, the Paddlewheel. She'd had a cancellation and needed a band, and this group, the Nodes, while not precisely the sort of group she usually booked in, had a reputation in the Midwest. So she'd come to hear them, and to talk to the leader.

Whose name, it turned out, was Jon.

"Yeah," Bob Hale said, as they sat at the bar on one side of the dance floor, yelling to be heard above the band, "it's that kid on the end, playing the organ."

She had looked at the kid, and he immediately seemed familiar to her.

"Nice enough kid," Bob was saying. He was a big, florid man in his forties, with reddish-brown hair and a childlike manner that gave him a certain immature charm. "You wouldn't know it to look at the squirt, but he's strong. Judas Priest, you should see him carry those amplifiers around, like they was pillows. The girls seem to go for him."

"Do they."

"Sure do." Bob grinned at her; he had big teeth. "Get you a drink, honey?"

"What did you say his name was?"

"Jon. I don't know what his last name is."

"Jon."

"Yeah. They're booked out of Des Moines. Or they were. Like I said, this is supposed to be their last night. But maybe I could talk to 'em for you and convince 'em that…"

She didn't hear anything else Bob said after that; she was walking away. Before that kid on stage got a good look at her.

Not that it mattered, at this point; she'd seen the flash of recognition—or *something*—on his face. He shouldn't have been able to recognize her, not at that distance; not with the blonde-streaked hair, the glasses, the businesslike suit and sweater she'd worn. But the feeling in her stomach said he *had* recognized her. Goddammit. God*damm*it!

Now she was out in the bar that connected the restaurant and club, which, like the rest of the Barn, was rustic—lots of rough barnwood decorated with an occasional horse-collar mirror and bogus wanted posters with Bob Hale's name and face on them. There were booths with baskets of peanuts and popcorn on either side of the dimly lit room, enclosed on three sides and affording enough privacy for people to sit and neck if they liked. Several couples were doing that now, and there were a few people sitting up at the bar, but otherwise the action at the Barn was clearly in where the Nodes were playing, rather obnoxiously, she thought. Which made her smile, and the smile felt like cement cracking. *If they play loud shit like that*, she thought, *I wouldn't have hired them anyway.*

She was sitting in a booth. The man she'd come with, Harold, looked over from the bar, where he was nursing a Scotch and water.

Harold was a big man, even though he stood only five-eight. He had the shoulders and thick arms, big hands, of a football player, specifically a guard, which was the position he'd played in high school and college, before he dropped out. His face, however, was surprisingly sensitive: heavy-lidded gray eyes behind black-rimmed glasses; a bulbous, flat-bridged nose that had never been broken; a full-lipped, sensual mouth, kept wet by nervous licking.

He came over to her. He was wearing a tan suit with a dark tie; his hair, a sandy brown, was thinning on top and cut short on the sides. He looked like a high school football coach who quit to sell insurance; but what he was was her business partner, co-manager of the Paddlewheel, their club in Gulf Port.

"What's wrong?" Harold said. He had a soft, hoarse voice.

"Sit down," she said.

Harold had left his Scotch and water behind; he sat across from her, hands folded. He licked his lips. He had that look she hated: the look as if he were about to cry.

"I should've gone to fucking Brazil," she said. She was sitting shelling peanuts but not eating them.

"I see."

"Give me one good reason why I should ever have gone back to you."

"Okay. I love you."

"Shut up."

"What's wrong?"

"Nothing. Nothing I can't handle."

"I see."

"Do you?"

"I think so."

"Tell me, then."

"You saw somebody. Somebody who knew you, before."

"How could you know that?" She never failed to be surprised by the big jerk's perceptiveness.

"It was bound to happen," he said with a shrug, hands still folded, "sooner or later. We're not that far from where you lived before."

She tore the shell off a peanut, rubbed the skin off the nut within. Added it to the little pile she was making.

"You should leave," he was saying. "Have you spoken to this person?"

"No."

"Then you should leave. Leave while he or she still is wondering whether it was you or not. It's that simple."

She threw a shell at him. "It's *not* that simple. God, you make me sick sometimes."

"Who is it? Who recognized you?"

"A kid in the band."

"A kid in the band?"

"A kid in the band. Remember the guy Logan I told you about?"

Logan was the name she knew Nolan by.

"Of course I remember."

"That kid in there, the organ player, that's Jon."

"Logan's partner."

"That's right."

"Who was in on the Port City thing."

"Right."

"I see."

"Quit saying that!"

"All right. What do you want me to do?"

"Go in there and see which kid I mean. Go in and get a look

at him. He's the short kid with curly hair and a good build."

"Okay."

"Then come back and sit in this booth and watch the door."
The double doors between the bar and dance area were just a
few feet away. "If he comes out and tries to use that pay phone
during the band's break, stop him."

"How?"

"Just do it. But don't come on like a strongarm. Say you're
expecting a call or something."

"All right. Then what?"

"Then nothing. Just keep an eye on him, when he isn't on
stage. The band only has one more break. They're playing their
third set now, which means they have one more set to play."

"After that, what happens?"

"We'll deal with that when the time comes."

"How?"

"However we have to."

He reached for the ashtray and with one thick hand brushed
the pile of peanuts and shells she'd been making into it. Then
he reached out and touched her hand. Held it.

"I don't kill people, Julie," he said softly. Eyes and lips wet.

"I know you don't."

"I'll do anything for you but that."

"I know you will."

"Anything."

"I know."

"But if it comes to…if it comes to that, I don't even want to
know about it."

She smiled at him sweetly, squeezed his hand, thinking,
*Fucking hypocrite! You don't care if somebody else does the
killing, though, do you? Just so you don't have to do it; just so
you don't have to know about it.*

She let go of his hand. "Give me some change. I have a long-distance call to make."

He half-stood in the booth, dug for some change, and gave it to her.

"Who are you calling?"

She got out of the booth. "You just stay put."

He licked his lips and nodded, then reached for the basket of peanuts.

She went over to the pay phone and dialed a number in Illinois direct.

It rang six times, then a slurry baritone voice came on, saying, "Yeah, what?"

"Ron?"

"Yeah."

"This is Julie."

"I know it is."

"I need you."

"Do you?"

"I have a problem."

"No kidding."

"I'm serious, Ron."

"So you're serious. I ain't heard from you in three weeks, and you're serious."

"I'm sorry. I really am."

"Why should I be surprised you're in trouble? You only come to me when you're in trouble."

"That isn't so."

"You only come to me when there's some shit job that old numb-nuts Harold won't do for you."

"Ron, you have to come here right away."

"Where's 'here'?"

"The Barn. Outside of Burlington."

"Yeah, I know the place. They got good rock 'n' roll there sometimes. Isn't this the Nodes' last weekend? That's a good band. Better than the shit you book in, anyway."

"Ron. This is serious."

"Yeah, okay. I can hear it in your voice, it's serious. Do I need to bring anything?"

"I think so."

"That serious, huh? It'll cost you."

"Money's no problem."

"Who's talking about money?"

"Ron. I'll make this worth it for you. I promise."

"Yeah, okay. I'm on my way."

The phone clicked dead.

She shivered and hung up.

She went back to the booth and sat across from Harold, who was eating peanuts, slowly, methodically.

"Ron's coming," she said.

"I see," he said. He pushed the basket of peanuts aside.

"Well, I can't depend on *you*, can I? If something ugly has to happen, Ron'll be up to it."

"How can you…"

"Because I have to," she said, biting off the words. "I'm supposed to be dead, goddammit…I ended up with $750,000 because Logan and Jon *thought* I was dead. If that kid gets to his friend with the news that I'm alive, that S.O.B.'ll come looking for me, *and* his money."

"I could handle him."

She laughed. "You couldn't handle Ron."

"Don't make fun of me, Julie."

"Harold, I'm sorry. You just don't know this guy Logan. He's like something out of a Mafia movie. Really scary."

"You've got money, Julie. Give him his share."

"He wouldn't be satisfied with just his share."

"Why not?"

"He's a killer. He tried to kill me, once, remember?" That was a lie, of course; it had been the other way around, but Harold didn't know that.

Harold was balling those thick hands into fists the size of softballs. "If he tries to hurt you, I'll…"

"What? What will you do? You don't kill people, remember?"

They could hear the muffled blare of the band in the other room: *"Scratch fever…Cat scratch…"*

"That would be different," he said.

"Would it?"

"You know it would."

"We'll let Ron handle it."

"But who'll handle Ron?"

"I will."

"Good luck."

She could handle Ron, all right, but the price was high: letting those hands rove across her body; letting those lips do what they wanted to. Sharing a bed with Harold was bad enough. Getting in bed with Ron was flat-out disgusting.

And, deep down, she was afraid of Ron. She was afraid of few human beings on this earth, but Ron was one of them.

But then, so was the man she knew as Logan.

The last song of the third set was "19th Nervous Breakdown," an old Stones song that Jon sang, and that tonight he was really identifying with.

He came down off the stage covered with sweat—not from nervousness: he was always wringing wet by the end of a set—and headed for the stage-right cubby hole behind the fake storefront, where he and Toni had spoken earlier. He grabbed a towel from the stack the Nodes always brought along with them. He wiped his face with it, rubbed his hair. Took off his shirt and ran the towel over his chest and back and arms, then put on a clean shirt. He went through at least three a night, and his sportcoat was always sopping by the end of the first set, discarded midway through the second. He worked hard at rock 'n' roll.

So did Toni, but she didn't seem to sweat at all. She stood in the doorway of the little room, leaning against the jamb, perverted pixie smile on her face. "How you doin'?" she asked him.

"Okay." Jon smiled back.

She came in and reached behind the amp and drum cases for her bottle of Cutty Sark. "Still got that old girlfriend on your mind?"

"Yeah."

She unscrewed the cap, swigged at the bottle. "Really sure it was her, are you?"

"I don't know. Maybe it wasn't."

Toni put the Cutty Sark away and took him by the arm. "Let's go have a look around."

Jon and Toni went out into the club and walked onto the dance floor. Les, Roc, and Mick were at a table, huddled together, making plans for the next incarnation of their band. The two factions of the Nodes didn't even exchange glances.

Their sound man/roadie, a twenty-year-old ex-DJ named Tommy, approached Jon and Toni. He looked like a pudgy, slightly dense Paul McCartney; he wore jeans and a T-shirt with the band's logo on it—THE NODES—in Art Deco lettering.

"Good set," Tommy told them, smiling and nodding, on his way to join the Les, Roc, Mick faction, of which he was a part. Since he got his paychecks from Jon, however, Tommy stayed civil where Jon and Toni were concerned.

From the back of the hall, where the stage was, to the other end was nearly the length of a football field, and Jon and Toni were stopped a dozen times as they walked along the edge of the dance floor, by the crowded tables. The Nodes had played the Barn three times before, and had a following here; word had gotten around that this was the band's last night, and the fans were complaining.

A table of girls who had all gotten in on fake I.D.'s grabbed at Jon as he passed; arms, hands reached out for him, like *Night of the Living Dead*, only pretty.

"You can't break up," a little blonde in a red satin warm-up jacket and Clash T-shirt said. She had him by the arm.

A pudgy but cute brunette in a blue satin warm-up jacket and T-shirt that said "Wanna Party?" had him by the leg; she was saying something too, but Jon couldn't make it out.

Two guys dressed like urban cowboys (and looking ridiculous, Jon thought, probably a couple of high school teachers who ditched their wives for the night) were standing talking to Toni, saying much the same thing the girls were saying to Jon, but without the touching. Relations between men and women may have changed, Jon noted, but it was still the women who did the touching without permission.

Bob Hale was still sitting on a stool over at the bar, stage right. Jon pulled away from the table of girls and went over to him, leaving Toni behind with her admirers in cowboy hats.

Bob extended a big, rough hand, which Jon shook.

"We're gonna miss you boys," Bob said. Considering the way Bob was always pursuing Toni, it was amazing he had included her as one of the "boys." Then, with a conspiratorial wink, Bob leaned in and said, "No other band pulls in the pussy like you guys." Bob was grinning like a junior-high kid who'd just discovered *Hustler* magazine.

"I appreciate that, Bob," Jon said, sitting on the stool next to him. "You know, the other guys in the band'll still be together, under another name."

"I don't give a shit about those guys. They play too fuckin' loud. It's you and little Toni that go over. The pussies like *you*, and the guys go for *her*."

That was nice to hear, and was true enough, but Roc, Mick, and Les had a following, too. But Jon went along with Bob, saying, "Well, Toni and I may have a new band ourselves in a while."

"You just give me a call when you do, and you got a booking."

"Thanks, I will. Say, Bob. Who was that good-looking blonde you were talking to?"

"You'll have to narrow 'er down," Bob said, grinning even wider; he was the kind of person who could make a caricature out of himself without trying. "I talked to half a dozen good-looking blondes tonight already."

"This one is old enough to be in here legally."

"Yeah, but is she old enough for me to be in her legally?"

"She was about thirty, wearing a white jacket and dress, black sweater. Nice tits."

"Oh, yeah, her. She'll never drown."

"Right, well, I didn't get a good look at her from the stage. Aw, but you know how it is, Bob. Sometimes the closer you get…"

"The worse they look! Damn if that ain't the truth."

"How does this one look, close up?"

"Well she ain't a ten."

"No?"

"She's a thirteen."

"No kidding. Who is she? Do you know her?"

"Yeah, I know her. Wish I could say I could fix you up with her, but I never been able to get anywhere with her myself, believe it or not. That's a high-class cunt. She's got money."

"Really?"

"Yeah. Name's Julie something. She runs a place called the Paddlewheel, near Gulf Port."

"Illinois, you mean? Across from Burlington?"

Gulf Port was a wide-open little town where the bars stayed open all night. When clubs on the Iowa side shut down at two, the "Wanna Party?" die-hards headed for Gulf Port.

"Right," Bob said. "Quite a place. Big gambling layout and everything."

"You're shitting me."

"I wouldn't shit a shitter. Little Las Vegas, they call it. You oughta see the place. Maybe you will—she wanted to talk to you about that, in fact."

"This Julie did?"

"Yeah. She needs a band. Somebody cancelled out on her. She was hoping you guys might want one last job, 'fore you call it quits."

"No kidding. Well, maybe I ought to talk to her."

"That's the funny part. She was asking me about the band—asked about you, in particular—then she just walked away. I wasn't even through talking yet."

Jon smiled at Bob; inside his head sirens were going off and red lights were flashing. "Well, be honest, Bob—when are you ever through talking?"

"Ain't that the truth," Bob said, and slapped the bar, and drinks all down the line spilled a little.

Jon thanked Bob and went back to Toni, pulling her away from her admirers.

"I was right," he said, taking her by the arm.

"About what?"

"It was who I thought it was."

"The woman?"

"Yes." And he told her what Bob had told him.

"So what now?"

"Now I call Nolan."

The pay phone was in the bar, on the wall around the corner from the pinball machines. He got change from the bartender. Toni was right with him.

"Do you have this guy's number?" she asked.

"Yeah. I memorized it."

"Memorized it?"

"In case something like this came up."

"Oh."

He had the receiver up to his ear and the coins poised to drop, when a hand settled on his shoulder, like a UFO landing. It was a hand that made Bob Hale's hand seem dainty.

Jon turned and looked at a guy just a few inches taller than he was but infinitely bigger. A sandy-haired man with sad grey eyes behind dark-rimmed glasses, and shoulders you had to look at one at a time.

"Excuse me," the man said. He licked his lips.

"Yeah?"

"I'm waiting for an important call."

"My call won't take long."

"I'd appreciate it if you'd not use the phone."

It wasn't a threat, exactly; the tone was rather kind—*Please do me a favor*. But the favor was being asked by a man who looked like the son of Kong in a business suit.

"Look," Jon said, "this is a public phone. You can't keep people from using it."

Which was a ridiculous thing to say. This guy could obviously keep people from using the phone. He could keep the state of Iowa from using the phone.

"I have a sick kid," the man said. Softly. "I'm waiting to hear about my sick kid."

Toni spoke up. "What the fuck are you doing here, then?"

Jon raised a hand to quiet her. "It's okay, Toni." He smiled at the guy. "It's no emergency on my end, mister. You can wait for your call. Be my guest."

Toni stood with fists on hips and glared at Jon, who pulled her away from there by the arm.

"Jon, why are you letting that asshole…"

"Shut up," Jon said, and took her back into the club.

He pulled her off into another of the cubbyhole rooms behind the storefronts; a couple was making out in this one, so Jon dragged her into the cubbyhole next door. She was fuming.

"Why d'you go along with that bullshit?" she demanded.

"I think somebody told him not to let me use the phone."

Toni thought about that.

"Look," he said. "I got to find out if that woman is still around. My guess is she split, but if she's still around, maybe I could corner her or something. I don't know."

"What good'll that do?"

"Maybe I can avoid a violent confrontation. I know how this woman's mind works. She'll figure if Nolan finds out she's alive, he'll come looking for her."

"Is she right?"

"Yeah."

"So what good does talking to her do?"

"I'll lie. I'll tell her Nolan's dead or in prison or something. That she has nothing to worry about from him."

"But what about from you?"

"I'll tell her I don't give a damn, personally, about her or the money she took."

"Is that true?"

"No."

"Well, let's go look for her, then."

They went back out through the bar, and noticed that the sandy-haired guy was sitting in a booth near the double doors to the club area, well around the corner from the pay phone, not an ideal place for somebody waiting for a call. Jon looked at him with a smile and a silent question, and he looked back and shook his head no, indicating that the call hadn't come yet. Jon shrugged at him, smiled again, and walked on with Toni.

Around the corner, a drunk in overalls was leaning against the wall, talking on the phone, slobbering at the receiver.

Jon said, "Looks like I'm the only one the worried papa wants to keep off the phone."

He and Toni casually walked through the bar and up through the restaurant, both floors of it, and the woman with streaked blonde hair and tinted glasses wasn't there.

"Either she split," Jon said, "or she's outside, ducking me. In her car in the parking lot, maybe."

"You want to go looking for her?"

"Not in a dark parking lot."

"You're not scared of her?"

"Of course I am."

"Why?"

"She almost killed me once. With a shotgun."

"Oh." Toni swallowed and followed Jon back into the club, where they immediately headed for Bob Hale, still perched at the stage-right bar.

"Bob," Jon said, putting a good-buddy hand on the big man's shoulder, "some drunk is tying up the pay phone."

"Well," Bob said, smiling, hauling himself off the stool, "let's kick his ass off, then."

"No, no. Listen, I have a kind of private call I'd like to make. Can I use the phone in your apartment?"

Bob grinned at Jon, then at Toni, then back at Jon. "You two can use my apartment for anything you want, if I can watch."

Toni laughed—a little tensely, but she laughed. She liked Bob, Jon knew. Considered him harmless, a teddy bear with a hard-on.

"No, really," Jon said, "I need to use the phone. How about it?"

"Sure," Bob said, and led them back around the bar to a hallway. They followed him down it.

Bob lived at the Barn. So did a German Shepherd about the same size as Jon. It stayed in the bedroom Bob kept, on the lower floor of the barn part of the Barn, in the rear, a bedroom Bob referred to as his apartment.

Bob unlocked the door, and the dog began to growl. It sounded like Mount St. Helen's thinking it over. Bob reached a hand down and grabbed the dog by the collar and pulled him away from the doorway, back into the bedroom. The dog was still growling, but that only made Bob laugh. Amid the laughter, he gave the dog a sharp command, and the dog sat, teeth bared, Rin Tin Tin with rabies. If Bob hadn't been there, Jon and/or Toni would have been dead by now.

It was a big, messy room: plush red carpeting with under-wear, shirts, other clothing carelessly wadded and tossed; a queen-size canopy waterbed with red satin sheets and black plush covers over at the right. No rough barn wood here: dark paneling, with built-in closet. At the near end was a bookcase wall with no books in it, just thousands of dollars' worth of stereo equipment, as well as a 19-inch Sony with videotape deck, and a library of XXX tapes.

Also the phone, which Bob handed Jon as he marched the dog out into the hall, closing the door as he went. Toni stood and watched as Jon touch-toned Nolan's number.

On the third ring, he heard Nolan's voice: "This is Nolan."

"Nolan! Listen…"

"You're talking to a machine. Leave your message at the beep."

Jon just looked at the phone.

"What's wrong?" Toni said.

"An answer machine," he said. "Now I've heard everything. Nolan's got an answer phone! I don't believe this."

The phone said, *beep*.

Jon left his message, Bob locked his dog back in the bedroom, and they all went back into the club, where Jon and Toni headed for the stage.

For the last set.

4

When she blew the words on "Heartbreaker," Toni *knew* she was scared.

Certainly not stage fright—she'd been singing with rock bands since junior high—but some *other* kind of scared, something in her stomach that was far worse than butterflies.

Something cold.

Something alive.

Fear.

When the song was finished, she rushed over to Jon and whispered, "Fill in with something. I need a few minutes."

Jon nodded, and away from the mike, stage-whispered to Les, Roc, and Mick to "forget the list—do 'Light My Fire' next," a song Toni didn't do anything on, which would give her a chance to take a break.

She stood inside the cubbyhole room stage right as the band went into the old Doors classic, Jon doing right by the elaborate pseudo-baroque organ break at the beginning. She was breathing hard. She wanted a smoke. She'd given it up two years ago and rarely had felt the urge since the first hard months, but now she wanted a smoke. She went out and bummed one off Tommy, the roadie, sitting at his sound board halfway down the dance floor, over stage left. Then she returned to the cubbyhole, sucking in smoke as if it was food and she was starving.

Mick was singing. He didn't sing very well, and in fact was incurably flat, but the Doors tune lent itself to that: the late Jim Morrison was known for many things, but singing on key wasn't one of them. Then the band went into the instrumental section of the song, Jon taking the organ solo, a sing-song thing that climbed the scale in mindless little would-be Bach progressions.

She wondered if that big sandy-haired guy—Jesus, was he big—was still in his booth, waiting for his mythical phone call. She decided to find out. She'd have plenty of time; this song went on for nearly ten minutes. She wandered back through the club, nodding as fans touched her arm and made comments about the sad fact that the Nodes were splitting, and then she was in the bar, where the big sandy-haired guy was sitting in the booth, talking intensely with a woman.

A woman in white with a black cardigan and tinted glasses and a beautiful face and—even seated in a booth it was obvious—a beautiful body.

Suddenly the cigarette was burning her throat. *I knew there was a reason I quit these fucking things*, she thought, and went up to the bar and put the cig out in an ashtray up from the bottom of which a little picture of Bob Hale stared. Standing next to her at the bar were two young women.

Toni had seen these women before; they had been to hear the Nodes at the Ramp in Burlington a few months ago, part of a group of half a dozen hard, hoody-looking bitches, one of whom had been attracted to Jon, and vice versa. She was one of the two at the bar, a lanky brunette about nineteen, in jeans and jeans jacket and a Nodes T-shirt; lots of eye makeup, and smoking a cigarette.

The other woman was in her early twenties, medium height, boyish build—nothing remarkable, other than the close-set beady eyes, the lump of a nose, the thick lips with permanent, humorless sneer, the dishwater blonde hair greased back in a ducktail, the black leather jacket and red T-shirt and jeans, cigarette dangling from the Presleyesque lips, a hand on the other girl's shoulder.

Toni couldn't remember their names, but she did remember that the night Jon and the brunette had spent a break in the band's van, the beauty with the ducktail had come up and smiled at Jon during the next break and, cleaning her nails with a switchblade, told Jon if he ever touched Darlene (*that* was the first girl's name; what was the second one's?) again, she would cut his balls off and hang 'em over her rearview mirror. Jon hadn't argued with her. He'd tried to make a joke out of it later, about what a cornball creep that dyke was, doing her Sha Na Na routine. But it hadn't come off: Jon knew the dyke had meant what she said.

Terrific, Toni thought. It wasn't enough somebody shows up from the part of Jon's past that included that thief Nolan; the dyke and Darlene had to turn up, too. Wonderful.

She ducked back into the club. Jon was still playing his organ solo, getting ready to let Roc take over on guitar.

"Light My Fire"—the baroque opening, anyway—had been the first thing she'd ever heard Jon play on the organ. She'd been in a music store in Iowa City—the Sound Pit—looking at PA equipment with some of those jerks in her old band, Dagwood, and Jon was playing a Crumar portable organ, asking the clerk if he knew anywhere he could find an old Vox Super Continental. The clerk was trying to sell Jon a Moog synthesizer, telling him *nobody* played combo organ anymore, and Jon was saying, "Bullshit, the punk and new wave bands are *all* using old Vox and Farfisas."

When she heard that she knew she'd found a kindred spirit. She started up a conversation with him, and soon they were having a drink at the Mill, a bar in downtown Iowa City, and then they were in bed at his apartment, or anyway the room he kept on the bottom floor of the antique shop he'd inherited from his uncle, a shop that had been closed since the uncle's death.

Rock 'n' roll, it seemed, was not Jon's first love. He lived in a cartoonist's studio, with drawing board, boxes of comic books, posters of comic strip characters like Dick Tracy and Batman and Tarzan, some framed original strips, making a gray-walled, cement-floored former storeroom a four-color shrine to comic art. Even the finely carved antique headboard of the bed they were in had some drawings tacked to it—Jon's own work, and good work it was, at that.

"Are you a musician or a cartoonist or what?" she'd asked him, letting the sheet fall to her waist as she turned to look at his drawings; she liked her breasts and liked having him look at them as she looked at his art.

"I don't know if I'm either anymore," he said. He was sitting up in bed with a pillow propped behind him. His chest was almost completely hairless, she noted.

"What do you mean by that?"

"I've been at this cartooning shit for as long as I can remember."

"Oh, and you're all of twenty."

"Twenty-one. I'd guess that's about how old you are, too. And I bet you aren't finding rock 'n' roll an easy life, either."

"You're right," she admitted. "I been at it eight years, and it's a hard go, even if you're good at it, and I am."

"Yeah, well, I'm good at cartooning and I'm not making it."

"It's hard to make it in any of the arts."

"No kidding. Oh, I've had a couple of things published in the undergrounds. Ever hear of *Bizarre Sex*?"

She smiled. "Try me."

"That's the name of an underground comic. I've done a couple of science fiction parody things for 'em. Doesn't pay much."

"It's a start."

"But it isn't a career. I don't know. I don't have much interest in commercial art, and the comic book field doesn't appeal to me; the pay sucks and they're doing the same old superhero junk, only badly."

"What about a newspaper comic strip?"

"Landing a syndicated strip is almost impossible, particularly if you don't do humor, which I don't."

"I thought you said you did two parodies for that underground comic."

"Yeah, but I doubt many newspapers would want to carry 'Dildos in Space.' "

"You may have a point. So where does music come in?"

"What do you mean?"

"I heard you play the organ. You're good."

"Aw, that's nothing serious with me. I played off and on with some bands when I was in junior high and high school. I don't think I could make a living at it. And I'm not sure I'd want to, if I could."

"Why?"

"My mother was in 'show biz,' and she had a shitty life, playing piano and singing in bars, on the road all the time, dreaming of being on Ed Sullivan someday, only he's dead now, and so is she."

"Do you have any kids?"

"Kids? Me? Hell, no."

"Then you wouldn't be doing anybody a disservice leaving 'em behind when you went on the road, would you? If that's what your problem is."

He thought about that a while. Then he said, "What kind of band would I be in? I hate disco. I hate country rock. I hate heavy metal. There isn't much I could stand to play, except old sixties stuff and maybe some of the new wave music coming out of England and the East Coast."

And that had been the beginning of it. She had told him

about her mock-Blondie band, Dagwood, which she wanted out of, and together they made plans to launch what became the Nodes. She knew about Roc, Mick, and Les, and they all got together in a friend's garage and jammed through some material, and two weeks later they had relocated in Des Moines, to be with the booking agency that had handled the now-defunct Dagwood.

Leaving Iowa City for Des Moines seemed to be slightly rough for Jon. He didn't say much about it but he was apparently very close to this guy Nolan, though they seemed to have had a minor falling-out of some kind lately, which made it easier for Jon to leave. So he said, anyway.

She had only seen this Nolan a few times. Actually, he seemed to be using the name Logan, but Jon always referred to him as Nolan. She didn't know if Nolan had ever even noticed her, really; to him she was probably just some twat Jon was shacking up with. They'd never exchanged a word.

But she had noticed him, all right. Looked him over good.

He was handsome, in an ugly way. A big, lean man with the slightest paunch, with dark, somewhat shaggy hair that was graying at the temples, and widow's peaked. He had high cheekbones, a mustache, and a mean look, but those eyes, those narrow, squinting eyes, had something else in them besides meanness. Intelligence, for sure. Humanity? Humor? Maybe not.

At the time, Nolan had been running some sort of restaurant in Iowa City, in which Jon was a partner, it seemed, though he didn't say much about that. When she saw Nolan, he'd be dressed in a sportcoat and turtleneck and slacks, something casual, in a country club sort of way, and the guy looked good, looked right. Only something was wrong; something about him made her think of a gangster.

She used to kid Jon about that.

"I wonder what your gangster friend's doing right now," she'd say, sitting up in bed in a motel room, watching TV, on the road with the Nodes.

"Probably sticking up a bank," Jon would answer, with a funny smile.

She and Jon had continued to share a room on the road, even though their romance had turned into a friendship, albeit a friendship that included sleeping together (but only occasionally screwing) and getting out of each other's way when an attractive member of the opposite sex came along. She had a feeling Jon could have been serious about her if she let him, but her insistence that she was not a one-man woman, that marriage and whatever were not in her plans *ever*, cooled him off a bit.

And he did seem to like the freedom to go after the bitches, like that Darlene she'd spotted out in the bar. Jon was a weird kid, in a way, so goddamn straight. He didn't even smoke dope —no drugs at all; no booze to speak of, either.

There was that one time, however, that he got good and plastered. It was at a party at some trailer out in the country, where a guy had a hog roast at three in the morning after the Nodes had played a particularly long night at a particularly rowdy bar. The girl Jon was with, a short little blonde in halter top and jeans, was the sort who wanted to drink but would not drink alone, and so Jon drank with her and later crawled off into the woods with her, too. But by the time he ended up back at the motel with Toni, he was plastered—plastered in the way that only someone who doesn't get plastered often can get plastered. And he started to talk.

And he told her the damnedest things.

About him and Nolan.

And bank robberies and shooting somebody called Sam Comfort, some crazy old man who was a thief himself who Jon and Nolan were looting, and wild goddamn things about some girl getting her head blown off by somebody called Gross, and shoot-outs in lodges up in Wisconsin. And the next morning Jon asked her to forget all that stuff he told her last night, and there had never been a word about it since.

Till tonight.

"Light My Fire" was almost over.

She got back up on stage, and Jon gave her a little smile and she gave him one back, nodding, and they went into the next song.

Playing tambourine and singing back-up, she glanced over at Jon, and he was into the music—not a sign of worry. And she felt better. Jon had left a message for Nolan, and the woman in white and her big sandy-haired stooge didn't know that. And that made Toni feel better; the cold feeling at the pit of her stomach was gone.

Then she noticed Jon flubbing the words on "Jailhouse Rock."

And at the back of the room, standing by the double doors, the big sandy-haired man waited and watched.

5

They got called back for two encores. One encore was typical for the Nodes; they were good enough to expect that. A second encore indicated to Jon that the word had spread through the crowd that this was the band's last night.

Some of Roc's followers were shouting for "Cat Scratch Fever" again, and even though Jon and Toni weren't featured on it, making it inappropriate for an encore, Jon went ahead and announced it and went off with Toni into the stage-right cubbyhole to wait it out.

"*That* fucking thing again," Toni said, shaking her head. Still not sweating.

"No accounting for taste," Jon said, smiling back.

"We better do one more and put this turkey out of its misery."

Jon nodded. "You okay?"

"I think so. I blew some words."

"I know you did. That's not like you."

"Yeah, well, I started thinking about the words, and that's deadly. As soon as you start thinking about 'em, you lose 'em."

"Right I blew a few myself. Lots of hamburger tonight."

Hamburger was garbled singing with the mouth right up against the mike, sounding like words but not words at all.

"Jon, that big guy's still hanging around. When I took that little break midway through the set, he was still sitting in his booth. Then he came and stood in back and watched for a while."

"Yeah, I know. I saw him."

"Yeah, well, your girlfriend was there, too."

"No kidding?"

"The one with the white outfit and the big tits? Yeah. Still here. Or she was twenty minutes ago, anyway."

"Jesus. So she didn't split."

"Nope. Somebody else was out there, too."

"Who?"

"Darlene."

"Who the fuck's Darlene?"

"You mean, which fuck's Darlene, don't you? Burlington, a couple of months ago? The Ramp? Lanky with brown hair and lots of eye makeup?"

"I think I remember."

"Had a dyke girlfriend who wanted to cut your nuts off?"

"I remember."

"Well, she's out there, too, cuter than Rod Stewart's mom. What's that dyke's name, anyway?"

"I don't remember."

"Me either. So, Jonny. Tonight's a real stroll down memory lane, for you, huh? Maybe they're all here 'cause it's the Nodes' last night."

"Maybe."

"Are you scared?"

"A little."

"Yeah. Me too. I'd take another hit of Cutty Sark if I thought I could keep it down. What should we do?"

"Get back on stage and play one more song, I guess." They did—"Johnny B. Goode" by Chuck Berry.

And it was the last song the Nodes ever played together, because the audience was too worn out and drunk to work up the applause for another encore, and Jon and Toni and the rest of the band came down off the stage and mingled with the crowd, as the Barn would be open for another half-hour before the lights would come up and the band's equipment would get torn down. The jukebox started up and an Olivia Newton-John record came on, a mild protest by someone not into the Nodes' brand of hard-core rock 'n' roll. Couples slow danced. Singles who hadn't scored shuffled toward exits, looking around one last time to see if somebody was left to come onto.

First order of business at the end of a performance was getting paid, and since Jon was listed as leader on the union contract Bob Hale had signed, it was Jon who followed Bob back behind the bar again, through a hallway and into a small office. Bob paid Jon in cash, shook his hand, reminded him to keep in touch if he and Toni put another band together, and went back to the table out in the club where a short-haired brunette waitress with a slender figure and a tired, pretty face waited to be the queen of Bob's waterbed this winter night.

Usually Jon waited till later to pay off the band members, but tonight he gathered them in the stage-right cubbyhole and gave them their shares, holding back his one-and-a-half shares (he owned the PA equipment and van and so got an extra half-share) as well as the agent's commission. These five people had worked and lived together for some seven months, and despite their differences, this was an awkward if not exactly poignant moment. Roc scratched the side of his narrow, faintly pockmarked face; he had some eye makeup on, which had always looked silly to Jon before. Now, for some unknown reason, Jon felt touched by the guitarist's show-bizzy affectation, out here in the Iowa sticks.

Roc extended his hand, and he and Jon—the two strong ones in the group, whose conflicting tastes had made this split inevitable—shook hands in a sideways, "soul" shake.

"It's been real," Roc (whose real name was Arnold) said, with a small, embarrassed smile.

"It's been real," Jon agreed, giving him back the same kind of smile.

There was a brief round of handshakes; the boys, except for Jon, each gave Toni a hug. Mick advised her to "watch the sauce—it'll catch up with you someday," and she advised him to "watch that dope you smoke or you'll wake up even dumber some morning," and they all laughed.

"We're not going to tear our stuff down tonight," Roc told Jon. "Bob said we could come back tomorrow and do it."

"I figured as much," Jon said. He knew that they planned to rent a trailer to haul their amps and guitars away. Usually the band traveled in two vehicles: Jon's van, with all the major equipment and room for two riders (invariably, Jon and Toni) and Roc's station wagon, which held the other band members and a few odds and ends of equipment

"We'll help take the PA and mikes down, of course," Mick added. "Help you load your organ and stuff, if you want."

"I appreciate it," Jon said, and everyone left the little cubbyhole and wandered out onto the dance floor, where the lights had just come up, bringing the usual groans and moans from the crowd, who, like a mole caught in the headlights of a car, preferred the dark.

"What now?" Toni asked Jon.

"I think I'll see if the phone's free."

"You already left your message, didn't you?"

"Yeah. But I'd like to see if I can get through to Nolan, and not his machine. I'd also like to see if Julie and the Incredible Hulk are still around."

They walked toward the outer bar.

"What if they are?" Toni asked.

"If Julie's here, I want to talk to her. Like I said, maybe I can defuse this thing. If that guy's still around and she isn't, I'm curious to see if he'll let me use the phone."

"And if he won't?"

"I'll talk to Bob. He's got a dog and a shotgun."

They entered the bar; people were getting one last drink, but the booths on either side were empty—nothing but moisture rings and ashtrays full of peanut shells.

No Julie.

No Hulk.

"Let's look around some more," Jon said.

"Like outside?"

"Like outside."

They went out on the wooden sidewalk that ran in front of the building. The night was cold; they could see their breath. It was November and it hadn't snowed yet. People were getting into their frost-frosted cars, most of the couples hanging onto each other, some because they were drunk, others because they were horny, and in a lot of cases both. No sign of Julie or her Hulk.

"Let's go back in," Jon suggested, and they did.

They took a booth.

"I don't know what to make of this," he said. "I know she spotted me. Shit."

"You got word through to your friend," Toni said, sounding as though she were trying to convince herself as much as Jon. "Why worry about it?"

"What, me worry? Look, let's go tear down the stuff and get the van loaded; the guys'll help us, and maybe Bob and his people'll pitch in, and we can get it done fast and head for Nolan's."

"Maybe he's already on his way here."

"You got a point. I'll try him again."

He went to the phone. He had a dime poised to drop in the slot when a hand rested on his shoulder. Not a big hand this time, but a smaller, softer one.

He turned and looked at Darlene, whom he suddenly

remembered very well. Her long brown hair was in a sixties shag, and she did have lots of eye makeup (even more than Roc); she reminded him of Chrissie Hynde, of the Pretenders. A smiling, skinny girl, taller than he was, with pert little breasts bobbling under a Nodes T-shirt; he couldn't remember that logo of his looking better.

She stroked his bare arm; he was wearing only a T-shirt, now, himself, also a Nodes T-shirt. She poked at the design on his chest, traced it with her finger.

"We look like twins," she said.

"Not quite," Jon said. "Hiya Darlene."

An image of that shaggy brunette hair buried in his lap flashed through his mind; the van back behind the Ramp. Oh yes.

"I'm sorry you guys are splitting up," she said. "You got a good band."

"We had a good band. It's over now."

"I'm sad."

"No big deal."

"I need a shoulder to cry on."

Your makeup'll run, he thought, annoyed with her and with himself, because she was making his jeans tight.

"You still got your van?"

"Sure, but right now I gotta help tear down, Darlene."

"This won't take long."

She had a whory mouth, but in a nice way, and though her teeth were faintly yellow, from smoking no doubt, they were nice teeth, and her tongue peeking out between the parted teeth was nice, too.

"How about another time?" Jon said. Polite smile.

"No time like the present." She had hold of his arm, hugging it, tugging at him.

He glanced back at Toni, in her booth; she was smiling at

him, amused. But then she mouthed something at him. He couldn't make it out and squinted and Toni tried again: *What about the dyke?* she was silently saying.

Jon turned back to Darlene, said, "What about your friend?"

She was still tugging him along, toward the door. "You're my friend, Jon boy."

"Please don't call me Jon boy. This is not 'The Waltons.' This is definitely not 'The Waltons.' "

She laughed, as if she understood him. "Come on. I got a present for you."

Jon didn't smoke. Jon didn't drink. Jon didn't do dope. But Jon did have a weakness. And Darlene was definitely part of that weakness.

He went outside with her.

"I said, what about that girlfriend of yours?" he said, pulling loose from her, getting an arm's length between them.

"She's not here."

"Well she *was* here," he said. "I *saw* her." He hadn't, really, but Toni had.

"So she was here," she said, "so what? She's gone now."

"Well, isn't she your…"

"She's just another guy to me."

"So I gathered."

"Come on, I got something for you," she said, tugging him toward the van, which was parked way down at the end of the tin shed that was the club portion of the Barn. The Nodes logo on their T-shirts was also on the side of the van, painted there, frosted over at the moment. Hugging his arm, she pushed herself against him, snuggled against him. As they walked, their footsteps sounded hollow on the wooden sidewalk. When they spoke, their cold breath hung briefly in the air, as though the words themselves were hanging there.

"What's her name, anyway?" Jon said.

"Who?"

"Your girlfriend?"

"Who cares?"

They were at the van. Jon unlocked the side door and they got in. There were some blankets on the cold metal floor of the van, which were used as padding between the amplifiers and such when the van was loaded for travel, and were also used for occasions like this, with Jon and Darlene falling on top of each other in the back of the van.

"It's a little cold," Jon said, reaching over and locking the door they'd just come in. "Maybe I should turn on the heater."

"It won't be cold long," Darlene said, pulling her T-shirt off. Her nipples were two red bumps in pink circles riding small, high breasts above a bony ribcage; Jon put his hands on the breasts, kissed the breasts, but his heart wasn't in it. His hard-on wasn't, either. It was, in fact, gone.

Because all he could think of what that dyke, whose name he couldn't remember, not that it mattered. He wasn't even thinking about Julie and that Hulk of hers, really, it was that goddamn dyke....

Then she was at his fly, and her head was in his lap again, and he was suddenly getting back into it when the side door of the van opened and Jon, angry, confused—*I locked that!*—said, "Shut that fucking thing!" and then saw who it was who opened it.

The dyke.

Terrific.

"Put your shirt on," the dyke said to Darlene. A low, but not exactly masculine voice.

Darlene, still blasé, did so, saying, "I only did what you told me to."

Like unlock the goddamn door when he wasn't looking, Jon thought, as the dyke crawled inside the van and shut the door behind her. In a black leather jacket and dishwater blonde ducktail and Elvis sneer, she was a fifties parody. A fifties nightmare.

"You don't scare me," Jon said, zipping up, scared. "Now just get out of here. Take your friend with you."

The dyke pulled at either side of her leather jacket, and the metal buttons popped open, and she took something out of her waistband. It was a gun. A revolver with a long barrel. Just like the one Nolan used.

"What is this?..." Jon started to say.

Just as the dyke was swinging the gun barrel around to hit him along the side of his head, the damnedest thing happened: he remembered her name.

Ron.

Two

6

It was a November afternoon that could have passed for September—not quite Indian summer, cooler than that, but with the sun visible in a blue, not quite cloudless sky. A nice day to be in Iowa City—if you liked Iowa City.

And Nolan didn't, particularly. Maybe that was why he moved out of here, a few months ago. That had certainly been part of it. That and Jon leaving.

Not that he and Jon had been particularly close. They had been through a lot together, but basically they were just part-ners—in crime, in business, if there was a difference—and had shared that old antique shop as mutual living quarters for a year or so. That was about the extent of it.

But without Jon around, Iowa City stopped making sense to Nolan. It was as though the town had an excuse being this way, with a kid like Jon living in it; now Nolan felt out of place, out of step, and more than a little bored in a college town perched uneasily between *Animal House* and Woodstock.

This downtown, for instance.

He was seated on a slatted wood bench. A few years ago, if he'd been sitting here, he'd have been run over: he'd have been sitting in the middle of a street. Since then, the street had been closed off so these college children could wander among wooden benches and planters and abstract sculptures, like the one nearby, a tangle of black steel pipe on a pedestal, an ode to plumbing, Nolan guessed. Some grade-schoolers were climbing on a wooden structure that was apparently supposed to be a sort of jungle gym; very "natural," organic as shit, he supposed, but the tykes seemed as confused by it as he was. A movie theater was playing something from Australia given four stars by a New York critic; people were lined up as if it was *Star Wars 12*. A boy and girl in identical U of I warm-up jackets strolled into a deep-pan pizza place; another couple, dressed strictly army surplus, followed soon after and would no doubt opt for "whole wheat" crust. Nolan hadn't seen so much khaki since he was in the service. One kid in khaki was playing the guitar and singing something folksy, as though he hadn't heard about Vietnam ending. Like Nolan, he was seated on a wood bench, and people huddled around and listened, applauding now and then, perhaps to keep warm. Nolan burrowed into his corduroy jacket, waiting for Wagner, feeling old.

That was it. Sudden realization: these kids made him feel old. Jon hadn't had that effect on him. Jon had, admittedly, looked up to him, in a way. But it hadn't made him feel old. Not this kind of old, anyway.

He glanced over at the bank. The time/temperature sign said it was 3:35. Wagner had been in there an hour-and-a-half already. Nolan had been in there, too, but only long enough to sign the necessary papers. He didn't feel comfortable in a bank unless he was casing or robbing it.

For nearly twenty years, Nolan had been a professional thief. His specialty was the institutional robbery: banks, jewelry stores, armored cars, mail trucks. He had gone into that line more or less as a matter of survival. He had been employed in Chicago, by the Family, in a noncriminal capacity, specifically managing a Rush Street nightclub; but a falling out with his bosses (which included killing one of them) had sent him into the underground world of armed robbery.

Not that he'd been a cheap stick-up man. No, he was a pro— big jobs, well planned, smoothly carried out. Nobody gets hurt. Nobody goes to jail.

It took almost the full twenty years for those Family difficulties to cool off—then, largely due to a change of regime—and it was during those last difficult days of his Family feud that Nolan teamed up with Jon. An unlikely pairing: a bank robber pushing fifty and a comic-collecting kid barely twenty. But Jon was the nephew of Planner, the old goat who pretended to be in the antique business when what he really was was the guy who sought out and engineered jobs for men like Nolan. It had been at Planner's request that Nolan took the kid on.

And the kid had come through, these past couple of years—the two Port City jobs; the Family trouble that included Planner being murdered; the heisting of old Sam Comfort. And more.

But Jon just wasn't cut out for crime. Oh, he was a tough little character, and no coward. He'd saved Nolan's life once. Nolan hadn't forgotten. But the kid had a conscience, and a little of that went a long way in Nolan's racket.

Fortunately, he and Jon had made enough good scores to retire, about a year ago. Or anyway, Nolan considered himself retired, knowing that his was a business you never got out of, not entirely; there were too many ties to the past for that.

Wagner was one of those ties: a boxman, a safecracker, who retired a few years ago and started up a restaurant in Iowa City, called the Pier. He'd made a real go of it but his health failed, and he invited Nolan to buy him out and Nolan had.

Only now Nolan was in the final stages of reversing that process: letting Wagner buy him out and take the Pier back over.

And there Wagner was—knifing through the crowd of window-shopping kids, moving way too fast for a guy in his fifties with a heart condition. But then, that was always Wagner's problem: he moved too fast, was too goddamn intense, a thin little nervous tic of a man with short white hair, a prison-grey complexion, and a flat, featureless face made memorable only by a contagious smile.

And then he was sitting next to Nolan, pumping Nolan's hand and saying, "You're a pal, Nolan, you're really a pal."

"I made money on the deal," Nolan said noncommittally.

"Not that much. Not that goddamn much. It was nice of him wasn't it?"

"Nice of who?"

"The banker!"

"Bankers aren't nice. Bankers are just bankers."

"It was nice of him, Nolan. To come down after hours to sign papers. That just isn't done, you know."

"Banks have been known to open at odd hours."

"Huh? Oh, yeah. I get it. Ha! Lemme buy you lunch."

"It's past lunch."

"Why, did you eat already?"

"No."

"Then let's have lunch. It'll make a great prelim to dinner. It's on *me*, Nolan."

"Okay," he said.

They walked across the bricked former street to a place called Bushnell's Turtle; it was a sandwich place specializing in submarines (its name derived from the fact that a guy named Bushnell invented the "turtle," the first submersible) and was in a beautiful old restored building with lots of oak and stained glass and plants. They stood and looked at the menu, which was on a blackboard, and a guy in a ponytail and apron came and wrote their order down. Then they were in line a while; the kid in front of Nolan was long-haired and in overalls with a leather thong around his neck and was reading, while he waited, a book called *Make Your Own Shoes*. Soon they picked their food up at the old-fashioned soda fountain-like bar, where the nostalgic spirit was slightly disrupted when a computer cash register totaled their order.

"The hippies did it right for once," Wagner said, referring to the restaurant. He was about to bite into a sub the size of one of the shoes the kid in line was planning to make.

"I agree with you," Nolan managed, between bites of a hot bratwurst sandwich, dripping with mozzarella cheese and sauerkraut.

"I love this town. Love it. Makes me feel young."

"Yeah, well, it makes me feel old, and you be careful or you'll have another heart attack before the ink is dry."

"Don't worry about me," he said, his mouth full of sub, "this pacemaker's made a new man out of me."

"You should've stayed in Florida. There's nothing wrong with being retired."

"Florida stinks! Nothing but old people and Cubans."

"And sunshine and girls in bikinis."

"Don't believe everything the Chamber of Commerce tells you. How's the Quad Cities thing working out?"

"Okay," Nolan said. "It's early yet."

"It's smaller than the Pier, I take it"

"Much. I can loaf with this place."

"You opened yet?"

"In a couple weeks. Still getting the inventory together. Still working with the staff."

"I'm sure you're working with the staff. Particularly the female staff."

"Just one." He smiled.

"Special, this one?"

"Just a girl. I knew her from before."

"Oh. What's it called?"

"Sherry."

"Not the girl, the joint."

"*Nolan's.*"

"No kidding? What was it called before that?"

"I don't know. I think it was always called *Nolan's*. It's been around for years. That's why I had to shut it down, for remodeling and such."

"Whaddya know. It must've been meant to be. So are you using the Nolan name there, then?"

"Yeah. I decided to. The coincidence of it was just too good to pass up. I still pay taxes and sign legal stuff with the Logan name. That's one good thing I got out of the Family—a legal name."

Wagner started on the second half of the massive sub. "You know," he said through the food, "I feel guilty about not giving you more money for the Pier. You're giving me a better operation than I sold you."

"I know. I didn't sell out entirely, remember. I still got half interest."

"Which you split with that kid, Jon, right?"

"Right. And the money you're going to be paying me monthly is sent in two checks, one for me, one for him."

"You see much of him lately?"

"No."

"So what's he doing? Where is he?"

"Playing with a rock 'n' roll band, of all things."

Wagner shook his head. "A nice kid, messed up in a business like that."

Nolan smiled, sipped his beer. "Yeah. When he could've stayed in heisting."

They finished their meal and walked out onto the street. "We still got work to do," Wagner said, hands in pockets, rocking back and forth on his feet. "The accountant'll be down at the Pier by now."

"Let's get it over with," Nolan said.

"You in a hurry or something?"

"Look who's talking."

"Then you'll stay the evening? The Al Pierson Dance Band's playing."

"Sure. Why not." He hadn't given Sherry a definite time he'd be back. There was no rush.

They drove down in Nolan's dark blue LTD.

The Pier was a former Elks Lodge, on the banks of the Iowa River, converted into a seafood restaurant. The bottom floor was the Steamboat Lounge; the main floor was the Mark Twain Dining Room; and the upper floor was the Captain's Ballroom. But Nolan and Wagner were headed for the Accountant's Den, which was to say, the office that had been Nolan's and was now Wagner's, where an accountant was waiting to go over the books, before the final changeover in management.

That took several hours, and by that time Nolan and Wagner were ready to eat again, in the dining room, where an illuminated aquarium built into the length of one wall gave a deep-sea effect. Nolan had the house specialty—pond-raised catfish—the one thing about Iowa City he missed.

Then they went upstairs to the ballroom, where the Al Pierson Band was playing. An eight-piece group in powder-blue tuxes, the Pierson Band had a good, solid sound; Nolan was amazed how full so small a brass section could sound.

About eight months ago, it had occurred to Nolan that in a town full of country-rock discos and live rock 'n' roll clubs, there was nothing for people of *his* generation—the sort of people who flocked to Iowa City for football and basketball weekends. He began providing Saturday night entertainment and soon added Friday, with groups like the Pierson Band. And it went over big—big enough to hire some top names; even the current Glenn Miller configuration had played at the Pier.

"How can you *stand* that shit?" Jon had demanded.

"What shit?"

"That…that *Muzak*!"

"You don't know what you're talking about, kid."

"It's worse than fucking *disco*!"

"I considered a disco, but that fad seems pretty dead to me. Besides, I'm not after the college crowd."

"Nolan, I got a piece of this place. What if I want to book a *rock* act in the ballroom?"

"No way in hell. You want the Ramones playing upstairs, while my businessmen and professors eat surf-and-turf downstairs? Sure."

"Well that music sucks, and that's all there is to it. I knew you were old, but I didn't know you were Lawrence Welk."

And the kid had stalked out.

It was probably the most hostile exchange they'd ever had. Soon Jon was gone, working out of Des Moines with his rock band.

He'd wanted to explain it to Jon. He'd wanted to explain that there were few things in this life that could bring a tear to his eyes, but one of them was Bob Eberley (or a good facsimile) singing "Tangerine." No kid brought up on the Beatles could understand that.

He sat at a side table and had a few drinks and listened to the music and watched the couples dance. The floor was crowded, and most of the people were in their forties, fifties, sixties. Lots of blazers and blue hair. It made him feel old.

He looked at his watch: almost one.

He went to Wagner's office and used the phone to call Sherry. She answered on the fourth ring.

"Hello," her voice said.

"Hi, Sherry. Glad you didn't have the damn answer phone on. I'm sorry I'm so late."

"That's okay."

"I'll be back in a few hours."

"Fine."

"Bye, doll."

"Bye, Logan."

He hung up.

He went back and sat at a table. He ordered another drink. Pierson was playing a Donna Summer song, and Wagner was out there shaking his bootie with some faded homecoming queen. Then the band began "Just the Way You Are," and Wagner came over, sweating, smiling, and sat with Nolan.

"Still determined to kill yourself, Wag?"

"I guess," Wagner grinned.

"Fuck!" Nolan said.

"What?"

He stood. "Logan she called me."

"Huh?"

"She called me Logan."

"What are you…"

"Someone's there with her. The girl's in trouble."

Wagner was saying something, asking him something, but he didn't stop to answer.

7

The first thing Sherry thought about when she got back to the house was putting out the dog. She'd been gone all day—shopping at both North and South Park with Sara, then sharing a pizza and a movie with her new friend (Sara worked at *Nolan's*, too, as a waitress). But she knew the dog wouldn't have made a mess. It was completely housebroken. Any dog that dared live with Nolan would have to be housebroken.

She pulled her little Datsun into the drive, parked it off to the side, leaving the way clear to the garage for Nolan when he got back. It was a chilly night, and she felt it: she was wearing the London Fog raincoat Nolan had bought her (it had looked overcast when she left the house that morning) and had as yet to hit him up for a winter coat.

She smiled to herself. Hours of shopping, and all she'd bought was one thing (some designer jeans, the ones Debbie Harry pushed on TV). Being a kept woman of a guy as tight as Nolan did have its drawbacks. Oh, he always came around, eventually; but being a Depression kid, he seemed to have trouble spending the kind of money it took to live in an inflated economy. But she wasn't complaining.

She went in the front door, opened the closet, and turned off the burglar alarm. The alarm was not connected to the local police station (Nolan was respectable these days, but not *that* respectable); it was just something that made enough noise to presumably scare burglars away and perhaps rouse some neighbors.

Actually, Nolan's house was about as isolated as a home in

the midst of a housing development could be. Of course, it was a small, exclusive development, of $150,000-and-up homes, of which Nolan's was easily the nicest and most secluded. The rest of the development took up one short street, which turned circular at its dead end and led back out again. Nolan's private drive was just to the right as you entered the street, and the sprawling, ranch-style home was surrounded by trees, the backyard dipping down to expose the lower story, which led out to a patio surrounded by more trees—two acres of them—with just enough yard showing to put a pool. Have to work on that, Sherry thought.

It was a four-bedroom house, two up, two down, with a spacious living room with a wall of picture windows looking out on the trees in back of the house. There were no paintings or other wall decorations to speak of, giving the place a blank look. There was one paneled wall, with fireplace, adjacent to the picture windows. The ceiling was slanted, open-beamed. It was a room of creams and soft browns, like the comfy brown modular couch that faced the TV and stereo area, the TV a 26-inch Sony, the stereo a component number on a rack, with records below—hers on one shelf (running to Barbra Streisand) and his on another (running to Harry James).

She hung up her raincoat and stretched. She was wearing a cream silk blouse and tailored brown wool slacks, very chic, but she'd been wearing them all day, and they were on the verge of rank. She'd kill for a shower.

But first, the dog.

It had not greeted her at the door. Had Nolan been there, and had she come in the door, the dog would have been yapping hysterically, jumping up on her, pushing at her thighs, then nipping her heels. Had she been a stranger, it would have attacked. But she'd come to know that the dog recognized her, by sound, smell, whatever, and when she came in without Nolan, the dog kept its place by the glass doors on the lower, basement floor.

That was because Nolan always entered that way. He never came in through the garage, even though he parked his car there and that would be the easiest way. He never came in through the front door. He always walked past the house down the stone steps into the backyard and unlocked the glass patio doors and came in that way. Because even at this "respectable" time of his life, Sherry had come to learn, Nolan retained an outlaw's paranoia. And entering his home the least expected way (actually, coming down the chimney or through a window would be even less expected, but...) seemed par for Nolan's course.

And there the dog was, curled near the glass doors on its circular rug, where it had been sleeping, looking up at her with bright eyes, tail wagging, a white-spotted black terrier about the size of a healthy rabbit.

She leaned down and petted it—got licked for her trouble— and unlocked the glass door and slid it open for the dog to go out. No need to chain it up: it wouldn't go far from where Nolan lived. It wouldn't go out of the yard, in fact.

The dog, like Clint Eastwood in an Italian western, had no name. Nolan referred to it only as "the dog" or "the mutt." It still seemed odd to her that Nolan would have a pet at all. She seldom saw him give the animal affection or attention, but it was clear the dog lived for Nolan's occasional pat.

It had taken her the best part of her entire first week back with him to worm the story out of him. Seemed the mutt had turned up at his back door, half dead; it had been in a bad dog fight or two, had half an ear chewed off, and hadn't eaten for days. "A skeleton with a tail," Nolan had described it.

Apparently the dog had touched a nerve in Nolan that Sherry hadn't known existed. He took the dog in; in fact, he took the dog to a vet—spent money on it! And, while saying Nolan nursed the dog back to health would be going too far, the dog had somehow survived. And somehow knew Nolan was responsible.

If Nolan sat in his reclining chair, reading a paper, watching TV, the dog slept on the floor near his feet. When Nolan slept, the dog slept under the bed. When Nolan ate, the dog sat politely nearby, waiting for the inevitable scraps. Every now and then, Nolan allowed the dog up on his lap; he'd pet it, grant it a smile, and it would curl up and sleep there. But only now and then.

Sherry was more openly affectionate to the dog, and the dog returned the affection; but it loved Nolan. It was, after all, a bitch.

She let the dog in, and it followed her upstairs, tagging after her as she undressed. Then she heard its claws clicking on the stairs, heading back down to wait for Nolan again, as she got in the shower and let the hot needles wash away the hard-earned sweat from a day of shopping centers, pizza, and Robert Redford.

Soon she was in a black Frederick's nightie, sitting on the couch, waiting for Nolan to come home and fuck her. She knew it sounded harsh, but that was what she was in the mood for: a good, hard, horny fuck. And she'd bet that Nolan would feel the same.

She was twenty and had a nice, if not busty, figure; she knew that her appeal to him was her youth, the suppleness of her body, the cuteness of her features, her California blonde hair (dyed or not). And she knew that his appeal to her (beyond this house and his affluence) was as a father figure. A coldly handsome, closed-mouthed father figure, perhaps; a father figure with bullet scars on his muscular body. A father figure who was great in the sack. But a father figure.

She'd first met Nolan at the Tropical, a motel he was running for the Chicago Family. Initially, she'd been a waitress there, and a bad one: it was when she got called on the carpet for spilling food in customers' laps that she ended up in Nolan's lap, and that pretty much was where she'd stayed the rest of that summer.

Then her father had called and told her her mother had had a stroke, and it was back to Ohio for Sherry. There would be no time to finish up college (she had a two-year community college degree and had hoped to get a four-year business degree) and the only job she could find was waitressing at a Denny's. Which was better than hell, but just barely. And when she wasn't waitressing at Denny's, she was looking after her mother, which she didn't mind, because she loved her mother, but it was sad. So very sad.

Three months ago her mother had died.

Sherry started back to college, and only a month in, she knew she couldn't hack it. It wasn't that she was stupid; she wasn't particularly *smart*, either, but it wasn't that she was stupid. More like bored. She was more bored than waitressing at Denny's. It was a rare week that she didn't think about her summer with Nolan. She had even cried herself to sleep a couple times, missing him, wishing she could have stayed with him.

Then, last month, he called. She didn't even know how he'd managed to track her down, but he had. And he wanted her to come live with him.

"I need a hostess at my new restaurant," he said.

"That's like a waitress, right?"

"Right. Only you don't spill shit on people."

"But Logan, that's my speciality."

"I know. And can the Logan stuff."

Logan was the name she'd known Nolan by at the Tropical.

"How come?"

"I'm using Nolan here. So don't call me Logan anymore. It'll just confuse people."

"Well, I'm already confused."

"That's how I like you."

"I'm also broke."

"I'll send plane fare."

"I'm on my way, then."

Their month together had been a lot of fun, if not a honeymoon. Nolan wasn't altogether humorless, though when he did make a joke, it was so dry, you could miss it if you weren't looking. They made good love together. They got along. He didn't insist that she cook—one thing he wasn't stingy about was taking her out to eat, though he did collect receipts to deduct the meals on his taxes, claiming he was "checking out my competition." And when she did cook, he didn't complain, even when the results (her Tuna Surprise, for instance) were less than spectacular. Memorable, yes; spectacular, no.

During the first week, the Nolan/Logan thing had been a running gag with them; she'd kept right on calling him Logan, till he finally threatened to turn her over his knee and spank her. She dropped her drawers and said go right ahead. And he had, and more.

But afterward he said, "Seriously—get used to calling me Nolan. I got to stick by one name in one place."

And from then on it was strictly Nolan.

She was watching a *Mission: Impossible* rerun when she remembered the answer phone: she hadn't checked for messages.

She went into the kitchen, and the red light was flashing on the little tape unit by the phone on the counter. She rewound the tape and played it back.

"Nolan, this is Jon. I'm calling from a place called the Barn, just this side of Burlington. I'm here with my band."

Jon. That was the kid Nolan was always mentioning. The one who was his partner or something, back when Nolan *wasn't* respectable. She'd never met Jon, but she knew he was someone important in Nolan's life.

"This is going to sound crazy," the voice was saying, sounding tinny coming out of the small speaker, "but I think I saw that bitch Julie. No, scratch that: I *did* see her, no mistaking it. She is *not* dead, Nolan."

What was this about? The kid sounded scared.

"Now the worse news: she saw *me*. Nolan, if she's been playing dead, she's not going to be happy I found out she's alive. She's going to cause trouble. So what I'm going to do is finish out the night—it's just before midnight, as I'm talking—and I'm going to confront her, if I can get the chance, and cool this down."

Very nervous, Sherry thought—even desperate.

"In the meantime, if you get home by, oh, twelve-thirty, get in your car and drive down here. Come via 61 all the way, so that if for some reason I end up coming after you, I'll spot you on the highway. It should take you about an hour and forty-five minutes to two hours to get here; the band quits at one-thirty, the club stays open till two, and then it's another half-hour or forty-five minutes of tearing down equipment and loading. Which means there'll be too many people around for her to try anything till three, I'd say. Or anyway, two-thirty. So if you can leave there by twelve-thirty, get down here. Otherwise, stay put and wait for me to get back to you."

It was a disturbing message. She didn't understand it, but

that only made it all the more disturbing; she rewound it, listened to it again, then rewound it again so that Nolan could hear it when he got home.

But one thing was certain: the twelve-thirty deadline was past; it was quarter till one now.

She went back to the TV, found an old crime movie with Cornell Wilde, which she started to watch, then switched to *Second City TV*. The crime movie was hitting just a little too close to home.

It took only about four minutes of *Second City* to get her laughing; she hadn't forgotten the disturbing answer-phone message, but it wasn't dominating her thoughts now. But she did wonder when Nolan would get here.

That thought had barely flicked through her mind when she heard the footsteps on the stairs and smiled. God, he was quiet coming in. Nobody was that quiet. Usually, the dog would have yapped at him, though, happy to see him. Not tonight. That was odd.

Still on the couch, she turned her head and glanced back at Nolan.

Only it wasn't Nolan.

It was two men: one of them, disturbingly, looked a little like Nolan, but a younger Nolan, about thirty-five, with no mustache and short, curly, permed hair that gave him a Caesar sort of look. He was in black—black slacks, black turtleneck, black gloves. The other man was coming up the stairs behind the Nolan clone, in shadows; she couldn't see him yet.

She reached for a heavy sculpted glass paperweight on the coffee table near the couch.

It exploded before she could touch it, shards of glass nicking at her arm. Choking back a scream, she clutched her blood-flecked arm with her other hand and glanced back at the men. The Caesar type had an automatic in his hand; there was an attachment on the end of it—a silencer?—and smoke was curling out the barrel. He was smiling faintly.

"I don't like shooting at Art Deco pieces," the man said. His voice was a smooth, curiously pleasant baritone. "Don't make me shoot any more furniture, dear. I'd sooner shoot you."

She felt very naked in her Frederick's nightie, and flashed onto an absurd thought: *Thank God I didn't go crotchless!*

Then she saw the other man. He, too, looked familiar. Then she placed him: he was a ringer for that guy that used to be on that Angie Dickinson police show. But, again, younger—perhaps thirty. He had curly, permed hair too, and a silly smile that scared her more than the tight, controlled smile of the other man. This one, too, was in black; this one, too, had an automatic with an attachment.

The first man came over to her, with a gloved hand brushed the glass from the coffee table, and sat down, the gun casual in his hand, but pointing at her. He was tanned. Handsome, in an unsettling way.

"Where's Logan?" he said.

"Logan?" she said.

"Or Nolan. Whatever he's calling himself here."

"He lives here," she said. Stupidly, she thought.

"We *know*," the other's voice said. She sat up, so she could see the other man. He was over turning off the TV, then crouching to look through the albums under the stereo. Looking through the records. Jesus. What kind of...

"Sally," the second guy said, holding up an album. "She's got Barry Manilow." Then to her: "You got good taste lady. How about Rupert Holmes? You got Rupert Holmes?"

"Uh, no," she said. *What the fuck...*

"Put some records on, Infante," the first one, Sally, said. "Put on the live Manilow album."

"That thing where he does the medley of commercials kills

me," Infante said. He had the slightest speech impediment: Elmer Fudd after therapy.

"Does it kill you?" Sally asked her, smiling, apparently amused by his flaky partner.

"I hope not," Sherry said.

"So do I," Sally said. "I don't like killing things, but I will if I have to. So will Infante, won't you, Infante? It was Infante killed the dog. I didn't have the heart to."

She brought her hand up to her face, bit her knuckles. She tried to hold back the tears, the trembling. It was no use. Barry Manilow was singing, "Even now…"

"Go ahead and cry, dear. Infante!"

Infante was right there, like a fast cut in a movie. "Yeah, Sally?"

"Check out the house. This Logan or whoever isn't here, but check out the lay of the land, and then get the lady some Kleenex. Her makeup's starting to run."

"Sure, Sally."

And Infante was gone.

Sally smiled; that the face was vaguely like Nolan's did nothing to reassure her—if anything, it only terrified her more. She had never been so scared; she'd never been so conscious of her heart, pounding in her chest, as if trying to get out.

Sally touched her arm; his touch was cold as a snake.

"If you rape me," she said, tightly, teeth clenched, "Nolan'll kill you."

Sally laughed; it was almost a gentle laugh. He patted her arm. "We're not going to rape you." Then Infante was there, holding the Kleenex out to Sally, who took it and passed it on to Sherry. "We're not going to rape her, are we, Infante?"

Infante looked at Sherry as though she was a slug. "Are you kidding?"

Sally held Sherry's hand; in the background Barry Manilow sang. Sally said, "All we want to know is where Nolan is."

Sherry said nothing.

"Is he coming back soon?"

Sherry said nothing.

"He's out of town, isn't he?"

Sherry said nothing.

Sally said, "Flick your Bic, would you, Infante?"

"Sure," Infante said. He got his lighter out. Sally held both of Sherry's arms down while Infante grasped both of her feet around the ankles and locked them in the crook of one arm as he held the lighter's flame to the bottom of her right foot, just under the toes.

She screamed. The pain was intense; it went on forever.

"Three seconds," Sally said to her. "You want to try for ten?"

"Please…"

"I don't get pleasure from this. Infante doesn't get pleasure from this. Do you, Infante?"

Infante, still gripping her ankles, grinned and said, "No."

"If we were sadists," Sally said, leaning in close, "we'd burn your face, not the bottom of your feet." He blew against her cheek; his breath was minty.

"There's nothing I can tell you," she managed.

"Infante. Flick your Bic."

"No!"

"Wait a second, Infante."

Barry Manilow was singing about the Copa; Infante was singing along, softly.

"Well?" Sally said to her.

"He didn't tell me where he was going. He just said he'd be gone most of the day, on business."

"Flick your Bic, Infante."

"That's the truth!"

The other foot, this time; the pain was searing, like a branding iron, lasting for days.

"Five seconds, that time," Sally said. "You want to get serious, dear? Or you'll never dance again."

Infante snickered at that, still singing to himself.

"I'm telling the truth!" she said.

Sally thought about that.

"Please," she said, "he didn't tell me, he didn't tell me, why should he bother telling me?"

"When will he be home?"

"I thought he'd be back by now. He said about midnight."

Sally let go of her arms, looked at his watch. "Jesus," he said to himself.

"Maybe she's telling the truth, Sally," Infante said, still gripping her ankles, the lighter in hand.

"Maybe. I wouldn't want him coming in on this, that's for sure."

The phone rang.

Sally looked at her sharply. "Could that be him?"

She nodded.

"Where's the phone?"

Another ring.

"In the kitchen," she said.

Infante said, "Extension's in the bedroom," releasing her ankles and running to the bedroom.

"Pick it up on the fourth ring!" Sally called out.

He was dragging her to the kitchen; she felt the skin on her burned feet catching and tearing against the carpet.

He pushed her toward the phone, and she picked it up on the fourth ring.

It was Nolan.

She answered his questions, Sally's automatic with its attachment kissing her neck.

Got to warn him, give him a sign, she thought.

"I'll be back in a few hours," he was saying.

"Fine," she heard herself say.

"Bye, doll."

"Bye, Logan."

She hung up.

Would he pick up on it? That she'd called him Logan? Had that been warning enough?

In the other room, Barry Manilow was singing, "This Time We Made It."

Sally dragged her back to the couch and she passed out.

8

Nolan left his LTD on the street, a block away, and made his way up behind the house, through the sloping woods. He stayed within the trees, not going across the lawn until he was parallel to the corner of the house—some lights on, upstairs— and then, keeping low, made for the sliding glass doors off the patio.

It had taken him just under an hour-and-a-half to get here; he'd come via Interstate 80, and no Highway Patrol had stopped him despite his speeding. He was grateful for that much. Whoever had Sherry in the house wouldn't expect him back this soon. He was grateful for that, too. But he wished he had a gun.

Somebody inside the house had a gun. He saw the concave pucker in the glass where the bullet had gone through. Beyond it he saw the slumped form of his small dog. The door's lock had been jimmied, so he didn't bother with his key. He just slid it carefully open. And stepped inside.

No lights on down here. But his night vision was in full force, and moonlight came in the doors behind him, and he could see the big open room, which would be a game room when he got around to putting a pool table in. There was a fire- place, as there was upstairs, but no furniture yet. Nowhere to hide, unless it was in one of the rooms off the hallway directly across from him: the two guest bedrooms, extra john, furnace room. He stood silently for a good minute. He heard muffled sounds upstairs. Nothing down here.

He slid the door shut behind him.

He knelt and gave his dog a pat.

He didn't have a gun. He didn't have a goddamn gun. He'd been in such a goddamn hurry to get here, he hadn't even stopped to ask Wagner for something. And he didn't have anything stashed down here, no weapon of any kind. He always went to the precaution of coming in the back way, but he hadn't bothered with stashing a gun. Stupid. He looked at the boxes stacked over against one wall. What was in those? Anything useful?

Still kneeling, he smiled to himself. Patted the dog's warm body. Got some blood on his hand but didn't wipe it off.

Some of that stuff in the boxes was Sherry's. She'd told her father she was getting an apartment when she moved here, so he'd given her some things: pots, pans, and so on. Also silverware.

He slipped out of his shoes and moved soundlessly across the carpeted floor to the boxes. Very carefully he sorted through the first box; the wooden case with silverware in it was under some Tupperware. He removed one stainless steel steak knife with a four-inch blade. He held it tight in a fist wet with the animal's blood.

There was only one way up, and that was the stairs, coming right up into the living room, at the back. Half a flight, a landing, then, to the left, another half a flight, and bam. If they were waiting for him, watching for him, he was dead. If they weren't, he had a chance. The stairs were carpeted, and he was quiet. He went up the first half-flight and waited, just one step below the landing. Listened.

Music.

"I think she's coming around, Sally," a voice said. An immature voice.

"Doesn't matter," another, older voice said. "She doesn't know anything else we want to know."

"Maybe we should ask her how he comes in. There's more than one way in."

"You may have a point."

"You want me to hold her feet again?"

"I don't think that'll be necessary."

Music—they were playing music on the goddamn stereo. Barry Manilow, wasn't it? Crazy.

"She's awake, Sally."

That name Sally, again. A man named Sally. Sal. Sal and Infante. The two bodyguards working for Hines, the local Family man.

"Which way does he come in?" he heard Sal asking.

"Front door," Sherry's voice said. Hurting.

"Maybe you better hold her feet again, Infante."

"No!" Sherry said. "It's the garage way. Doorway's in the hall."

"You telling the truth? Hold her feet, Infante."

"It's the truth!" Sherry all but screamed.

Actually, Nolan would have preferred Sherry really tell the truth. That would send at least one of them down here. Well, maybe there was a way....

He stepped onto the landing. Looked up the stairs. No one at the top. There appeared to be only the two men here with Sherry, and they were in another part of the living room above.

He went up a few steps. Peeked over the edge of what was the living room floor, at left, through the black latticework railing.

Sherry was on the couch.

Infante's back was to Nolan, and the guy was apparently holding Sherry by the ankles. The other one, Sally, was pinning down her arms, questioning her, his back partially to Nolan.

"Better flick your Bic, Infante," Sally was saying. "Don't burn the same spot."

Nolan's hand tightened on the steak knife as the pain made

Sherry jerk up, into a sitting position, while Sally covered her mouth with a hand to stifle her scream.

But when Sherry jerked up, her pain-widened eyes met Nolan's. He was visible from the shoulders up. He gestured: raised a finger and pointed downward, thinking *Send them to me, doll. Send them to me.*

Then he ducked down out of sight. Sat on the steps.

"All right!" Sherry said. "All right. It isn't the front door. It isn't the garage way, either."

"What way is it, dear?" Sally said.

Nolan slipped back down the stairs.

"He comes in the way you did," she said.

"The basement!" Infante said.

Brilliant, Nolan thought. He was standing with his back to the wall, just at the bottom of the stairs, to the right.

"I better move that dog," Sally said. "Shit! And he'll see the bullet hole, too. Damn!"

"What'll we do, Sally?"

"Shut off the fuckin' music, for one thing. He could be here in fifteen, twenty minutes. Christ! I'll go down and get rid of the dog."

The music stopped.

Infante said, "He won't notice the bullet hole, or that we broke in through there, till he gets up close."

"Yeah, you're right. So if I'm watching for him down there, I can nail him right through the glass door while he's standing out in the yard. Yeah. Okay. You stick with the bitch here, in case he varies from pattern and comes in up here."

"Okay, Sally."

"Just shoot him. Don't talk to him."

"Yes, Sally. Sally."

"Yeah?"

"You be careful. I wouldn't want nothing to happen to you."

There was a pause.

Then Sally said, "Yeah. You, too."

Nolan heard Sally on the stairs. He stepped off the last step, and Nolan put a hand over his mouth and the steak knife in his back, lower right.

Nolan eased him to the floor. Sally gurgled and died, getting blood on Nolan's hand. Nolan wiped his hand on Sally's shirt. Then he took the man's silenced 9mm from a limp hand and left him there, the knife handle sticking out of his back like something to pick him up by.

Nolan went slowly back up the stairs, gun in hand.

Infante was sitting on the arm of the couch, his back to Nolan, blocking Nolan's view of Sherry, who was still lying there. He couldn't risk a shot, for fear of hitting her. He should probably try to lure Infante downstairs...but Infante would likely drag Sherry along, not wanting to leave her unattended, so that was out.

Nothing to do but try to come up behind him slow.

Nolan was halfway between the top of the stairs and the couch when Infante turned and with a startled expression that was only vaguely human, shot at Nolan three times with the silenced 9mm's twin. Nolan dove for the floor and rolled into the entryway area by the front door while a plaster wall took the bullets, spitting dust.

The kitchen was off the entryway, and Nolan ducked in there, as it connected to the living room and would allow him to enter on the opposite side, which should confuse Infante and give Nolan a better look at where Sherry was, to take a shot at Infante and still keep Sherry out of harm's way.

And Sherry was on the couch, all right, but Infante was heading down the stairs, into the basement, shouting, "Sally! Sally!"

Nolan went to Sherry, who reached for him, hugged him.

"Are you okay, doll?"

She was smiling, crying. "My feet are killing me."

"I better go after him."

"No! Stay with me."

There was an anguished cry from downstairs—a wail.

"I'll kill you!" Infante's voice, muffled but distinct, came from below.

"Maybe he'll come up after me," Nolan said.

But the next sound from below was the glass doors sliding, slamming shut.

Nolan ran to the picture windows. He saw Infante scurrying across the yard, off to the right, into the woods.

"Stay put," Nolan told Sherry.

"Nolan…"

"Stay put!"

"Where would I go?" she yelled at him, angry for a moment.

Nolan went out the front door, fanning the gun around in front of him. The full moon was keeping everything well lit; there was a pale, eerie wash on the world. But no sign of Infante.

Then he heard an engine start, a car squeal away.

He stood there a moment and let the cool air cool him down.

Then he went back in. To Sherry.

He examined her feet. "Sons of bitches," he said.

"They hurt. They really hurt."

"Second-degree burns. You're lucky."

"Oh, yeah. Lucky."

"They've started to blister. Third degree would've been trouble. I'm going to get you some cold water to soak them in."

"Please."

He got a pan with ice and water in it and eased her to a

sitting position, and she slid her feet in, making a few intake-of-breath sounds, but seeming to like it, once done.

"I should get you to a hospital," he said. "I should get you to an emergency room."

"How can you do that?" she said. "They'll want to know how it happened. I don't know what this is about, but I know you. And I know this isn't something you'll want the police or anybody in on."

He scratched his head and said, "Right. Burns on the feet are dangerous, though. You need a doctor."

"Sara's boyfriend is a doctor."

"Sara? At the club?"

"Right."

"Will he keep his mouth shut? Will he make a post-midnight house call?"

"He's a *married* doctor. He'll do anything Sara asks him."

"Good. What's Sara's number?"

"It's in the back of the phonebook."

"I want you to stay with her for a few days."

"Where will you be?"

"I don't know yet. I don't know what this is about, either."

He got up to go to the kitchen to call Sara.

"Did you know those two men?" Sherry asked.

He turned and looked at her. For all she'd been through, she looked terrific, sitting there in a short black nightie, soaking her feet.

"Yeah," he said. "A couple of guys who work for Hines."

"Hines. Isn't he connected?"

"Yeah, Hines is Family. That bothers me. I haven't had any Family trouble for a long time."

"You going to talk to Hines?"

"He's out of town. And anyway, those two were Family, out

of Chicago, before they got assigned to Hines. They could've got their orders from somebody other than Hines. With Hines out of town, that almost seems likely."

"You've got Family friends."

"There's Felix, that lawyer I always dealt with. But if I call him, he'll lie to me, if I'm on the shit list again. I don't know. I think I'm going to have to go out and knock heads together and see what's going on."

He went to the kitchen.

"Nolan!" she called out

He came back out and said, "What?"

"I almost forgot. There's a message for you on the answer machine. A long one."

"Oh?"

"It's from that friend of yours."

"Jon?"

"Yes. It sounded like he was in trouble. Maybe this has something to do with that."

But before she had finished her sentence, Nolan was in the kitchen playing the message. He listened to it twice.

He came back talking to himself, saying, "Julie, alive? If so, how is she connected to anybody Family? I don't get it." Then, to Sherry: "Did those guys hear that message? Did they get that out of you?"

"No," she said. "I kept thinking they'd want to know, if they'd known to ask. But they didn't ask, and I was happy to keep it from them."

"Good girl."

"You missed your deadline, you know. You were supposed to go after your friend if you got home by twelve-thirty."

"Well, I didn't. And he isn't here yet, so I'm going after him anyway. It's my only lead."

"Did you call Sara?"

"Not yet. Listen. Tell her nothing. Nothing about how you got the burns. Nothing about the shooting. I'll let her know I'll make it right by her, for helping, no questions asked. Then I'll have to bandage your feet up, best I can, till her doctor friend can apply proper dressings at her place."

"Okay."

"Then I got to bury something in the woods, and I'm off."

"You mean that guy downstairs? Sally? You killed him?"

"Yeah, I killed him. But I don't mean him. I'll dump him someplace. He doesn't rate a burial. I'm talking about my dog."

Three

9

Jon came to.

He knew three things immediately: he was in the back seat of a car, on his side; it was dark, so it wasn't morning yet, or anyway the sun wasn't up; and his head ached so bad, his eyes hurt.

He sat up; it took some doing, but he sat up. His hands were behind him, and he could feel the cold steel of handcuffs; his legs were bound at the ankles with thick, heavily knotted rope, like the handiwork of a very ambitious, sadistic Boy Scout.

Or Girl Scout.

He looked out the window to the left. The dyke, Ron, black leather jacket, ducktail, and all, was standing in an arrogant slouch, listening to Julie talk.

Julie.

She was still wearing the white outfit, but the tinted glasses were gone, an affectation she presumably dropped during more private moments. She was gesturing as she spoke, and occasionally she would reach out and touch Ron's face, casually.

The two of them were standing in the midst of a big open graveled area, a parking lot. This car Jon was in the back of was one of only two cars parked in it. The other one was a low-slung sportscar, a Porsche, Jon thought, the color of which he couldn't make out—something light pastel—and the owner *had* to be Julie.

Behind them was a building that appeared to be an old brick warehouse, but there was a neon sign, which wasn't on, over a covered entryway, indicating it had been converted into something else. A restaurant or a club, maybe. He couldn't tell, exactly; he couldn't really see that well.

He tried to make out what they were saying, but it was muffled; they were a good twenty feet away. He pressed his ear to the glass of the car window and listened. He began to pick up some of the conversation.

"Just hold onto him for me," Julie was saying.

"You want him to disappear forever, he can," the dyke said.

"Not yet. In a day or two, maybe."

"It don't matter to me. I'd soon cut his throat as look at him."

A sick feeling swept over Jon—not nausea: hopelessness. A physical sense of hopelessness.

Then he didn't hear anything. He took his ear away from the glass and looked out the window, and Julie and the dyke were kissing. There was a full moon tonight, but it didn't lend much romance to the scene, the way Jon saw it.

Then the big sandy-haired guy with glasses, the Incredible Hulk guy, came out of the warehouse, and Julie and Ron broke it up; Julie walked to meet the guy, and the dyke just stood there, hands on her butt, looking sullen. Julie and the guy talked for what seemed forever and was maybe five minutes.

How the fuck could she be *alive*, anyway?

He and Nolan had driven to Ft. Madison and seen the twisted, burnt wreckage of the car she'd been in. Or was supposed to have been in. Didn't make sense.

But what did make sense, where Julie was concerned? The only thing you could count on was she'd use her looks to manipulate those around her. Like she had with that poor dead bastard Rigley, the Port City bank president.

She'd put him up to it. They didn't know it at first but it became obvious as soon as she came into it. Rigley could never have done it on his own.

Rigley had come into the Pier, about a year ago, and announced to Nolan that he recognized him as one of the men who had held his bank up two years before. Rigley then blackmailed Nolan, and Jon, into helping him rob his own bank, to cover up an embezzlement. The robbery had gone off without a hitch, but when it came to making the split at Rigley's cottage on the Cedar River, he and his beautician girlfriend, Julie, put a double-cross in motion.

But at the last minute, the banker panicked, and when Julie fired a shotgun meant for Nolan, Rigley got in front of the blast. Nolan dove for the girl, but she swung the now-empty shotgun around and whacked him in the head, and he went down.

Jon was under the dead banker. He pushed the corpse off and grabbed for the girl's arm as she fled, but she caught him in the gut with the gunstock, and then again on the back of the neck, when he doubled over.

Moments later he came to, grabbed his .38 from off the floor, and went out after her.

Julie was in her yellow Mustang, the laundry bag of money sitting in back like a person.

He had her in his sights, but he couldn't do it. He couldn't shoot. Couldn't kill her.

So he shot at her tires; maybe hit one.

Then she was gone.

And minutes later he and Nolan were pursuing her. There were only two ways she could go: back to Port City, which on the heels of the bank robbery was unlikely, or toward West Liberty, a little town near where she'd lived before moving into Rigley's cottage.

On the outskirts of West Liberty, they saw it: the Mustang, with a flat tire, pulled over on the shoulder. In front of it was a blue Ford that said WEST LIBERTY SHERIFF'S DEPT. on the side. Julie was in the back seat of the Ford. So was the sack of money.

The sheriff or deputy or whatever, a pudgy-faced guy with a weak chin, close-set eyes, five o'clock shadow, and a western-style hat, sat in front, getting ready to pull out on the highway, into town. He apparently had stopped Julie for driving recklessly in a car with a flat tire, and stumbled onto something a bit bigger.

Julie saw Nolan and Jon as they drove by, but didn't alert the sheriff. Nolan and Jon drove back to Iowa City to sit it out.

That night, back at the antique shop, in the upstairs living quarters, they kept the radio on and the TV too, waiting for news of the West Liberty arrest. It never came.

"I think we been snookered," Nolan said. "I think that West Liberty hick was in on it with her."

"Nolan, that's nuts," Jon had said. "She couldn't've planned ahead for a flat tire. She couldn't've put something that complex together."

"Yeah," he said. "You're right."

"So now what?"

"We keep waiting."

The next morning it was on the news: on a narrow bridge on the highway outside Ft. Madison, a gas tanker truck struck a car, head on. There had been an explosion. The two men in the truck were killed, as was the woman driving the car. Several thousand dollars in burnt bills in Port City bank wrappers linked the young woman driving the car to yesterday's Port City bank robbery. In the days to come, the woman, though burned beyond recognition, was identified as the dead bank president's mistress. The cops put a scenario together for the robbery and its aftermath that did not, thankfully, include Nolan and Jon.

But Nolan had not been satisfied. He went to Ft. Madison and looked at the burnt wreckage of the Mustang.

"I think we been snookered," he said again.

Again, Jon said, "You're nuts. She was running, and it all caught up with her."

"You mean God killed her?"

"Well…"

"He doesn't have that good a sense of humor."

There was one thing Nolan could still do, and Jon drove him, after a good month had passed, to West Liberty. The weak-chinned deputy sheriff—whose name was Creel—lived in a little white frame house a few blocks from the outskirts of town—a few blocks from where he stopped Julie's Mustang. So at two in the morning one night, with Jon at his side, Nolan knocked on Creel's door.

Creel answered in his pajamas. Nolan, wearing a ski mask, put a gun in Creel's neck.

Within the house, a female voice from upstairs called, "Honey? Is something wrong?"

Nolan said softly, "Nothing's wrong."

Creel looked at Nolan wide-eyed, slack-jawed; he looked at Jon standing just behind Nolan, also in a ski mask, also with a gun.

"Nothing's wrong, honey," Creel called back. "Just some sheriffing!"

And Nolan walked the deputy around back and had him sit in a swing on a swing set. Creel had kids, apparently.

"Tell me about Julie," Nolan said.

"What?"

"Tell me why you didn't turn Julie and that money in last month."

And Creel did something amazing: he started to cry. He sat in the swing and cried.

Then he talked.

"I was nuts about that cunt. She had a beauty shop in town. For two years I tried to make her. I usually don't cheat around, but that cunt was s-o-o-o-o-o-o beautiful. And she laughed at me when I came onto her. *Two years* I tried making her."

"Get to the point."

"There's not much to tell. I saw this car driving wild. Flat tire. Pulled it over and it was this Julie. She had a shotgun, but it was empty. And she had a bag of money. All that fuckin' money. She said, 'You hear about the Port City bank job this afternoon?' I said yeah. She said, 'This is the money. Hundreds of thousands here. Nobody knows I got it but you.' Jesus, I said. She says, 'You want to be rich and fuck me whenever you want?' I didn't say nothin'. She says, 'Rich,' and reaches for my dick. 'Nobody's home at my place,' I says. My wife and the kids was at her mom's in Des Moines, for Christmas. She says, 'Drive us there, then. Now.' And I did."

Creel started laughing.

"We parked the Mustang in back here, in the garage, and took the bag of money in and plopped it on the kitchen table. She and I sat and played with the money and laughed. Then we went upstairs to the bedroom and, sweet Jesus, I fucked her. Three times, and it was…nothing like it, ever. We was in bed together, and I drifted off to sleep, thinking it was a dream, a crazy dream. I woke up a couple hours later, handcuffed to the bed. Alone in the house."

Creel sat there, swinging.

"You believe she's dead?" Nolan asked.

"If she isn't, I'd like to kill her." He laughed. "Or fuck her." Then he just sat there blankly. Swinging.

"We never had this conversation," Nolan said.

"Right," Creel said.

And Nolan and Jon went back to Iowa City and forgot about it.

Now, a year later, Jon was in the back seat of a car, hand-cuffed like that dumb asshole Creel, while Julie and some dyke named Ron talked about whether or not to kill him.

Right now Julie was still talking to that sandy-haired guy. If only they'd go into that warehouse for a while, maybe he could *do* something…

The car he was in was an old souped-up Ford, with tuck 'n' roll upholstery, four-on-the-floor, stereo speakers on the back ledge. He was locked in, of course, but maybe…

On the other side of the car, the one facing away from Julie and Ron and the Hulk, Jon bit the tip of the locking knob on the door. He pulled up with his teeth. It clicked.

He glanced over to see if the figures out in the parking lot had heard it. It had sounded incredibly loud to him. But they still stood there, Julie and the guy, talking, Ron doing her James Dean slouch.

With his back to the door, he used this cuffed hands to grasp the door handle. He pulled. The latch gave, but he didn't open the door. He was still watching the people in the lot. To see if they'd heard the sound—which seemed to him to echo across the world like a shout in the Grand Canyon. But they didn't seem to. Ron glanced over, but just momentarily.

He waited a minute or so.

Then he pushed the door open a bit, hoping the dome light wouldn't go on. It didn't. One small break. He edged it open and slipped down out of the car onto the gravel and eased the door shut.

On his belly, he looked under the car, toward Julie and the Hulk and Ron. He saw their legs; they hadn't moved.

He looked off, in the opposite direction. Another twenty feet of parking lot, then trees. If he could make it to the trees, and perhaps hide, then eventually work the ropes off his ankles, and find a highway...

He crawled on his belly. The gravel was rough; it scraped him. He was only in T-shirt and jeans. His mouth, already tasting like an old gym sock, took in dust.

He could hear them talking. They hadn't noticed him. Trees ahead, a few yards.

Then a voice. Ron's.

"Hey!"

Feet ran on gravel.

He tried to get on his feet; maybe he could hop faster than he could crawl.

He never found out.

A foot was on his back, and then he heard Ron say, "You ain't goin' noplace," and she grabbed him by his bound ankles and dragged him, face down, back to her car.

Harold took off his glasses and rubbed his eyes. He was sitting behind the metal desk in the small paneled office at the rear of his and Julie's club, the Paddlewheel. He was waiting for the phone to ring.

The Paddlewheel was a big place, an old converted warehouse near the banks of the Mississippi, in Gulf Port, Illinois; it contained a restaurant, several bars, several dance floors with stages, and a casino. But Harold's office was small.

Harold, of course, was big, a big man who felt uncomfortable in his small office, physically uncomfortable, psychologically uncomfortable. This small office was just another unspoken insult in his life with Julie. But he loved her. He loved her. And if she didn't love him back, well, she didn't love anybody else, either. Except Julie, of course.

Julie had a large office upstairs, with a huge wood-topped desk, bulky old-fashioned safe, file cabinets, chairs, bar, television, stereo, a couch where she slept sometimes. Almost an apartment, and she did use it as a place to go, to stay, even overnight—when she wanted to get away from him for a while, Harold knew.

They lived together in a big white house with pillars, a near-mansion built ten years before by a wealthy farmer for a beloved wife who divorced him a year later. The place was several miles outside Gulf Port, in the midst of rich farmland that Julie now owned, one of several investments she'd made with the money they were earning from the Paddlewheel. It was a four-bedroom home that required a housekeeper to come in three times a week, filled with antiques Julie picked up (her only hobby); they slept in separate bedrooms, though he was allowed to join her in her bed for love-making a few times a week.

As for his small office on the basement level, she claimed it was a ploy of sorts; it was obviously necessary to keep considerable cash on hand for the casino and, she said, she wanted a certain amount beyond that in case the day came that they should need to leave in a hurry. So the big old safe in her office, in which a few thousand was kept, was a decoy; the safe containing over $100,000 was in the floor of Harold's small office, a little vault in the corner, under the carpet.

It had been a long and disturbing evening. What it should have been was a pleasant night out—dinner at the Barn, followed by scouting the band there for possible fill-in at the Paddlewheel. But then this Jon kid turned up out of Julie's past.

Julie had taken the money from that bank job and turned it into the Paddlewheel, from which had come land holdings and a sporting goods store in Burlington and…and Jon and Logan would want their share, now that they knew she was alive. Julie claimed they'd want even more—revenge, she said. But Harold didn't really buy that. He knew Julie well enough to know that if there was one thing Julie loved besides Julie, it was money; that was the only fever in her, and she wouldn't do the smart thing, the right thing, and call this Logan and the kid Jon in and admit her deceptions and cut them in for a share. No way in hell. She'd do anything but that. Harold knew that only too well. He knew only too well what Julie was capable of, for money.

He sat rubbing his eyes, waiting for the phone to ring. It was almost two in the morning, and he was exhausted. He wanted to go to his room at the house and sleep. Just sleep.

But he had to wait till the phone rang.

Those two guys Julie had contacted, the ones her Chicago connection put her onto, should have called by now.

He didn't like being part of this. He didn't like being any part of killing. It wasn't the first time she'd got him into being part of something that was directly opposed to everything he'd ever been taught, that he'd ever believed in. He didn't understand it, how he could have come to believe in one thing, live for one thing: Julie. The few nights a week in her bed, doled out like a child's allowance; the occasional tender look; those few times a week she'd squeeze his arm and smile, or touch his face. He lived for those. He didn't believe any of them, but he wanted to. And he took what he could get.

And then there were those rare, real moments when she got blue and came to him for some emotional support. When she needed a man to lean on, and for a while, a short while, he'd be a man to her, and to himself.

The phone rang.

It was the long-distance operator with a collect call for anyone from Mr. Smith. Harold accepted the call.

A young, out-of-breath voice said, "This is Infante."

"I was told I'd be speaking to a Sal," Harold said.

"Well, you're speaking to Infante!"

"I better speak to Sal."

"You can't! You can't...he's dead. Sally's dead."

Dead. So it was starting, Harold thought. It was starting again.

On the other end of the phone, Infante seemed to be sobbing.

"Are you all right, Infante?"

"I'm fine!" the young voice said with defiance.

"Where are you?"

"Some restaurant. I'm at a restaurant. Denny's."

"Where?"

"I don't know. Port City? I'm using a pay phone."

"In a booth?"

"It's a kind of stall."

"Well, keep your voice down, then, Infante."

"Yeah. Okay."

"What happened?"

"We had the guy's girlfriend. We were waiting for him. But he came in and surprised us. He killed Sally. With a knife! With a goddamn knife!"

"Please. Why did you leave the Quad Cities?"

"I couldn't stay! He knows who I am, this Logan or Nolan or whatever. He'd come after me."

"Then you better go someplace where you have friends who can hide you."

"I'm not *hiding* from that son-of-a-bitch! I *want* him. He killed *Sally*! Don't you get it?"

"Look. Infante, is it? Go to your friends—"

"*Sally* was my friend. He was all I had! That fucker Nolan, I'm going to *kill* him!"

You better decide whether you're going to kill him or run from him, Harold thought But he said, "What are your plans, then?"

"I'm coming to you."

"Infante, I wouldn't…"

"I don't care what you'd do. I'm coming. You owe me money."

"That'll be taken care of…"

"It sure will. And you can put me up somewhere. While we wait."

"Wait for what?"

"For Nolan."

Harold rubbed his eyes again.

"Yes," he said into the phone, "I suppose you're right. He will be coming, won't he?"

Harold gave Infante some directions and hung up the phone. Harold rarely drank. It was a holdover from his football days; he'd taken training very seriously. And he still took vitamins, watched his diet, worked out at a spa. He was into his thirties, and most men of his physical type would have gone to fat by now. Not Harold.

But right now he felt like a drink. He'd have to go out to that parking lot, where Julie was dealing with that crazy lez, and tell her about Infante. Thinking about her with Ron gave him a sick feeling; thinking about what Infante had told him, and how Julie would react to it, made him feel sicker. He went to the bar just outside his office and unlocked the booze and mixed himself a Manhattan.

Despite his not drinking much, he could make a hell of a mixed drink. He'd been a bartender for three years, after all. That's what he'd been doing when Julie came back into his life a century ago. Last year.

Of course he and Julie went back a lot farther than a year ago. She had been the high school cheerleader, the homecoming queen candidate, the local beauty contest winner, who had caught the eye of the local football hero—Harold. His eye wasn't all she'd caught: on the eve of his freshman year at State, she announced she was pregnant.

No problem: he had scholarship money, and an extra job. And he loved her. Very, very much. So they married. They had a beautiful little girl, Lisa. They were happy. Or at least he was. Julie seemed moody, but it wasn't a bad first year for a marriage. Then his grades got bad.

He hadn't been in Vietnam long when he got the "Dear Harold" letter.

He didn't see any action in 'Nam. He'd had two things going for him: bad eyes and the ability to type. He was a clerk typist, in the rear area, and never heard a shell go off. It was an easy war for Harold.

Peace had been another matter. He was divorced from a woman he still loved. He was a football hero without a college degree and had few qualifications for anything outside of clerical work or a factory job. He ended up a bartender, in an all-night joint in Gulf Port, across the river from Burlington, where he'd gone to work in a college buddy's office as a clerk. He'd thought about bettering himself. He'd considered going back to college and trying again; he'd considered going to a business school, for a two-year degree at least, to bolster his clerical credentials.

But he gave that up after one of the two-week summer visits he had yearly with his daughter. She was being raised by Julie's younger sister and her husband, an executive with a public relations firm in Minneapolis; she was very happy with them. They were her parents, for all intents and purposes. And while Lisa—who was thirteen now—loved her father, enjoyed their visits together, she made it clear she was happy where she was. And one thing Harold wouldn't do was make his daughter unhappy.

There were only two things Harold wanted in life: his daughter, Lisa, who was lost to him, except in the "Uncle Daddy" sense, and his ex-wife, Julie, who had gone into business, with a beauty shop in a small Iowa town called West Liberty, and who wanted nothing to do with him—though she did call him on the phone now and then, when she was feeling low.

So Harold had settled into life-as-existence. He worked at menial jobs. The bartending gig was about the longest-term employment he'd had since the service. He took an odd pride in his ability to mix a good drink, any drink, and talked sports with customers till all hours. Harold did still get some pleasure out of watching sports on TV. That, and listening to old Beach Boys and Beatles albums from his high school days, was about all Harold had.

Till that afternoon last year when Julie showed up at the bar.

She had looked strange. And beautiful, of course. She was wearing a clingy blood-red sweater and slacks. She had a wild look, her eyes aglitter, her hair slightly disarrayed. An animal look. And there was good reason: she was on the run.

"Do you want me back?" she whispered. Just like that. Leaning across the bar. There were only a few customers in the place. Jody's, like most Gulf Port establishments, was a night spot primarily. But she whispered.

"You know I do," he said.

"Can you get somebody to relieve you here?"

"For a few minutes?"

"For until I say different."

"I'll make a call." He did. "The relief guy will be here in twenty minutes. Can it wait till then?"

"Yes," she said, and took a table near the bar.

The new girl, Doris, a blonde of about twenty-five with dark roots and a nice frame and a pleasant, pockmarked face, waited on Julie; Julie ordered coffee. While Doris was off getting it, Julie came to the bar.

"Who is she?"

"Just some transient gal."

"Transient?"

"Divorcee. No kids. Got an ex-husband in Ohio she's on the run from."

"Why?"

"Cause he still loves her. Ever hear of that?"

"What did he do, beat her?"

"I guess."

Julie nodded and went back to the table. Doris brought the coffee.

Julie said, "You're new here, huh?"

Doris smiled, said, "Just collecting a few paychecks, honey. I'm on my way to California."

"Oh. Relatives there?"

"No. My folks are gone and I was the only one. I got a couple of old boyfriends out there, though. That's better than relatives."

"Any time. How's your paycheck collection coming along?"

"What do you mean?"

"I'm on my way to Los Angeles. Just stopped here to look up my ex-husband. He's that good-looking bartender over there."

"Harold's your ex? No kiddin'!"

She sat down.

"Say, I was mostly saving for my bus fare and such. If you can use a rider, somebody who can help you drive, I'll turn in my apron and hop in your car."

Julie smiled and extended a hand. "It's a deal."

Shortly before three o'clock that morning, Harold was in the Mustang, and Doris was behind the wheel. Harold, in the passenger's seat, was steering, because Doris was unconscious. Julie had put Seconal in some coffee Doris drank a few hours before. Harold was off on the shoulder, waiting for Julie. There was some snow on the ground, but no ice on the highway. It was cold. Harold was sweating.

She came over the bridge, driving his old sky-blue Dodge Charger, the one he'd had since college, and she blinked her brights. That meant the truck was coming. He pulled the

Mustang across the mouth of the narrow bridge, left it in park, got out and ran to hop in Julie's waiting car. They were half a mile away when the small bridge behind them seemed to blow up, in a huge orange ball, as though a shell had hit it.

He finished the Manhattan and went out to her. It was chilly in the parking lot; there were no lights on out here, but the full moon provided some unreal-seeming illumination. She was standing with Ron, standing close. He pulled her away from Ron, who stood and watched them, that permanent, pouty snarl on her face.

He told Julie about the call from Infante.

They were talking about it when Ron noticed that kid, Jon, making a break for it, crawling away from her car toward the woods. The lez ran after the kid, dragged him back to the car, tossed him in.

Then Ron came back and said to Julie, "You oughta let me…"

"No," Julie said. "Take him to your place and sit on him."

Ron shrugged. "Okay," she said, and sauntered off to her '57 Ford and rumbled off.

"You're not going to kill that boy, are you?" Harold asked Julie.

"No."

"You mean Ron'll do it for you."

"I need him alive at the moment. Till we find out what Logan's up to."

"He'll come here. He's probably on his way right now."

"I can handle him."

"I don't think so. He sounds like one man you can't handle."

"We'll put this Infante to use."

"He doesn't sound like much. Some poor sappy kid. I'm afraid his partner was the smart one."

"He's the dead one now."

"True. Very true."

"Well, Harold. There's always you."

"I won't kill for you, Julie."

"Right," she said. She put her arm in his. "Let's lock up and go home. We can talk about it."

11

Cool cloth touched his face. It was soothing. Jon opened his eyes.

And looked into Ron's face.

For a moment the face looked almost human: the pouty mouth, the close-set eyes, were in a sort of repose, the nastiness set aside. Then she saw that he was awake and, with just a subtle shift, the features turned ugly again.

She stopped dabbing his face with the damp washrag; she pulled back.

"Don't stop," Jon said. "Feels good."

"You got bunged up," she said. Her tone was strangely apologetic. And almost a whisper. "I was cleaning off the dirt."

His face did hurt; even without touching it, he could feel the raw patches.

"Go ahead," he said. "That felt good, what you were doing."

She shrugged, with her shoulders and mouth both, and started touching his face again. Her touch was gentle. Which struck Jon as weird.

"I...I don't remember passing out," he said.

"You hit your head," she said.

"When?"

"When I tossed you in back of my car, after you tried to crawl off. You hit your head on the door. You got a bump."

He tried to feel his head, and his hand jerked, like a dog on a leash. He glanced over and saw that the hand was cuffed to the headboard of an old brass bed. His left hand was free, however, and he touched the bump on his head; it was sore, but it wasn't a big bump. On the side of his head, though, where she'd hit him with the gun barrel earlier, there was a real goose egg.

"You don't got a concussion or nothing," she said.

He was beginning to get his bearings. He was on his back, on the bed; his right hand was cuffed, and his left leg was, too, by the ankle. She was sitting on the edge of the bed, tending him. The room was dim: the only light on was a shaded lamp on the nightstand. This appeared to be a room in an older home. There was yellow floral wallpaper, faded, and paint was coming off the ceiling in spots, from water damage. Opposite the foot of the bed was an old dresser with mirror; on top of the dresser was a row of trophies of some sort. There was a door to the right; a window over to the left. It was an average-size bedroom. Nothing remarkable about it.

Except maybe for the pictures. The mirror over the dresser was covered with them, pin-ups taped to it, but not of girls: Elvis Presley, James Dean, Eddie Cochran; fifties teen faves, mostly dead. Some of the pictures were faded pages clipped from old magazines, the Scotch tape yellowed and dried; others looked more recent. It was a mirror you couldn't look into. But the faces on it looked back at you, peeking over the row of trophies.

She yanked the cloth away from his raw face. "What are *you* lookin' at?"

"Just the pictures. On the mirror."

"What about 'em?"

"Nothing. They're fine. They're fine."

Her face lost some of its nastiness, and she said, "Your name's Jon, huh?"

"Right. And you're Ron."

"Yeah. Sounds like a poem, don't it? Jon and Ron." She laughed.

He found a little smile for her somewhere and forced something out of him that he hoped sounded like a laugh. *God*, this dyke is *nuts*, he thought.

"I'm, you know…sorry about this," she said. Sullenly.

"Sorry?"

She dragged it out of herself. "I…got nothing against you, really."

"You don't?"

"I used to come listen to you. Your band. You guys were good."

"Thanks."

"You played too much sixties. I like fifties."

"Uh, well, there's lots of requests for sixties stuff these days. But I like fifties music myself."

She smiled; the sullenness was gone. "I know. I heard you do 'Whole Lotta Shakin'.' Anybody that can do Jerry Lee that good is okay by me."

"I'm…glad you liked it."

"Look, I know I probably made a…bad impression that time, few months ago, when I got on your case for being with Darlene. I know it's not your fault. Darlene, she's always hitting on people."

He tried to think of something to say to that, but couldn't. He was trying to stay low key and calm, trying not to scream at her. She seemed relatively calm herself at the moment, and he had a feeling that keeping her that way might be to his benefit.

"Are you hungry?" she asked suddenly.

"I…hadn't really thought about it."

"Well, are you?" Nastier.

"Sure. Sure. If it…wouldn't be too much trouble."

"Naw! Not at all. How 'bout a ham sandwich and a beer?"

"That'd be…great."

"No problem," she said, smiling, rising. She sauntered over toward the door and out.

What a fucking fruitcake! he thought, and began to take toll of his situation. He took a look at the headboard of the bed. He was cuffed to one of its brass posts; there didn't seem to be any way to slide the cuff off the thing. And he certainly couldn't pull his wrist through the cuff.

He was able to get into a sitting position, but he could stay that way only by supporting himself with his free hand. It allowed him to see that his ankle (his shoes were off; he could see them over on the floor, by the dresser) was cuffed to the brass end rail of the bed.

For having an arm and a leg free, he was pretty goddamn helpless.

If he didn't feel so weak, he could try to overpower her; maybe knock her out with a punch when she got close, or kick her in the head or something. But then what?

Then she was there with the sandwich and beer, a Coors.

She'd taken off the leather jacket; she was in T-shirt and jeans now, her smallish breasts poking at her T-shirt in a reminder that she was female.

She handed him the sandwich and a paper napkin and said, "I put hot mustard on it."

"I like hot mustard."

"You got beer to wash it down with." She put the beer on the nightstand, since he didn't have a hand handy to take it.

He ate the sandwich. He was starving. He didn't realize it till he got the food in front of him, but he was starving.

She was smiling as she watched him eat. And not at all in a sinister way. The dimness of the room, with its single source of light, threw shadows on her and everything else, but the effect was softening.

When he was finished, she said, "Use another beer to wash that down better?"

"Uh. Sure. That'd be great."

This time she left the door open as she went, and he could see her going out into the hall and taking a right down some stairs; he could hear her feet on the stairs, and then again, a couple minutes later, coming back up.

She gave him a second Coors; she'd brought a beer for herself, too, but in a glass. She had an empty coffee can under her arm and set it on the floor by the bed.

"What's that for?" he asked.

"You can't buy beer, you can only rent it," she said.

"Oh."

"Can you reach it there?"

"I don't think so."

"With your hand, stupid."

He reached over with his left hand and could feel the lip of the can.

"Yeah," he said. "Thanks."

She sat on the edge of the bed again.

"How old are you?" she asked him.

"Twenty-one," he said.

"How old you think I am?"

Thirty.

"Twenty," he said.

"Twenty-five," she grinned, with a slight foam mustache.

Thirty.

"Fooled me," Jon said.

"I live right," she explained.

"Uh, Ron?"

"Yeah?"

"Why am I here?"

"How the fuck should I know?"

"Well. You did bring me here."

"Yeah. So?"

"Well, why'd you do it? Why am I tied up like this?"

"That's between you and Julie."

"Julie."

"Yeah. I'm only doing this 'cause she asked me to. I don't get no pleasure out of it."

"You don't."

"Fuck, no. You're a nice kid. You sing good. I like you."

"You do."

She smiled again—a real smile, with some gums showing, and disarming, in a weird fucking way. "Yeah. I don't always like guys, you know."

"You don't?"

"Nope. But I don't always like girls, either." She touched his leg.

He couldn't think of anything to say.

"You thought I was queer, didn't you?" she said.

"Oh. I don't know."

"I like girls. I like guys, too, sometimes. I don't know. Sometimes, it's…well, it's easier for me with girls."

"Is it easy with Julie?"

He'd crossed some line he shouldn't have. She pulled her hand away from his leg, and the nasty look returned. "Don't get cute, prick," she said.

"I didn't mean anything by it."

"You just better stay on my good side."

"Hey, I'm not here because I asked to be, you know."

"Yeah. I know. You got a better temper about it than I would, I guess."

"Do you work for Julie?"

"I do stuff for her. I'm kind of a night watchman at the Paddlewheel. Most of Gulf Port is all-night places, but Julie closes up at two. So I keep an eye on the place most nights."

"Not tonight."

"No. Tonight I'm keeping an eye on you."

"I see."

"If Julie wants me to sit on you, she's got her reasons. It's between the two of you. I got nothin' to do with it."

"How much do you know about her?"

Ron smiled. "I know her pretty well."

"She tried to kill me once. With a shotgun."

"Sure," she said, sipping her glass of Coors.

"We were in on a bank job together, and she tried to kill my partner and me."

"You? A bank robber? Don't make me choke."

"She took the money. Where do you think she got the money for the Paddlewheel, you dumb cunt? Then I saw her at the Barn, tonight, and she figures I'll tell my partner about her, and she's afraid he'll come after her."

That stopped Ron. For some reason—Jon's near-hysteria, perhaps—it had rung true to her.

"What'll he do, this guy?" she asked.

"I don't know. Now that she's kidnapped me, I don't know what he's liable to do."

"Kidnapped. Who's kidnapped?"

"I'm handcuffed to the goddamn bed, lady. What the fuck do you *think* this is?"

Ron got up, walked around.

"Julie said sit on you," she said. "I'm doing what she asked me to and that's all."

"I heard you. And I heard you say back at that parking lot you'd as soon kill me as look at me."

Ron turned and looked at him, and there was an expression on her face that could only be described as a mixture of pain and embarrassment. She came over and sat on the edge of the bed and picked up the washrag from the nightstand and touched a couple places on his face again. Then she put the washrag down and said, "That was just bullshit."

"Was it."

"I'm sorry about your face getting bunged up, and your head. I hit you with the gun pretty hard. I…"

She lowered her head.

"I show off sometimes," she said. "When somebody like Darlene's around…or somebody like Julie, especially Julie…I show off. I get tough. Act tough. Talk tough. Overdo it. Don't ask me why."

Why is she telling me this? Jon wondered.

"She's going to ask you to kill me," Jon said.

"Naw. It'll never happen."

"You've done things for her before."

"I roughed some people up for her before. Big deal."

"You kidnapped me tonight for her."

"Kidnapped! Nobody's been kidnapped."

"Ron. Let me go, before you get in this any deeper."

"Yeah, and you'd go to the cops."

"I can't go to the cops."

"Why, 'cause you're a bank robber? You're funny."

"Ron, Julie's going to call your bluff. She's going to ask you to kill me. Are you up to that?"

Ron thought about that.

"I'm tired of talkin'," she said, rising. "You get some sleep."

She switched off the lamp and left the room.

For about an hour, Jon worked at the cuffs, tried to see if the headboard of the bed could be unscrewed or otherwise come loose from the bed itself.

Then sun was coming in the window, and Ron was coming in the door. She was still wearing jeans and T-shirt and had a plate of eggs and ham in one hand and orange juice in the other.

"Did you sleep?" she asked.

"I guess," Jon said, not sure.

"If I give you this stuff, will you be good?"

"I won't try anything," he said.

"All right," she said, and gave him the food. She stood over by the dresser and leaned against it while he ate. She fingered one of the trophies on the dresser.

"This was my brother's room," she said. Out of nowhere.

"Really? Where is he now?"

"Dead."

"Uh. I'm sorry."

"Stock car accident. That's what the trophies are."

"I'm very sorry."

"He was about your age when he cracked up."

"Really? When was this?"

"Fifteen years ago, June."

"You must've loved him."

"Yeah. I thought a lot of him. He was what kept this place going."

"Oh?"

"I had three little sisters. My mom and dad drank, and Billy... my brother...he was tough. If Dad tried to hit one of us, he'd belt him. From about thirteen on he could beat the crap outa my old man."

"No kidding."

"When Billy got killed, I...kind of took over. Stepped in. Otherwise my old man would've started in on us again. Boy, did it shock the shit out of *him*."

"What did?"

She laughed. "When he found out his little girl could beat the crap out of him too. He only stuck around about a year after that."

"Where's the rest of the family now?"

"Mom's dead. Bad liver. The girls are all married. One of 'em just this last summer. Too young: sixteen. I didn't raise her right, maybe. Pregnant. Oh well. Maybe she'll be happy."

In the distance, bells were sounding.

"It's Sunday," she said. "I'm gonna be gone a while. Think you can get along without me?"

"Do I have a choice? Where are you going?"

"Mass, stupid," she said.

She went out, shutting the door this time.

"Light a candle for me," Jon said.

James Dean and company stared at him while he struggled with the cuffs and the headboard. About fifteen minutes later, he heard her go out; he wondered what she looked like dressed for church. Then he got back to his struggling. And got nowhere. He fell asleep after a while.

He woke and it was dark in the room. It wasn't night: the shades were drawn. A little light crawled in under the shade and from around the edges, but the nightstand lamp was off, and there was no other light in the room.

She was standing near the bed. She wasn't wearing anything. Her body wasn't great, but it wasn't bad; she had a square-ish frame with modest breasts, but there was no fat on her. It was a supple, vaguely muscular body. She had a tattoo of a black rose near her right hipbone, just above her pubic thatch. Her pouty face didn't look pretty, exactly, but she wasn't ugly.

He didn't say anything as she undid his pants.

"No man ever made me come," she said. "Do you think you can, Jon?"

"I'll try," Jon managed.

She sat on him.

Four

12

Nolan almost missed the sign.

It was over to the left, a barn-wood sign about four by four, with the following words painted on in faded red: "THE BARN, Turn Right." This was lit from beneath by two small floods.

He turned right, off the highway onto gravel. The road was narrow, its ditches deep, and to stay out of them, Nolan slowed to about thirty. He could see the structure up ahead, beyond the flattened cornfields, up to the right. It was stark in the moonlight, a barn with a tin shed growing out of it, like an outstretched arm.

In front of the barn was a graveled parking lot, and he pulled into it. There were no other cars in the lot. He got out of the little red Datsun, which he'd gotten from Sherry, tucking the silenced 9mm, which he'd gotten from dead Sal, into his waistband. He hadn't taken time to change clothes—he was still wearing the corduroy jacket and turtleneck and slacks he'd worn to Iowa City today, though that seemed like a year ago—and he felt less than refreshed.

The drive from the Quad Cities had drained him. He'd had a long day, too much of it spent behind the wheel of a car, and the rest poring over the books with Wagner and the Pier's accountant, and drinking a little too much afterward. And then the shit had hit the fan, and he'd pulled the energy out of somewhere; the adrenalin had pumped and he'd managed to save that nice ass of Sherry's and rid the world of that cocksucker Sal, whose body he'd dumped on a side road between the Quad Cities and Port City.

Right now he felt every one of his fifty-odd years, after a cramped hour-and-a-half in a small car, on a rolling, narrow two-lane highway, watching for speed traps, popping No-Doz to force his alertness to an artificial edge.

He stood and stretched and looked at the barn that was the Barn, letting the chill air have at him. Between the full moon and a number of tall posts with outdoor lights, the exterior of the structure was well lit, though its windows were dark. He didn't bother trying the front, restaurant, entrance, but walked around to the side door.

He could see the rustic bar, with its booths and wanted posters, through the steel-cross-hatched window of the door; there were enough beer signs lit to get a look. Not a soul. He walked around the long tin shed—it seemed a block long—and found some more empty parking lot at the rear.

On the other side of the building, though, in still more parking lot, were several vehicles.

There was a big four-wheel drive, a Land Rover, two-tone tan; a snow plow; and a van.

The van was light blue with a painted logo on it that said "THE NODES."

Jon's group.

Jon's van.

Nolan slipped out of his shoes.

It hurt to walk on the gravel in his goddamn socks, but it was quiet. The van had no side windows, but there were windows in back. On his toes (ouch—fuck!) he could peek in. He saw a lumpy bundle on the floor, a blanket over some stuff, he guessed. *Could* be a small person sleeping. He couldn't tell.

He looked in the front windows; the driver's and rider's seats were empty. He quietly tried the doors on either side. Locked.

Now what?

Somebody was in the Barn. There had to be, or the owners were goddamn dumb. A big place like this, stuck between a couple of cornfields, full of booze and other inventory, not to mention furniture and fixtures—hell, there *had* to be a sleep-in watchman. Without one, you'd go broke in a week.

So somebody was in there—somebody who belonged to the tan Land Rover.

Which meant Nolan could go to a door and start banging his fist till somebody inside answered. And that somebody *might* know something about the abandoned Nodes van. Julie couldn't have grabbed the whole goddamn *band*, could she?

He went to the nearest door, which wasn't far from the parked Land Rover, and stopped.

Jon's phone call had brought him here, but Jon was, obviously, in trouble. The kind of trouble Sherry had been in, no doubt, or worse. What guarantee was there that Nolan wasn't walking into some setup right now? Knocking, announcing himself, could be very stupid....

He went to the Land Rover and lifted the hood.

It took about thirty seconds for the sound of the sticking, blaring horn to get a reaction inside the building. A dog barked; some lights went on; movement within. Nolan was waiting, his back to the building, to the right of the door, 9mm in hand, as the man looked out—a big man, tall, wearing a hunting jacket over a bare chest and shiny blue pajama bottoms. He had a shotgun.

The man was only partway out, the door open, leaning toward the Land Rover and its blaring horn; he didn't see Nolan, who was behind the partly open door. That was good.

Not good was the snarling dog on the other side of that door, a big dog, from the sound of it, who may not have seen Nolan but obviously sensed him, and knew *exactly* where he was.

Fortunately, the dog was unable to transfer its knowledge to his owner, who said, "Stay back, Queenie—I'll let you know if I need you."

But Queenie had a mind of her own, and as the man stepped out of the doorway onto the gravel, Queenie lurched forward.

Just as she did, Nolan shut the door on the bitch, hard, catching the snapping animal by the shoulders, lodging it there.

"Order it back!" Nolan said, shoulder pushing against the door. The dog, which had shut up for a second, caught by surprise and pain, was barking hysterically, trying to get its big German Shepherd head around to where she could bite off Nolan's left hand, on the door knob. Above it all, the Land Rover's horn was going as though this was a jail break.

The guy was standing there, his back to Nolan, but partially turned, glancing over his shoulder to see the gun in Nolan's right hand. His own shotgun was slack in his hands.

"Order it back, I said," Nolan said, straining against the door.

"Queenie," the man said. "Get back."

The dog's snapping turned into a quiet growl.

"Get back, Queenie."

The dog pulled back.

Nolan shut the door. Behind it the dog still growled. Even the blare of the Land Rover's horn couldn't drown it out.

The big man in hunting jacket and pajama bottoms twitched, as if about to turn.

Nolan said, "You can't turn fast enough."

The guy kept his back to Nolan but turned his head just enough to give Nolan a "Fuck you" look.

Nolan said, "Toss the shotgun. Toss it good."

The guy tossed it.

"Go fix your horn," Nolan said.

The guy walked slowly toward the Land Rover. Nolan followed. The guy lifted the hood, stopped the blaring. He shut the hood, then turned and looked at Nolan and said, "I'm gonna..."

"You're going to shut up," Nolan said.

The guy did.

"I'm not a thief," Nolan said, which wasn't exactly true, but in this case was. "I'm not here to cause you any harm."

"Go to hell."

"Lean back against the four-wheel. Put your hands on the hood."

He did.

"What's your name?" Nolan asked.

"Fuck you."

"Don't be stupid. This isn't a contest."

"Bob Hale."

"You the watchman?"

He bristled. "I *own* the damn place."

"No offense. This van here."

"What about it?"

"It's the band's, isn't it? The band that played here tonight, correct?"

"Yeah. Correct."

"What's it doing here?"

"I don't know. I'm surprised it's still here myself."

Nolan was afraid of that.

"Some of 'em loaded some equipment in a trailer and left," Hale was saying. "They said the other guy would probably be by tomorrow for his amplifiers and shit, which is still inside."

"The other guy."

"Jon. The leader. Had a chance to get laid or something and bugged out. He'll turn up for his stuff tomorrow."

There was a sound behind Nolan; he turned, quick, and saw the rear doors of the Nodes van open up.

"Get out slow," Nolan said. He was standing with his back to the building, which he didn't like doing, but it allowed him to keep an eye on both Hale, by the Land Rover, and whoever it was climbing out of the Nodes van.

"Let's see your hands," Nolan ordered. "Over your head."

It was a girl. A young woman in a denim jacket and jeans. So the bundle under the blanket *had* been a small, sleeping person.

"I wanted to make sure it was you," she said. She was staying near the van. A busty little brunette with a pretty, heart-shaped face.

"You're Jon's girl, aren't you?" Nolan said.

"Not his girl, exactly," she said, shrugging. "But I'm who you think I am. I think."

"Toni, isn't it?"

"Yes," she said. She seemed surprised that he remembered her name. And a little pleased. "Can I put my hands down?"

"Yes, and come over here."

She went to Hale.

"Bob," she said, putting a hand on his arm, which was still leaning back so he could keep his hands on the Land Rover's hood, per Nolan's instructions, "this is a friend of Jon's. I didn't want to worry you before, Bob…but something's happened to Jon."

He looked confused. "What are you talking about?"

"Somebody's kidnapped him, I think," Toni said.

"Did you call the cops?" Hale asked.

"Can't," Toni said.

"Better be quiet," Nolan told her.

"Why can't you?" Hale asked.

Nolan raised his gun.

"Just asking," Hale said.

Nolan looked at Toni. She nodded. He looked at Hale. He said, "Jon and I are involved with some people who wouldn't like the police involved. You don't want to know any more than that."

"You're right," Hale said.

"I'll put my gun away if you'll take us inside and keep your dog off."

"Okay." Hale shrugged.

"Go get his shotgun," Nolan told Toni.

She did.

Nolan broke it open, handed the shells to Hale, then handed him the empty gun as well.

He turned to Toni. "Get my shoes, would you?"

"You're in your stocking feet!"

"That's why I want my shoes." He pointed to them.

She got them for him. He put them on.

Then Hale led them into the Barn, commanding his surly dog to heel, which it did, reluctantly.

Hale took them out into the bar, where he turned on some lights. The dog headed for a nearby pinball machine and curled up beneath it and slept; even in repose, it looked like a killer. Nolan asked Hale if he had some coffee. Hale asked if instant was okay and Nolan said fine.

While Hale got the coffee, Nolan got the story of what had happened here, from Toni's point of view.

"When Jon never got back," she said, "I went out and found the van was still here. I couldn't think of anything to do but hope you got Jon's message, and wait for you to show up."

"So you waited in the van."

"Yeah, but I fell asleep and didn't hear you get here. Didn't hear you prowling around, either. You say you tried the doors on the van?"

"The ones up front, yes."

"And I slept right through it. I'm not very good at this, am I?"

"Well, you're new at it. And I'm quiet."

"Yeah, you sneak around in your socks. I didn't wake up till that horn started in. Scared the shit out of me, too."

"So Julie runs a gambling joint," Nolan said. "That explains the Chicago connection."

"What?"

Nolan shushed her, as Hale joined them in the booth with the coffee. The big man seemed almost friendly now. He had even taken the time to put some money in the jukebox; Charlie Daniels was singing something mournful at the moment. But it did serve to give a social flavor to this forced meeting.

And Hale clearly liked Toni; he looked at her with an obvious, though somehow childish, lust.

"Why'd you stay out in that van?" Hale asked her. "If I'd known you was in trouble, you could've come stayed in my pad."

"I never thought of that," she said with a straight face.

"Toni says this woman—this Julie," Nolan said, as if he didn't know who Julie was, "asked about Jon."

"Yeah. She was interested in booking 'em over at her club."

"His band, you mean."

"Yeah. She has quite the place, over there by Gulf Port."

"Tell me about it—the Paddlewheel."

"I suppose I could. I could also call Julie, after you leave, and tell her you was asking about her, you know."

Toni touched Hale's arm again. "Please don't."

"You don't want in this any deeper than you already are," Nolan told him. It wasn't exactly a threat.

Hale thought about that.

Then he said, "Okay, you convinced me. Ask me what you want and get out of here. I want to get back to bed. Listening to that dog is making me sleepy."

Over under the pinball machine, his dog was snoring.

"You know," Hale said, "you could just as easy killed that bitch of mine out there. But you didn't. Maybe that says something about you."

"Maybe it does," Nolan said.

13

The double bed, covered by a garish green and red floral spread, came out of the wall at right; a TV and dresser with mirror were against the wall at left. There was just enough room between for Infante to pace.

It was a dingy little room, with smudged-looking yellow plaster walls and a green shag carpet speckled with dirt; over the bed was a picture of two horses running. Tacky, Infante thought. Just the sort of depressing room he *didn't* need right now. But he had no choice but to be here; this was where that guy Harold said to come. Besides which, there wasn't any other motel in Gulf Port.

Infante had rolled in just after three and had driven around a little bit, checking it out, and found Gulf Port wasn't a town at all, not really—just a collection of trailers and shacks, no business section or anything. If there hadn't been a full moon, he wouldn't have been able to see the town, hardly, which would have been okay with him.

Scattered along the outskirts of Gulf Port, though, were eight or ten bars, all thriving, and that explained it: Gulf Port wasn't a town, it was a watering hole, a place to go when the bars across the river closed up at two.

The motel was down the road from a place called Upper's, a big one-story brown brick country rock joint with a hundred cars in the lot. The neon sign in front of the motel said "EEZER INN" in pulsing orange. Cute, Infante thought. The woman at the check-in desk was chubby and about fifty-five, with a lot of makeup and perfume and a frilly white blouse unbuttoned enough to show the start of big, withering boobs. Sickening. Ex-whore, he supposed. She was reading a Harlequin paperback. She'd tried giving him a sexy smile as she handed his room key over to him, and it all but made him barf.

There were ten units in front and another ten in back, and about half of them were full up. He'd asked for one in back, and now he was pacing around inside the dreary little cubicle, feeling as unappealing as the desk clerk and as dirty as the room itself.

He hadn't had time to grab any of his things before leaving. He was still in the black outfit he had worn with Sally when they went in after Nolan's bitch. He felt dirty. He needed a shave. He considered taking a shower, but then he'd just have to get back in these sweaty clothes, and he couldn't stand the thought of that.

He'd shower after his employers, the man Harold and the woman Julie, had come and gone. He had called them as soon as he got in the room, which was five minutes ago; they should be here any time now.

He stopped pacing. He sat on the double bed, with his back to the running horses. The silenced 9mm in his waistband nudged him, and he took it out and put it beside him, on the bed. Then he sat leaning forward, his elbows on his knees, forehead against the palms of his hands. He felt very alone. He missed Sally.

"I'm going to kill that fucker," he said. To himself. Through his teeth.

He sat up. He could see himself in the dresser mirror. He looked bad—scroungy. But he looked at himself, pointed a finger at himself, and said, "Understand? *Kill* the fucker!"

There was a knock at the door.

He got up, took the gun with him just in case, cracked the

door (there was no night latch), and it was a sandy-haired man in dark-rimmed glasses, big—not tall, but big—and good-looking, in a rough way. He was wearing a yellow sports shirt and tan slacks. Smelled of Brut.

"You're Infante," the man said.

"You're Harold."

"Right." The big man turned and motioned to somebody in the car pulled in next to Infante's jet-black Mazda. The car was a cream-color Porsche. Which said class. Which also said money. Maybe this wasn't such a bad crowd to be in with after all, Infante thought.

A woman got out. She was wearing black slacks and a silky blouse, tits flopping. Handsome enough woman, he supposed. Nice clothes, anyway.

The guy went to her; he had a fluid walk, like an athlete. Put an arm around her. He was a muscular sort—big shoulders. *Works with weights*, Infante bet.

The two of them came in.

Infante closed and locked the door and stuck the gun back in his waistband and said, "This place is a dump, in case you missed it."

The woman, Julie, turned to him and smiled. It was an attractive smile, not that he gave a damn. "I'm sorry we couldn't do better for you," she said. "Gulf Port isn't exactly Las Vegas, you know."

"That's not the way I heard it," Infante said.

"If you mean the Paddlewheel, it's not in Gulf Port proper. It's a few miles from here, on the river."

"You wouldn't think people running a classy place like that would stick a friend in a dump like this."

The man, Harold, sat on the bed. "Infante, this is only tem-porary...."

"Put me up in the Holiday Inn across the river, then, back in Burlington. I'm allergic to cockroaches."

Julie touched his arm, and he batted it away.

"Excuse me," she said, searching his face. "You see, we need to have you close at hand. We need you here."

"Yeah, well, we'll see."

"I think we have mutual interests. Sit down, won't you?" She gestured toward the space on the double bed, next to Harold. Infante sat down.

"Harold said your partner was killed," the woman said.

"Yeah. Yeah he was killed. Goddammit."

"This man Logan…"

"His name is Nolan."

"Nolan, then. He did it."

"Yeah he did it."

"And you want even."

"Of course I want even. What kind of guy do you think I am?"

She seemed to think about that for a moment, then said, "We're going to pay you what we promised, even though you and your partner didn't exactly…succeed."

Infante sighed. "Look. I gotta admit something. Sally handled the business end. I don't even know what you promised us. Sally was the brains, I have to say."

The woman walked back and forth, slowly, thinking, smiling. "Then why don't we just start over? Why don't we pick a new figure? How's ten thousand dollars?"

"Ten…"

"That's a lot of money, isn't it?"

"It sure…"

"Enough for you to disappear for a while?"

"Sure."

"Then you'll do it?"

"Do what?"

"Kill Nolan."

"Try and stop me!"

"Oh," she smiled, not pacing, stopping in front of him, "I'm not about to do that."

Next to him, the big guy seemed glum. Sensitive face, Infante thought.

"Now," she was saying, "when can we expect him to arrive?"

"Nolan? I'd say…couple days. Late tomorrow at the soonest."

Harold said, "How do you figure that?"

"He's got Family friends. He'll want to check with 'em about who sent us. They'll be able to find out too, pretty easy."

"Couldn't he do that with just a phone call?" Julie asked. "Couldn't he be on his way here right now?"

"I don't see how," Infante said. "All he knows is two Family boys tried to kill him. He's going to figure, at first, that he's on the shit list for some reason. Which'll send him off in the wrong direction. He'll go to Chicago and hit on a few people in person till he finds out what's going on."

Julie was nodding. "You're right" she said. "I know this man; that's what he'd do."

Harold said to Infante, "How long will it take him?"

Infante shrugged. "Once he knows the Family didn't send us, he'll find you. No question. He's in tight with some pretty high-up people. A few phone calls, and they'll have you cold."

"Julie," Harold said, "*you've* got Chicago connections. That's how we got hold of Infante and his partner. Couldn't you…"

"Sorry," Infante interrupted, "but any connections you got are much smaller shots than the people Nolan's tight with. The guy I work for, Mr. Hines, who is in the Bahamas at the moment, didn't like it when this Nolan came to the Quad Cities, opening up a club. He complained and pretty soon there was a phone call. From a guy named Felix. He's nobody you ever heard of, but what Sally told me is he's like the corporate lawyer for the

Family. And he told Mr. Hines that Nolan was a personal friend. So Nolan's well connected, all right."

"Shit," Julie said. She wasn't smiling now.

Harold said to her, "That means you can't turn to your Chicago friends for help."

"I don't dare to, no, dammit," she said. She had a hand on one hip and rubbed her forehead with her other hand.

"If Nolan's connected," Harold continued, "killing…killing him might cause you trouble. Family trouble."

She shot the man a look that said he was saying too much in front of a relative outsider like Infante.

But Harold pressed on. "You could leave," he suggested.

"Don't be silly."

"He's right," Infante said. "Just take off. Your boyfriend and me can handle Nolan." Infante patted Harold's shoulder. "We'll let you know when the smoke clears."

She laughed. "I told you I *know* this man, Logan, Nolan, whatever. He's not easily handled. But he does have a weakness."

"What's that?" Infante said.

"Harold," Julie said, "I'm kind of parched. Get us some Cokes from the machine, would you?"

Harold shrugged, rose; Infante watched the man walk to the door. Graceful for a big guy. He went out.

She sat on the bed next to Infante. She didn't touch him, but kept her distance.

"Harold's a bit squeamish," she said.

"A lot of big guys are soft at the center," Infante said.

"Harold has his strong points."

"I bet he does."

"I just don't want him hearing what I'm going to tell you."

"Okay."

"Nolan's got this friend. This close friend."

"Yeah, so?"

"It's this kid, about twenty. Muscular, curly haired little guy. Cute."

"Yeah?"

"And they're close friends. You catch my drift yet?"

"You mean…Nolan and this kid…?"

"Right."

"He's living with a broad, for Christ's sake."

"So what?"

Infante thought about that, said, "Yeah, right. So he's double-gaited, so what about it?"

"So I got the kid."

Infante grinned. "No shit?"

"None at all. I'm keeping him at a place just a few miles from here."

"He's your guest, only it wasn't his idea, you mean."

"Right. A friend of mine's sitting on him."

"I'm liking the sound of this. Go on."

"I'm not leaving. Or hiding, or anything. I'm waiting for Nolan to show up, and then I'm going to use the kid on him."

"How?"

"I'll make Nolan an offer. He figures I owe him, from a past thing. And he won't be thrilled I sent you and your partner after him. But he likes money. He can be bought. And he likes this kid."

"So, you'll settle up with him?"

"I'll offer him money and give the kid back; all he has to do is just go away."

"Will he buy that?"

"He'll do what he has to to get the kid. And the money won't hurt."

"I take it he doesn't know yet that you have this kid?"

Julie smiled. "We grabbed him before he had a chance to get a message out."

"Where do I come in?"

"When I hand the kid over to him, you'll kill them both. Any problem with that?"

"No. How's it going to work, exactly?"

The door opened.

Harold was back with the Cokes. He passed the cans around, and everybody sipped at them. Julie took two slow drinks of hers, then put it on the dresser.

"I'll be back in touch," she said.

Harold looked a little confused.

She headed for the door, and Harold, looking back at Infante suspiciously, followed.

"Get some sleep," she told Infante, and they were gone.

He sat on the bed. The gun nudged his belly again, and he took it out of his waistband and laid it on the bed, next to him, gently. Ten thousand dollars. He smiled.

He took his shower. Hot, steaming shower. He was starting to feel better. Every few minutes, though, he had a grief pang; he came out of the bathroom, towel wrapped around him, and saw the empty double bed and couldn't hold back the tears.

He sat on the edge of the bed and cried, his body trembling. Now and then rage would flood through him and he'd say, "*Kill the fucker.*"

He was doing this when another knock came at the door.

He rubbed his hand across his face.

So the woman was back. She ditched the hunk and was going to fill him in on the details. Fine.

He took the gun with him, just in case it wasn't Julie, and went to the door and cracked it open, and it wasn't Julie.

It was Nolan.

14

It was well after four in the morning when Nolan let Bob Hale and his dog go back to sleep, and headed out for Sherry's Datsun in the Barn parking lot. The girl, Toni, followed him. He opened the door on the driver's side, and the girl grabbed his forearm.

"I'm going with you," she said.

He didn't say anything.

"I'm not going to argue with you. I'm going. And that's the end of it."

He didn't say anything.

"You need me. I been to Gulf Port before—know my way around the bars. I know how to find Darlene. That's the little cunt that tricked Jon into going out to the van for a quickie. She had to be in on it, or at least see what happened, see who grabbed him."

He didn't say anything.

"I can find her. I know she hangs around the bars in Gulf Port. Seems to me she might even live there; if not, across the river in Burlington. I can find her. And if you find her, you find Jon. So I'm going. You need me, and I'm not going to argue with you."

"Get in," Nolan said.

"What?"

"Get in. We're wasting time standing here yakking."

"I'm going?"

"Of course you're going. I wouldn't have it any other way." He smiled at her, just a little. "Get in."

She got in.

It was only ten minutes to Burlington, a city on rolling hills overlooking the Mississippi, an industrial town of thirty-some thousand, whose various facelifts did not conceal its age. A freeway, lined with shelves of ivy-covered shale, cut through the old river town, and after paying the thirty cents round-trip toll, they were rumbling over the steel bridge, to Illinois and Gulf Port.

The sign just beyond the bridge directed them to the left, but the road curved around to the right, finally depositing them in a pocket below the busy interstate, where Gulf Port rested like a wound that hadn't healed properly.

On first impression, Gulf Port was nothing but bars. Bars with big parking lots full of cars and trucks. Even just driving by, it was clear just how rowdy these places were, drunks and loud music constantly tumbling out the doors. In the background, among trees that hid the river, he could make out the towers of a grain elevator, which seemed to be the only business of any consequence in Gulf Port that didn't serve beer. He drove through the narrow, unpaved streets and found that this was little more than a trailer court, with an occasional sagging house thrown in for variety. No grocery store; no business section at all. He hadn't even seen a gas station yet, though there probably was one among the bars.

"Shitty place to visit, and I wouldn't want to live here," the girl commented. It was the first thing she'd said since they left the Barn.

Nolan nodded. "Welfare ghetto, looks like."

He drove back toward the bars.

"According to Hale," he said, "these bars'll be open till five. That doesn't give you much time to spot this Darlene."

"It should be enough. There's a bar on the farthest end of

town, about the nicest one. It's called Upper's. Turn here."

He did.

"It's down there. See the sign?"

He saw it: a standing metal sign that in blue neon said "UPPER'S" at the front of a large parking lot. He pulled in. The lot was eighty percent full. A few well-plastered customers, men in their twenties in jeans and western-style jackets, with the long hair that once would have branded them hippies but now probably meant young blue-collar worker, were pushing each other around and laughing, just outside the front door. The building itself was a low-slung brick building, brown, with a tile roof; a big place, despite being only one story. The front door was closed at the moment, but it didn't entirely muffle the country-rock music within.

"She'll be in there if she's anywhere," the girl said.

"If she isn't?"

"If she isn't, she's in the sack with some lowlife. That's my guess, anyway."

"Hooker?"

"I think a few beers is all she costs. But it's possible she's hooking."

"How sure are you she lives here?"

"If she doesn't, she lives back in Burlington. She and that dyke I told you about were at the Burlington gigs the Nodes played."

"Okay. I want you to go in and see if she's in there."

"And?"

"And then we're going to wait and follow her home."

"Why don't I just corner her in the ladies' can or something?"

"Once we've talked to her, we'll have to shut her up."

The girl winced. "You don't mean…"

"No, I don't mean that. But we got to tie her up and gag her.

Which if she's hooking is probably part of her scene anyway."

She smiled. "You're funny."

"A riot."

"We're going to get Jon, aren't we? He's going to be all right, right?"

"I don't know. I'm not promising you anything."

"He'll be all right. I know he will."

"Listen. Toni, isn't it? You got to face something: he may be dead right now."

She swallowed hard; her eyes looked wide and wet. Pretty little thing, Nolan thought.

"That's the kind of people we're dealing with," he said. "I'm sorry it's the case, but it is the case. Now. Go in there and see if that bitch is getting beers bought for her."

She nodded, got out. She had a nice rear end on her, Nolan noted clinically.

He sat and waited. He was tired. He rolled the window down, and the cold air felt good. He'd trade his left nut for an hour's sleep. But the stream of drunks and near-drunks coming in and out of the place, plus the country-rock music in the background, served to keep him from dropping off, and then the girl was back.

"She's in there," she said. Smiling like a conspirator.

"Fine."

"What now?"

"We wait."

"And follow her home."

"Right."

They sat there for ten minutes.

"Are you okay?" she said.

"I'm fine. Why?"

"You look like you're ready to fall asleep."

"That's because I'm fifty years old and been up a like number of hours."

"Well, I can watch for her. You sleep."

"Thanks, no thanks."

She patted his arm. "Jon's going to be all right."

He said nothing.

Five minutes later, a rather tall, heavily made-up girl with shaggy brunette hair, wearing a black down-filled jacket over a Marshall Tucker T-shirt and tight jeans, walked out arm in arm with a big, somewhat drunk guy in a cowboy hat, padded cowhide vest, and jeans.

"That's her," Toni said.

The couple swayed to a red truck, one of those hotrod pickups on the other side of the lot and the big guy stumbled behind the wheel as she got in on the rider's side and they pulled out. Nolan followed.

It wasn't far; in a "town" the size of Gulf Port, it couldn't be. The trailer was one of half a dozen others on a desolate, somewhat shaded block two blocks from Upper's. This apparently allowed Darlene to do her local bar-crawling without taking her car, because a several-year-old green Maverick was parked in front; rust was eating it. She guided the cowboy out of his pickup, up the couple of steps and inside.

"Well?" Toni said as they drove past.

"Let's wait till the pickup leaves," Nolan said.

"Shouldn't we…?"

"We'll talk to her by herself. We don't need to involve any civilians. This is complicated enough as is. We know where she lives. We'll come back later."

"That guy'll be there all night!"

"Right." He pulled over. "I'm getting in back," he told her. "I'll keep down. I want you to drive to that motel down from

Upper's and get a room. It's the only motel in town, and they may be watching for me for Julie. So you get the room."

She nodded, and they got out, and he got in back and she got behind the wheel.

Soon they were in the motel room, a dingy little yellow room with a double bed and a picture of a ship at sea over the bed. Toni appraised the latter and said, "At least it isn't on black velvet."

"What?" Nolan said.

"Nothing. What are we doing here?"

"I'm getting some sleep. You can do what you want."

"But what about Jon? Shouldn't we be…"

"If they've killed him, it won't matter. If he's alive, they'll probably keep him that way. But if I don't get a couple hours sleep, I'm liable to fuck up. Okay?"

"Don't pretend to be such a cold fucker, Nolan. You aren't fooling anybody."

"Then I'm not fooling anybody." He lay on the bed and closed his eyes.

"When should I wake you up?" she said.

"I'll wake up in a few hours. Why don't you sleep, too?"

"How can you sleep at a time like this?"

"It's hard with you talking."

"What about Darlene?"

"The cowboy'll be out of there by noon, probably. We'll call on her then."

"What if she gets up before then? What if she leaves?"

"Where would she go? Church?"

"She could go somewhere in the afternoon. Shopping in Burlington."

"She'll be back, then. Are the bars open here on Sunday?"

"Yeah."

"She'll be back."

"Yeah. I suppose you're right. Nolan."

"What?"

"Can I lay down on the bed?"

"There's only one bed."

"Does that mean yes?"

"It's a double bed, isn't it?"

"That means yes." She lay down.

A few minutes went by.

"You're not asleep yet, are you?" she asked him.

"Apparently not."

"Am I bothering you?"

"No." His eyes were closed.

"You're tense."

"I'm fine." He rolled over on his stomach.

He felt her hands on his shoulders, on the muscles between his neck and shoulders. She began rubbing.

"You are too tense," she said.

It felt good.

"Well, maybe I am," he said.

"Does that feel good?"

"Keep doing it," he said.

She rubbed. Then she untucked his shirt and reached her hands up under it and scratched.

"How's that feel?"

"Good."

"Just good?"

"Very good."

"I thought you were human."

"Why, is that news?"

"I just never knew a man who didn't like his back scratched."

She stopped and he turned over and leaned against his elbow

and smiled at her. She was a cute kid; nice tits with the nipples poking at the Nodes T-shirt.

"Turn over," he said.

She grinned and got on her stomach.

He rubbed her back a while; then he reached his hand under the T-shirt and scratched her back. She made contented sounds, like a purring kitten.

He slapped her butt and she yelped.

"Looks like you're human, too," he said.

She turned over and smiled up at him; took his hands and put them up under her shirt, in front this time.

"Hey," he said.

"What?" she said.

He didn't pull his hands away; he liked them where they were.

"You're Jon's girlfriend," he said.

"I'm not his girlfriend. I'm his friend."

"Just a fellow band member, huh?"

"That's right."

She kissed him. Slow, sweet kiss.

He looked at her, pushed her away from him, hands still under her shirt; she had a scared look.

"I need to be close to somebody right now," she said. "And I don't think it would hurt you, either."

She pulled her T-shirt off; her breasts looked just as nice as they felt.

He turned off the light. He took off his clothes, and she took hers off, too. They got under the covers and made love; it was slow and rather sweet. Like the kiss. She was right: it was exactly what he needed right now.

Afterwards, he sat up in bed and said, "Are you sure you're not Jon's girlfriend?"

"I care about him a great deal."

"You've never slept with him?"

"I didn't say that."

He shook his head, smiled disgustedly. "I been had."

"Me too," she said. "Listen, I'm thirsty."

"There's a pop machine a few doors down."

"I'd rather have Cutty Sark."

"I bet you would. Will you settle for a Coke?"

"Sure," she said. "You don't really mean you're going to go get it for me?"

He shrugged. "You scratch my back..."

He put his clothes on. As an afterthought, he stuck the silenced 9mm in his waistband.

"Do you need that?" she asked, wide-eyed.

"No," Nolan said, meaning it. "I'm just being paranoid."

The night air—actually early morning air—was still cold, and he still liked the feel of it, the alertness it gave him. He hadn't managed to get any sleep yet, after all. But the girl had done him good. She had released some of his tension, though he found himself feeling guilty, as if he'd somehow betrayed Sherry. Which was crazy. He wasn't married. But he didn't suppose this Toni could understand how he felt, not with the strange sense of morality she and that generation of hers seemed to have.

As he was nearing the Coke machine, he noticed a car parked in the stall in front of one of the other rooms: a shiny black Mazda. Sporty little car, but it wasn't the car that caught his eye—it was the license plate. Even though this was Illinois, most of the plates on the cars in the motel stalls were Iowa ones; this one was Illinois, specifically Rock Island County.

Infante.

Nolan had left his LTD home, with its Rock Island plates,

296 MAX ALLAN COLLINS

for just this reason; he'd suffered the discomfort of Sherry's little Datsun because its Ohio plates wouldn't lead anybody to him.

But Infante was dumb. Which became even more obvious when Nolan found the car unlocked. He checked the registration; the car belonged to Carl R. Hines, Infante's boss.

Nolan took the 9mm out of his waistband.

He went to the door of the room the Mazda was parked in front of. He knocked.

Infante answered the door wearing a towel, which he held around him with one hand; in the other was the twin to Nolan's 9mm, but he was too startled and slow for it to do him any good.

Before Infante knew what was happening, Nolan slapped him across the face with the automatic, knocking him back into the room, the 9mm's twin tumbling out of Infante's hands, leaving him sitting on the floor with the towel a puddle across his lap, rubbing his face and saying, "Shit! Shit!"

Nolan shut the door.

Infante said, "You fucker!"

"Shut up."

Infante started to get up.

Nolan pointed the 9mm at Infante's head. "Keep your seat," he said.

Infante's eyes darted around, looking for his 9mm.

"It's under the bed," Nolan said. "I don't think you can get to it in time."

"I'm going to kill you, you fucker."

"I don't think so."

"How did you get here so fast?"

"Weren't you expecting me?"

"Not for a couple days. I figured first you'd go to Chicago and check on why we tried to hit you."

"That's pretty smart—for you, Infante. But, no, I already know who sent you: a bitch named Julie, with a heart as big as all indoors."

"She'll kill you if I don't, Nolan. She's smart. Too smart for you."

"We'll see. Where's Jon?"

Infante grinned. "Your lover boy?"

"My what?"

"Julie told me about you two. I'm gonna kill him, too. I'm gonna feed him your dead dick, first. He'll like that."

Nolan laughed. "Julie is smart. She's been pushing the right buttons where you're concerned, obviously."

"What do you mean?"

"Never mind. What was the plan, Infante? Was she going to wait for me to show up, then try to trade Jon to me, in return for leaving her the hell alone?"

Infante looked disappointed. "Maybe," he said.

"And then she was going to have you hit us both."

Infante grinned again. "Maybe."

"Where's Jon?"

"Fuck you, fucker."

"Don't tell me. I don't want you to tell me. I'd rather tie you in a chair and burn the bottoms of your feet till you tell me."

That made Infante nervous. "I tell you, I don't know where he is. Somebody, some friend of hers, is keeping him. All I know is it's not far from here."

"Is that the truth? Believe me, I'd get a kick out of burning your fucking feet."

"It's the truth! I don't know where the fuck he is."

Nolan nodded; he believed Infante. Goddammit.

And Infante whipped the towel off his lap and at Nolan's face, and it stung, stunning him, and the naked Infante was on him, and Nolan went over backwards.

Then Nolan was on his back, and Infante's hands were on Nolan's throat squeezing, and the world was turning red.

"You shouldn't have killed Sally, you fucker! You shouldn't have killed Sally!"

Nolan fired the 9mm, and Infante took it in the gut; his hands loosened around Nolan's neck, and Nolan pushed him off. Infante lay on the floor like a fetus, clutching his stomach, looking up at Nolan, dying.

"You shouldn't have killed Sally," Infante whimpered.

"You shouldn't have killed my dog," Nolan said.

15

By midafternoon, Jon wasn't afraid of her anymore.

She was really just this poor, sad person, Ron was, somebody who got stuck with the responsibility of her family in such a way that it, well, made a man out of her. She wasn't stupid, though smart wasn't the word for her, either. Just this poor, uneducated, pathetic case, who he'd feel very sorry for if she didn't have him handcuffed to a bed in what was apparently an old house out in the country somewhere.

He guessed he'd been raped. It was a new experience for him, maybe even a learning experience: he understood better what women had been going through all these years. Still, he had a hunch he could put up with being raped better than most women would, as long as it wasn't a man doing it.

If he'd been pressed about it he'd have to admit that he'd found some enjoyment in it. This strange, hungry, mannish woman sitting on him, grinding, coming like crazy, which was the good part: that made her beholden to him, in a way. Afterwards, still on top of him, she'd smiled and stroked his cheek and then suddenly her face had fallen and she seemed embarrassed or something, and got off him and ran out of the room, scooping up her clothes as she went.

She came back in T-shirt and jeans, with breakfast.

"It's afternoon," she said, shrugging, "but I figured maybe you oughta have something to eat, and…I don't know…this seemed right."

She'd made him sourdough pancakes and link sausages and American fries. On a nice plate, with a big glass of orange juice.

It looked great. She had it on a tray, which she handed him.

"How about undoing this?" he said, nodding toward his cuffed hand.

She shook her head no. "Can't do that." She seemed embarrassed about that, too.

She went over and let up the shade, and sun came in.

He ate the breakfast.

"This is terrific," he said.

She sat on the edge of the bed, watching him, smiling just barely; saying nothing.

When he was done, she took the tray away and was gone for over an hour. At one point he heard water running. Was she taking a bath? Then he heard a hair dryer.

When she returned, she was wearing a white peasant blouse, lacy in front with long sleeves; and jeans. She had a little makeup on: pale lipstick; blush on her cheeks. Her head was a mess of curls: ducktail no more; she had hot-curled her hair, evidently, after washing it. The perfume she had on was a little strong, an evergreen fragrance, like a room deodorizer, and it hit him as soon as she stepped in the room. But it wasn't an unpleasant smell, and he found it kind of touching.

She came over and sat on the edge of the bed.

"Who are you, anyway?" she asked.

"My name's Jon. I play rock 'n' roll. You know that."

"No," she said, not looking at him, still embarrassed, "tell me about you. I want to know about you."

He told her about himself. About living with various relatives while his mother, the "chanteuse," worked the Holiday Inn circuit or whatever; about his aspirations to be a cartoonist, which really seemed to interest her.

"My brother used to read *Spider-Man*," she said, grinning. "I still got some of the books."

"No kidding?"

She got up and went over to the dresser. She opened a drawer and took out a three-inch stack of comics, then came back and sat on the edge of the bed and put them in Jon's lap.

They were early issues of *Spider-Man, The Fantastic Four, The Avengers*, well read but not in bad shape; not the very first issues, but within the first twenty of each. Toward the bottom of the pile he found *Amazing Fantasy* 15, which had the first Spider-Man story.

"Do you know what this is worth?" Jon said, holding it up for her to see the cover, which showed Spider-Man dragging a bad guy to justice in the sky.

"I'd never sell it."

"It's probably worth five or six hundred bucks."

She shrugged. "It was my brother's. I wouldn't sell it."

"Well, if you ever need a few bucks, these books are worth something. Particularly the *Amazing Fantasy*."

"You can have it if you want."

"I can have it?"

"Sure. My brother would want you to."

"Ron. I might not be alive tomorrow."

"Don't be stupid."

"Let me go, Ron. You can't keep me here like this."

She frowned. "I don't want to talk about it."

He let it pass. For the moment.

"Listen," she said. "Before, when we…you know."

"Yeah?"

"It wasn't so bad, was it?"

He smiled. "It wasn't so bad."

"You mean, you…liked it?"

"I liked it."

"You're not just saying that?"

"No."

"You're not just trying to get on the good side of me?"

"No."

"Are you sure?"

"Yes."

She sat there and thought about that.

Then she undid his pants again.

She stayed beside him in bed a while, curled up next to him in peasant blouse and panties, till it got dark. This time of year it got dark early, so it was probably only about five or five-thirty. He hadn't been here a full day yet, and to his knowledge, Julie hadn't been in contact with his keeper yet, either. As Ron lay sleeping beside him (or pretending to be asleep, he didn't know), he considered again the possibility of overpowering her. He could slip an arm around her neck, but unless he was prepared to kill her, that wouldn't do him any good. Not unless the key to the handcuffs was in the pocket of those jeans of hers, tossed over on the dresser. And there was no guarantee he could drag himself, by somehow dragging the bed with him, over there to find out. And the way she was softening to him, maybe keeping up the good behavior was the best way to go. But just how long he could—well, keep it up—he didn't know.

Pretty soon she rose and stretched and smiled at him, without embarrassment now, and went and put her jeans on, moving with a lack of shame and a confidence that seemed more like the old Ron, but not at all masculine.

At the doorway she stopped and turned and said, "I'm not much at cooking, except breakfast and sandwiches and that. I usually eat my meals in the kitchen at the Paddlewheel. It goes with the job. But I can stick a TV dinner in the microwave for you."

Somehow it seemed incongruous to him that she would have a microwave.

"That's fine," he said. "Anything."

She was on her way out when he called to her. "Ron?"

"What?"

"I want you to let me go."

She sighed.

"Things are going to get rougher than you know," he said. "I wasn't lying about the bank robbery. I wasn't lying about Julie trying to kill me that time. And I wasn't lying about my partner, either."

"He's a real bad-ass, this partner of yours?" There was no sarcasm at all in Ron's voice.

"That's one of the best descriptions of him I ever heard," Jon said.

She stood poised in the doorway like something in an arty photo. Then she said, "I'll think about it," and was gone.

He grinned at the door, which Ron had halfheartedly pulled shut. Only partially shut: he could hear her footsteps on the stairs very clearly.

He felt good, considering. She was going to let him go, he knew it. He'd won her over. He felt like Burt Reynolds. He'd fucked her over to his side; turned the dyke into a woman. What a man. He sat there, grinning, handcuffed.

A few minutes later, there was a banging sound downstairs: somebody at the front door. Pounding the hell out of it.

He heard the door being opened.

Ron's voice said, "What is it?"

"Things are falling apart, Ron. I need you. I need your help." A woman's voice.

Jesus fuck. No.

Julie.

"Come in, come in," Ron said. "Is it raining out?"

The door shut.

"Drizzling," Julie said. "Cold. Icy. Maybe snow, I don't know. Listen, that kid."

"What about him?"

"I'm going to have to go away for a while."

"Yeah?"

"But I'll be back. I'll be back for you, Ron."

"You will?"

"I'm dumping that asshole Harold, and we're going to be together, you and I. But first I have to go away for a while."

"I don't understand...."

"I'll have five thousand dollars in cash for you, in just a few minutes. I'm going to the club to get it, before I leave."

"Five thousand dollars?...For me? Why?"

"It's time."

"Time?"

"You said you could make that kid disappear for me, any time I wanted. Well, it's time. And I want it."

"What?"

"You to kill him, what do you think?"

"Kill him? I don't know...I don't mind sitting on him for you, but..."

"Ron! What's the matter with you? You said last night you'd as soon cut his throat as look at him! Since when did you care whether some goddamn man lived or died?"

There was silence.

"I want more," Ron said.

"What?"

"I want more than five thousand. I want ten."

"Well, Ron...we'll be together..."

"Maybe we'll be together and maybe we won't. I want ten."

"Okay. You got it."

"You go get the money. It'll be done when you get back."

"No. You do it now, Ron. I want it done now."

He could hear the shrug in Ron's voice. "All right."

He struggled with the cuff his wrist was in, as he heard her footsteps on the stairs, but it didn't do any good, it didn't do any goddamn fucking good, and then she was in the doorway, with a .38 in her hand.

She shut the door behind her.

"You bitch," he said, his free hand a fist.

He didn't have to swing it: his words struck her like a blow.

"Please, no," she said. Whispering. Her eyes looked wet.

She set the gun on the nightstand.

She fumbled in her front pocket. The jeans she wore were tight; she had trouble finding it but then she brought it out: a small key.

She unlocked the cuff at his wrist.

"We're only one floor up," she whispered. "There's just ground under the window, not cement or anything. Hang out the window and drop."

"Ron…"

"I'm going to tell her you got away. I came up here and you were gone. I'm going to tell her I had you tied, and you got loose. She doesn't have to know about the cuffs."

She was undoing the cuff at his ankle.

He got up; she helped him. He was dizzy. Hard to keep balance. He started unsteadily toward his shoes.

"Never mind that," she said irritatedly, pushing him toward the window.

He grabbed her by the small of one arm. Looked at her. Touched her face.

"Get out of here," she said.

She opened the window for him, and he climbed out into the darkness, hanging by the sill, facing toward the house, and the night air felt cold, the drizzle felt good. He dropped.

The ground was hard, and one of his ankles gave, twisted. Fuck! He fell backward but was up in a second, and hobbled across the cold ground, wishing he had his goddamn shoes. This wasn't as clear a night as last night, but he could still make out the general shape of things. The old two-story farmhouse. The bare yard going back to what was apparently a plowed cornfield. Trees off to the left, which he was heading toward now.

His ankle hurt like hell, but he was so glad to be out of there and maybe, just maybe get out of Julie's grip, that the pain felt good, as good as the cold, wet air. The pain meant he was alive.

Then he was in the trees, and he could see the road: there were trees on either side of it, so it would be easy enough to head for cover if a car came. And since a car could mean Julie again, he didn't dare flag one down, so he hobbled in the road, because with his turned ankle it was better than moving through the trees and bushes and high grass. And he heard a noise behind him, back at the farmhouse. Something that could have been a shot.

He stepped up the pace, coming as close to running as a guy with a bum ankle can get; sort of a drunken jog.

Pretty soon headlights were coming up behind him, and he headed to the right, into the trees, and dropped to his stomach in the tall, wet grass; the car slowed, as if the driver had thought she (and this was certainly a she: Julie) had seen something moving in the road ahead but wasn't sure. Then moved on.

He waited what seemed forever and was possibly a couple minutes.

Then he made his way back to the road. He listened very

carefully before he started his drunken jog again, listened for an idling motor, in case Julie had pulled over and cut her lights up ahead. He heard nothing, except the sound of the rain—the drizzle had already turned to rain—against the ground, the trees, the road.

He started moving again.

Should he stop at a farmhouse? There'd surely be one soon.

He didn't know if he could come up with a story that could get him safely out of this area without the cops getting into it. A guy with no shoes, looking bruised and beat-up, coming to a farmer's door for help? Assuming he didn't get shot first, what could he say?

Better to get to a town, if that didn't take forever; if luck had headed him the right direction down this road, he might end up at Gulf Port before long. A tavern there would ask no questions about his appearance, and he might even be able to bum a dime to try to call Nolan again.

But he felt sure Nolan would be on the way. He just didn't know how to connect up with him.

Up ahead there was a curve in the road. He got off to the side, so he could make a quick move off into the trees if a car came unexpectedly around it. And just as he jogged around the bend, the beams of headlights hit him like a spotlight, and he knew he'd never make the trees in time.

16

When Nolan got back to the motel room, the girl was asleep.

He sat on the bed next to her and watched her. She looked young. Very peaceful, her breasts rising, falling, with an easy rhythm. He hated to wake her. He hated to let her in on what had just happened. But he couldn't think of any way around it.

For one thing, it wasn't fair to her not to let her know what was going on here. She had to know just how rough it was getting, so she could have the option of getting out. He hoped she'd decide to stay; he could use her help.

He shook her, gently.

"Oh," she said, scratching her head, her brown hair a pleasant mess. "I was dreaming."

"What about?"

"I don't remember. But it wasn't a nightmare."

"That's something, anyway."

"Right. Didn't you go to get me a Coke?"

"Yeah. I forgot it."

"That's all right. I probably shouldn't be putting any caffeine in my system anyway, not if I want to get some sleep. What's that on your shirt?"

Nolan looked down at the front of his turtleneck. "Blood," he said. "Powder burns."

"Jesus. What's going on?"

"There are some things you need to know. Sit up."

She did, and he told her about Sally and Infante breaking into his house, how they tortured Sherry, how he came in on them, killing Sally. She listened with a wide-eyed expression that tried to be interest but was mostly fear.

"Why didn't you tell me this before?" she said. No anger, just curiosity.

"I didn't want to scare you off," he said. "I thought I could use you."

She managed a smirky little smile, smoothing a hand over the bed. "I see."

"That isn't what I mean."

"I know it isn't."

"Telling you about my killing Sally makes you an accessory after the fact," he said. "That's the main reason I didn't tell you. There's always a chance, in a situation like this, that you can end up in the hands of the cops. So you were better off ignorant. I wanted your help, but I wanted to protect you, too."

"You didn't get blood on your shirt from killing Sally. That's new." She reached her finger out and touched the front of his shirt, like a kid checking if paint was dry. "That's wet."

He told her about spotting Infante's car, about the confrontation in the motel room.

She looked ill.

"This screws things up a little," he said. "I didn't intend killing Infante—not at the moment, anyway. I wanted him alive, so I could use him, to get to Jon, and handle Julie, as well. Dead, he's a problem."

"Why?"

"When Julie tries to contact him and finds him gone, she may figure I'm in town, which takes away the edge I need."

"What can we do about it?"

"Well, if Julie finds Infante's body in his room, we're as dead as he is."

She nodded. "And so is Jon."

"Right. We're better off if we get rid of the body."

"Oh, Jesus."

"There isn't much to it, really."

She shuddered. "Yeah, I know. It's the second body you've dumped today, after all."

Nolan shrugged. "It's got to be done."

"Well, give me a second."

"It's almost five. We better get this done while it's still dark."

She got out of bed and followed him out of the motel room. Neither one wore a coat, and it was cold. There was no one around; the sky was just hinting at dawn.

Nolan handed her some car keys. "These are to that little Mazda over there. It's Infante's. Back it around, right up to the edge of the sidewalk in front of the door to his room, and open the trunk."

She nodded, and went to the car, and did as she was told.

Nolan unlocked Infante's room, silenced 9mm in hand; it was faintly possible that Julie might have showed up in the few minutes he'd been back at his own room, explaining things to the girl.

But there was no one in the room except Infante, and he was just a sprawl of leaking flesh on the carpet by the bed. Nolan took the spread off the bed and rolled Infante up in it; it was harder than it sounds. Then he went to the doorway, and the girl was standing by the open trunk.

"Nobody's around," she said, glancing from side to side, her breath visible in the air. "You need any help in there?"

"No."

"Good," she said, hugging her arms to herself, shivering, only partially from the cold.

Nolan went back and lifted the mummylike Infante into his arms, carrying him like a bride over a threshold, only Infante was going out, not in. When the girl saw the bundle in Nolan's arms, she covered her mouth.

"Shut the door," he said.

She shut the door to Infante's motel room.

"Go get the other car."

She walked down toward the Datsun. Briskly.

He laid Infante in the Mazda trunk, which was empty except for a spare tire. He had to stuff Infante in there, and bend parts of him around, as though he was fitting a piece into a puzzle, but the wrong piece. Infante would have been uncomfortable, had he been alive. Nolan shut the trunk.

The girl was there with the Datsun. It had frost on it, as did the Mazda.

He went over to where she was leaning out the rolled-down window and said, "Just follow, me," and got behind the wheel of the Mazda.

He led her down a country road lined with trees on either side. About fifteen miles out of Gulf Port, Nolan pulled the Mazda into an access inlet to a cornfield. The field was flattened and desolate looking. There were no farmhouses or barns in sight. Nolan took a handkerchief and wiped everything he'd touched: steering wheel, trunk lid, even the car keys, which he pitched out into the field. Then he left the Mazda where it was and joined the girl in the Datsun, waiting in the road nearby, motor running.

"Turn around as soon as you can," he said, "and head back to the motel."

She nodded.

When she was pulling into the stall in front of their room, Nolan said, "Now let's check Infante's room again."

"Why?"

"Don't want to leave a mess."

They got out of the car. Nolan went down and unlocked Infante's room. She followed him haltingly inside. There was a reddish-brown spot about the size of a saucer, but not as perfectly round, on the floor by the bed.

"Get a towel," Nolan said, "and get it wet and soapy."

"You want me to clean that up?"

He just looked at her.

She frowned. "Woman's work is never done," she said, and went into the bathroom.

Nolan looked under the bed. The twin to the 9mm was there.

He reached under and got it.

By this time, the girl was on her hands and knees scrubbing. She stopped for a moment, looked at the reddish-stained towel in her hands, and said, "I think I'm going to be sick."

"That's good enough," Nolan said, nodding toward the spot on the floor. "You don't want to rub it bald."

"I'll get another towel with just water and kind of rinse the area."

"Good idea."

Nolan went to the dresser and found a notepad and pen. He wrote the following on the top sheet: "Got hungry and bored. Going to Burlington for some food and a movie. Be back in a few hours." He didn't sign it, but left it out on top of the dresser. The girl looked at it.

"You think that'll hold 'em off for a while?" she asked.

"It might."

He went to the phone. He dialed the desk.

"I'm in room thirteen," he said. "I'm just getting to bed now, and I don't want to be disturbed. So don't bother sending a maid around at all today. I'll be sleeping."

"Sure," a disinterested female voice on the other end said.

"You write this down or something. I don't want to be disturbed, got it?"

"I got it," the voice, now irritated, said.

"There'll be a tip in it for you."

"Oh! Well, sure. I'm writing it down now."

"And hold my calls. I'll pick up any messages at the desk later. Just say I'm not in."

"Glad to. My name's Frances, by the way."

"Fine, Frances."

"So you'll know who to tip."

"I'll remember, Frances."

He hung up.

"Is that going to work?" the girl asked.

"It might. Take another towel and wipe off anything we touched. I never knew anybody who actually got nailed by fingerprints, except on TV. But I don't want to be the first."

He gathered Infante's clothes and the damp towels used by the girl to clean the blood up, and on the way back to their motel room, dumped it all in a trash barrel, shoving it under some other garbage.

"The sun's up," she pointed out.

"So it is," he said. "Let's get some sleep."

It was late morning when he woke and found her sitting on the edge of the bed.

"Are you okay?" he asked her.

"I don't know. I don't feel so good."

"How so?"

"My stomach hurts. I feel kind of weak."

"You're hungry."

She made a face. "Please. I dreamed I cleaned up blood with a mop and bucket all night."

"All morning. How long since you've eaten?"

"I don't know. I had lunch yesterday. I never eat a meal before a performance, so…"

"So you haven't eaten for a long time. You're hungry. Here." He dug in his pocket for some money and gave her two twenties.

"What's this for?"

"I want you to drive over to Burlington and find a McDonald's or something. Someplace where you can get a breakfast to go. Eat yours there, if you like, but bring me something."

"How can you eat at a time like this?"

"The same way I can sleep, or screw."

She gave him a long, sarcastic smile, then said, "Forty bucks for breakfast is gonna buy you a truckload of Egg McMuffins, you know."

"I also want you to stop at one of those big discount stores and pick me up a shirt. Something similar to this, but without the blood and powder burns."

"Anything else?"

"Some clothesline."

"Clothesline?"

"Just enough to tie somebody up with."

She grinned. "Got ya."

"And get some toiletries. Toothbrushes, toothpaste, a shaver, shaving cream. Like that."

"Okay."

"Go."

She went—slowly, glancing back at him, afraid to go out on her own, he guessed. But she went.

He lay back on the bed and slept till she got back.

When she did, they both ate breakfast; she had waited to eat hers with him. It was McDonald's, some pancakes, sausage, eggs. Cardboard food, but since neither of them had eaten for many hours, they wolfed it down.

Nolan took a shower, used the toothpaste. Shaved.

"The shirt's a little big," he said, getting into it, "but it'll do."

"I got extra-large," she said.

"I take a large."

"Are you complaining?"

"No. I'm grateful."

"Well. You better be."

"Where's my change?"

She shook her head, and got the change out of her jeans, then handed it to him.

"It's almost two," she said. "Shouldn't we be checking on our friend Darlene?"

"Take a shower first."

"Don't be shy, Nolan. If I stink, say so."

"You'll feel better. Clean up, and we'll go."

When they did, they found the cowboy was still there; the red hot-rod pickup hadn't moved an inch.

"Shit," Nolan said, slamming the heel of his hand into the steering wheel.

"What now?"

"This is getting messy. I don't want to involve anybody else. I want the girl by herself."

"They're probably still asleep. It was after four in the morning when they got here, and they probably didn't get to sleep till five or six."

Nolan nodded. "Good point. We better just wait."

There were a few people out walking around on what was turning into a dreary, overcast Sunday afternoon. Some kids playing, none of them wearing warm enough clothing, considering the chilly weather—looking a bit ragged, in fact. A woman in a parka walking a shaggy mutt. An occasional blue-collar hippie on a motorcycle. Just enough action to make it awkward to park somewhere nearby and watch and wait.

"Back to the motel," he said.

"Jesus, I'll go stir crazy."

"It's okay. We can keep an eye out the window and see if Julie or somebody shows up knocking at Infante's door. That'd get us to Jon, too, you know."

She sighed. "I'm getting worried."

"Don't be. Wherever Jon's being held, it's likely we'll want to wait till after dark to get him anyway."

"After dark? Jesus!"

"It's dark by late afternoon this time of year. Don't worry. If he's dead, he's..."

"Dead. Yeah, I know. You're real comforting, Nolan."

Nolan watched a football game on TV, with the sound down; the girl sat by the window near the door, peeking through the partly drawn curtains, watching for anyone who might pull into the motel lot. It was a quiet afternoon. The only action was a few people checking out late: a couple in their twenties, dressed in an expensively casual way, walking arm in arm toward a Corvette, in an easy, worn-out fashion that bespoke a fun-filled night before; some college kids—guys—heavily hung-over, shambling out to a station wagon like the survivors of a train wreck. Otherwise nothing—no Julie. Nothing.

At five they went back to Darlene's. It was misting out; it was dark already. The red pickup was gone; but her rusting green Maverick was there. And so, presumably, was Darlene.

As soon as they got out of the car, they could hear it: a loud buzzing sound coming from within the trailer. Nolan and the girl exchanged glances, the girl shrugging, indicating that she had no idea what the sound was, either.

Nolan went up and knocked on the door, Toni at his side. He had a Bible in his right hand, supplied by the Gideons to the motel room and by the motel room to him. In his left hand, held at the moment under his jacket, was the 9mm.

He kept knocking till the buzzing stopped.

She opened the door about halfway, looking down at Nolan (it was three steps up to the door of the trailer) with sultry, suspicious, and heavily made-up eyes. Her hair was piled high and tousled, in a calculated way, and she had on a black T-shirt with white lettering that said "STIFF RECORDS" curved over the smaller "WORLD TOUR," curved in turn over a globe, underneath which it said: "WE CAME, WE SAW, WE LEFT."

"What do you want?" she said. Her voice was flat, disinterested, her expression a bored smirk.

"We're with the Jehovah's Witnesses," Nolan said, showing her the gun in his left hand, which was hidden from view from any passersby by the Bible in his right hand.

She tried to shut the door, but Toni hopped up the steps and pushed against it with a shoulder and held it where it was, smiling at Darlene, who immediately recognized her and, after a moment, retreated into the trailer. Toni went in first and Nolan came after, shutting the door and locking it behind him.

Nolan kept his gun in hand, but tossed the Bible over on the counter in the kitchenette, which was off to the right, where a pile of unwashed dishes and beer cans and such indicated that a slob lived here. The living room was barely furnished at all: just a couch against the facing wall, a component stereo spread out on the floor over at the left, with a few big, brightly colored pillows scattered around as if the place had been ransacked. There were LP's scattered, too, and rock group posters taped to the walls. Nolan didn't recognize any of the groups; they were just so many sullen faces staring out at him. The only poster he recognized was a country performer, Willie Nelson.

In the middle of the floor, standing on newspapers, was a gray poodle; at the poodle's feet were clumps of its hair, and a clipper on a long black cord lay on the papers nearby, as well.

That explained the buzzing: Darlene had been giving her poodle a haircut.

And the poodle was going nuts, barking, yapping.

Nolan walked over to it, pointed a finger at it, and it sat and shut up and looked up at him and whimpered.

"Some watchdog," Darlene said, sitting on the couch, trying to be sullen, like the faces on the posters around her. But her fear was showing. There was a pack of cigarettes on the couch next to her, and she lit up.

"You're the bitch that sings with the Nodes," Darlene said between puffs, "that much I know. Who's the guy with the gun and the Bible? And what's it all about, Alfie?"

Toni went over and grabbed a bunch of the front of Darlene's T-shirt and pushed her back against the wall. Darlene, startled, dropped her cigarette and her sullen pose; the fear in her wide, mascara-thick eyes was as apparent as the whimpering dog's.

"*You're* the bitch," Toni said. "The bitch who set Jon up."

Toni let go of her, and Darlene slid back down onto the couch, where she fumbled for her cigarette—and her pose—and said, "Don't know what the fuck you're talking about."

"Tell me about last night," Toni said. "Tell me about Jon and the van."

Darlene found a nasty little smile somewhere. "Will the Jehovah's Witness get embarrassed if I said I gave the kid a blow job, and sent him on his way?"

"You're lying."

"Go fuck yourself."

Toni swung a small, sharp fist at Darlene and sent her sprawling across the couch. Darlene, on her side, felt her mouth.

"I'm bleeding," she said.

"Maybe it's just that time of the month," Toni said. She had a much more convincingly nasty smile than Darlene had mustered. Toni, taking the lead, amused and pleased Nolan.

"You fuckin' assholes," Darlene said, sitting up, trying to act mad but coming off scared. "I don't know what the fuck this is about, but you better get your asses outa here. My boyfriend's gonna be back any minute."

Toni and Nolan exchanged glances. Nolan shook his head no.

Toni said, "You're bluffing."

"Eat it."

"You set Jon up. We want to know what really happened last night. We want to know who's got him and where he is now. And you're going to tell us."

Darlene blew a smoke ring; she seemed to be getting her act together finally.

Toni motioned to Nolan, and they went over to the kitchenette area, Nolan keeping the gun pointed Darlene's way. The poodle was sitting in the midst of the papers, staring up at Nolan.

"I think I can make her talk," Toni whispered.

"You're doing fine."

"You don't mind if I handle this?"

"No. I'm enjoying myself. I'm not into knocking women around, but I don't mind watching one knock another one around."

"How about tying her up for me?"

"Fine."

Nolan got a kitchen chair and dragged it into the living room area; the poodle scooted away, running down the narrow hallway toward the bedroom to hide.

Toni pointed at the chair. "Sit in it," she told Darlene.

Darlene just sat on the couch and smoked her cigarette.

Toni grabbed her by one arm and slammed her down in the chair.

Nolan picked up the cigarette Darlene had just dropped and

put it out in an ashtray on the floor near the couch. Then he took the small bundle of clothesline out of his jacket pocket and tied Darlene into the chair, and she swore at him. He ignored her; he sat down on the couch. The poodle skulked back in. It jumped up on the couch and lay next to Nolan and looked up at him pathetically; he scratched it around the collar a few times, and it rested its head on his leg.

"What's your dog's name?" he asked Darlene.

"Quiche Lorraine," she said.

"What kind of name is that?"

Toni explained. "It's from a song." She jabbed a finger at Darlene's STIFF T-shirt. "Really, Darlene, you should make up your mind. You can't be into both the B-52's *and* Willie Nelson. It just doesn't make sense."

Darlene didn't respond; she looked nervous. Being tied up didn't agree with her.

"I suppose you like to be flexible," Toni said. "It's nice to be able to come on to guys in both camps. Shitkickers and rock 'n' rollers, too. But I really think you should make up your mind, one way or another. I'm going to help you."

Toni reached down for the poodle clippers. She hit the switch, and the buzz filled the room.

"What are you doing?" Darlene shouted.

"I'm gonna give you a poodle cut," Toni said.

"No!"

"Sure. It'll be real punk. A skinhead, like in England."

"You fuckin' bitch!"

Toni grabbed a handful of the shaggy hair on top of Darlene's head and held her that way as she got behind her and started to shave at the base of her neck.

"Stop it! Stop it! I'll tell you what you want to know! Just stop it!"

Toni switched the clippers off but left the flat, wide nose of them against the base of Darlene's neck.

"What happened last night?" she asked.

"You…you know who Ron is?"

"That dyke you hang around with."

"Yeah. She paid me a hundred bucks to get that Jon to come out to the van."

"And?"

"She hit him over the head and put him in the back of her car."

"A hundred bucks. You helped kidnap somebody for a hundred goddamn bucks?"

Darlene managed to shrug, despite Toni's grip on her hair. "It wasn't kidnapping. She said somebody had it in for the kid and was paying her to rough him up or something. That's all I know."

Toni looked at Nolan, who was still on the couch, the poodle beside him.

Nolan said, "Can you tell us where this Ron lives?"

Darlene turned her head, which, tied in the chair as she was, was all she could turn, and looked at Nolan and said, "Sure. Why not."

Toni let loose of Darlene's hair but stood by, clippers in hand, as Darlene gave Nolan directions.

Then Nolan went to the kitchen, poodle following along after him, and found an unused dishrag in a drawer. He gagged Darlene with it. He made sure the dog had bowls full of food and water, and he and Toni left.

"That was smart," Nolan said, getting in the car, behind the wheel.

"What?"

"The poodle clippers. How d'you know that'd do the trick?"

"She's vain as hell. Didn't you notice? Sunday afternoon and she's got her makeup on, to the hilt. What for, just to give her pooch a trim? *That's* vain."

"Would you have done it?"

"Skin her? With pleasure."

They drove out of Gulf Port and down that same tree-lined road they'd been down earlier, to dump Infante. As they drove, Toni filled Nolan in on what little she knew about Ron. Nolan was doing barely forty; the mist was turning to rain, and visibility was poor. As they were coming around a curve, Nolan saw a figure, caught in the glare of his headlights, scurry off toward the side of the road, toward the trees.

"That's Jon!" he said.

He hit his brakes, threw it in park and jumped out.

"Hey, kid! It's me."

The figure stopped, turned. Across the darkness and through the rain a voice came back uncertainly: "Nolan?"

"Yeah."

Jon ran to him, grabbed him by the forearms.

"Nolan! Nolan!"

The kid was in T-shirt and jeans and socks; his face looked bruised, and his clothes were wet and dirty.

"You look like shit," Nolan said.

"You look great!"

The girl was out of the car now, and had run to Jon. She hugged him, and he hugged her back.

"Get in the car," Nolan said, "both of you." They got in the car, Toni in back.

Quickly, Jon told Nolan what had been happening.

"You figure Julie passed you on the road here, then?" Nolan said.

"I didn't see the car, but it had to be her."

"She's probably headed for the Paddlewheel. To grab some money and run."

"I want you to drive down to that farmhouse, Nolan."

"Why?"

"I think I heard a shot. I want to check it out."

Nolan glanced at Jon.

Then he said, "Okay. There's a gun in the glove box."

Jon opened the glove compartment and took out the long-barreled .38. There was a box of shells, too, but the gun was loaded already, and Jon didn't bother with them.

Leaning forward from the back seat, her hands on the seat between Nolan and Jon, Toni said, "Let's leave. Let's get out of here. Let's go home."

Jon turned and said, "We can't. If we don't catch up with Julie now, she'll just turn up again sometime, and we don't need that shit."

"He's right," Nolan said. "We'll keep you out of it as much as possible."

"Gee, thanks," the girl said.

There was a gravel driveway leading into a larger gravel area next to the farmhouse; a barn and silo were off to the right. Nolan pulled in. There was only one car around: a vintage fifties Ford. The farmhouse was peeling paint—looked a bit run-down—but it was no hovel. There was a porch. Nolan, gun in hand, walked up the steps, and Jon followed. Toni stayed in the car, behind the wheel, windows up, doors locked.

The front door was ajar.

They went in; prowled the bottom floor, found it empty, not touching anything (though Nolan did pocket a ring of keys from a table). There was a living room, a dining room, a kitchen, a barely stocked pantry. Everything was neat, though the furniture was rather old, worn. There were a number of family portraits displayed. Unlike Darlene, Ron wasn't a slob, at least.

Upstairs, in the room Jon had been kept in, they found Ron. She was on the floor, in her peasant blouse and jeans, between the bed and the dresser. She was dead.

There was a gun in her hand, and she had a head wound. In the right temple, out the left.

"Julie never stops maneuvering, does she?" Nolan said, bending over the body.

"What?" Jon said. He looked shaken.

"Faking this as a suicide. I don't think that's a close-range wound. I think Julie shot her from the doorway. That's judging from the angle of it, the powder burns, the entry and exit wounds. But the local people may not figure it out immediately. Hard to say."

Nolan rose.

Jon knelt over the body. He touched the dead woman's cheek. He closed her eyes.

"Kid. Let's go."

"Yeah. Okay, Nolan." He rose, slowly.

"You might as well put on your shoes."

"Huh? Oh. Yeah."

His shoes were between the body and the dresser. He got them, then sat on the edge of the bed and put them on. The kid had been through a lot, Nolan thought. Maybe the girl was right; maybe they should just get the hell out. Go home.

Next to Jon on the bed was a stack of comic books.

"It never fails," Nolan laughed. "You always manage to turn up some funny-books, don't you?"

Jon looked at them. He picked them up and took them with him as they left the house. He held the comics under his shirt to protect them from the rain, as they went to the car.

Toni climbed in back and Jon got in front on the rider's side. Nolan took the wheel again. Jon handed the comics back to Toni. "Put those on the floor or something, will you?" he said.

"Okay," she said, smiling.

Both she and Nolan were amused by Jon's managing to come away from this situation with a stack of old comics.

"Any of these valuable ones?" the girl asked, kidding him.

Jon didn't seem to pick up on the kidding. "Very," he said.

"What are you going to do with 'em?" Nolan asked. "Sell 'em?"

"I wouldn't sell them. I wouldn't ever sell them." Jon opened the glove compartment and took out the box of .38 shells; he stuffed a handful of the shells in his pocket, put the box back.

"Let's go find Julie," he said.

17

She would have to run.

There was no other choice. Nolan was here; his breath was on her neck; and this time he wouldn't go soft and spare her, like that time at the cottage. This time he would kill her.

She knew that, and she could accept it, and she would eventually deal with it—deal with him—but now she had to run. She didn't even know where she would go. Mexico, she guessed. Money still went a long way in Mexico. And when some time had passed, she could hire somebody to do Nolan, and Jon, as well. Some other expatriate American, maybe, who could sneak back in the country and get it done.

Or something. There'd be some way out of it. There always was. Plenty of options.

But right now, running was the only option she could come up with.

The Porsche slid going around a curve, and she slowed down; the blacktop was slick with rain. *Don't panic now*, she told herself. But the rain and the darkness, crowding her on the narrow blacktop that led to the Paddlewheel, seemed to be on Nolan's side.

She had been so sure she was on top of this Nolan situation, it made her smug; so sure she was in control of things, it made her complacent. When she thought about how she'd spent the morning and afternoon, she could kick herself: sleeping till noon, sitting in Harold's study with a gin and tonic, explaining to him her plans for Nolan, playing down the role of that slug Infante. (In the version she told Harold, Infante would be on hand only as protection, in case Nolan didn't uphold his end of the swap she would propose.)

Still, Harold had seemed morose; it was almost as if he had seen through what she told him, that he knew she really intended having Nolan and Jon killed. He had sat in his study all afternoon, listening to an old Beatles album, *Revolver*; he seemed to enjoy feeling sorry for himself, and the world, his lips moving to the lyrics of "Eleanor Rigby," for Christ's sake. What a jerk. She didn't know why she'd put up with him for so long.

On the other hand, there was a part of her that liked him and his self-pitying ways. He wasn't a stupid man—he certainly came in handy at the club, doing the books, handling the staff—and she liked having a big, reasonably competent man around, who depended on her, whom she could mother into submission. She'd always had a knack for finding men who needed a mother in a woman, and having all but raised most of her brothers and sisters, she was used to playing mother— though it occasionally struck her as ironic that she had never spent enough time with her own kid to really qualify in that department.

So as Harold sat in his study, listening to old Beatles records, she felt a weird mixture of contempt and affection for him—a man his age, sitting there feeling sorry for himself, losing himself in memories of high school. It was fucking pathetic....

Around three she had called the motel to talk to Infante. She needed to go have a talk with him, alone, without Harold around, to fill Infante in on what her plans really were where Nolan and Jon were concerned. But the woman on the desk said Infante was out. It struck Julie as strange, but not suspicious, particularly, at least not at first. When she called back around quarter to five and got the same response from the desk

clerk, she put aside her gin and tonic and her book on refin-
ishing antiques and grabbed her coat. She stuck her little pearl-
handled automatic in her purse and told Harold she would be
back soon.

She knocked on Infante's motel room door and got no answer.

The woman at the desk, a thin, plain woman about forty,
doing the crossword puzzle in the Sunday paper, shrugged
without looking up, saying all she knew was the night clerk had
left a note saying the man in room 13 had requested not to be
disturbed, and that if anyone called, to say he was out. Julie
asked to speak to the night clerk, and was told she wouldn't be
on duty till midnight. When Julie insisted, the woman gave her
the night clerk's phone number, and she called her from a
booth outside the motel.

"That's right," a sleepy female voice said. "He wasn't *really*
going anyplace. Just wanted some sleep. Like I do. Do you
mind?"

"So he wasn't going out?"

"I was supposed to say he was out and take messages."

"I see. Tell me. Did anybody check in last night after two?"

"*Everybody* checked in last night after two. Couples, mostly.
Get the idea?"

"Any singles? A man maybe?"

"No single men. There was this girl."

"Girl?"

"Pretty brown-haired girl. Not real big."

"What was she wearing?"

"I don't know. T-shirt and jeans, I guess."

"Do you remember anything specific? There's money in it if
you do."

"Well. The T-shirt had the name of a rock group on it."

"Oh?"

"Not some big group, like Kiss or something. A band from around here, whose name I recognized."

"What was it?"

"The Nodes. Ever hear of 'em?"

Julie went back to the check-in desk and, for twenty bucks, the clerk tore herself away from her crossword long enough to give her the key to room 13. There Julie found a note, presumably from Infante, saying he'd gone out for a bite to eat and a movie. She looked around the room carefully. She noticed two things: there were no towels in the bathroom, and there was a damp spot on the floor near the bed.

She was driving back to the house, down the tree-lined country lane along which Ron also lived, when she noticed a car, apparently abandoned, pulled into one of the access in-roads to a cornfield. She must have passed it before, on her way to the motel, but hadn't noticed it. Now she did: a Mazda. Infante's car.

She stopped and got out and had a look, not touching anything. It was empty; the keys weren't in the dash. But she had a feeling the trunk wasn't empty.

She got back in her Porsche.

Somehow that kid Jon had gotten a message to Nolan. Maybe there was another phone at the Barn, one she hadn't known about. Maybe Jon had used Bob Hale's private phone. That was probably it. Damn! Whatever the case, the kid had obviously got to Nolan, because Nolan was here already; Infante was dead, most likely; and she was shit out of luck.

She pulled into the driveway of her house and stood poised in front of the pillared structure like the heroine on the cover of a gothic paperback. There was no sign of Nolan yet. The only other car around was Harold's Pontiac Phoenix, in the garage, where it was supposed to be. She went in the back way, through the kitchen, gun in hand. But there was nobody in the house except Harold, still sitting in the study, listening to Beatles records: "All the lonely people…"

"What are you sneaking around for?" he asked, turning down the stereo, eyeing the little automatic in her hand.

"He's here," she said, putting the gun back in her purse. "Nolan's here."

"Jesus Christ."

She went upstairs and started packing a bag. He was at her side as she did.

"I'll get in touch with you," she said. "It may be a few months."

"I'm not going with you?"

"No. The Paddlewheel is too good a thing to throw away. We're going to try to hold onto it. You're going to hold onto it for me."

"Where will you be?"

"I don't know yet. And when I do know, I won't tell you. If you don't know, you can't tell anybody."

That hurt him. "*Tell* anybody? What…"

"Look. Nolan will show up, and when he does, the less you know, the better, because you're probably going to have to take some heat from him. But he's not going to kill you or anything."

"Well, that's nice to know."

"Harold. Just play dumb. You can handle it."

"Your confidence in me is overwhelming."

The bag was packed.

She put a hand on his shoulder. "You'll come through for me. You always have."

He smiled wearily; he nodded.

"Now," she said, carrying the bag out of the room, heading down the stairs, Harold trailing after, "you go to the Paddlewheel. I'm going to need that getaway money."

"The hundred thousand?" Harold said.

"Yes. I can live a long time on that."

She was at the front door. He grabbed her arm. Softly.

"Don't leave me," he said.

"Harold," she said, pulling away, "I'm not going to leave you. I'm just getting my butt out of here before it gets shot off. I'll be back. I like my life here. I'm not giving it up easily." She kissed him on the mouth, hastily, and said, "I'll meet you at the Paddlewheel in twenty minutes, half an hour."

"Where are you going?"

"To Ron's."

He grabbed her arm again, hard this time. "Why?"

"To tell her to let that kid go, that's why. That should cool Nolan off a little."

He let go. Licked his lips nervously. "Oh," he said.

"See you at the club."

The person who answered the door at the farmhouse seemed to be Ron, but Julie couldn't be sure. It was a not unattractive woman with makeup on and a peasant blouse and jeans; also a choking cloud of perfume. Yet this apparently *was* Ron.

And Ron's attitude didn't seem to have changed: she was more than willing to kill the kid, for a price.

Only when she went upstairs to do it, she was gone too long, and Julie followed up after her.

Ron was alone in the room. She was busy undoing handcuffs that were hanging on the bedposts. Her gun, a long-barreled revolver, was on the nightstand. The window was open; cold air was coming in.

Ron seemed startled when she noticed Julie in the doorway.

"Little bastard got away," she explained.

"I see," Julie said.

"I don't know how he got out of these things," she said, taking the handcuffs over toward the dresser, turning to lay them on top of it, facing a mirror all but obscured by taped-on pinups of Elvis Presley and others.

"Neither do I," Julie said, and picked up the revolver and shot Ron through the head.

She put the gun in Ron's hand; with some luck, it would pass for suicide. Ron would just be that sullen lesbian who finally ended it all.

And now Julie was pulling her Porsche into the unlit Paddle-wheel lot. Harold was already there; his Phoenix was over by the front door. They were closed Sundays, so there was no problem with staff or customers being around. There was no sign of Nolan, though that didn't mean anything. She got the little automatic out of her purse. Her suitcase was in the trunk; she was ready to go. All she needed was her money, and no Nolan.

She walked to the front door and unlocked it, glad Harold hadn't left it open. At least he was thinking. She went in, locking the door behind her. Harold had turned on a few lights, just enough for her to navigate, and to get a look at some of what she was leaving behind.

She walked through the entryway, past the hat check area and the rest rooms, and stood for a moment at the top of the few steps that led down into the dining room. It was a big room, full of tables with red cloths and candles; a mural of a paddlewheel boat extended along the wall at left; and a huge picture window stood across the room from her—with a magnificent river view—though with this rainy, murky night you couldn't see much of it now. The room otherwise had been left the natural (though sandblasted) brick of the warehouse it had been; the kitchen was off to the left.

She was proud of what she had accomplished here. When

she took over a year ago, the restaurant had barely been breaking even, though of course the casino downstairs (which then as now was open on Friday and Saturday nights only) had been doing a good business. If she hadn't seen the potential of the place, that time Harold brought her here to eat when she was staying with him after the Port City robbery, she wouldn't be in this mess, she supposed; she wouldn't have settled so dangerously close to where she lived before. But she'd seen the potential, all right. And found from Harold that the original owner—a guy named Tree, with mob connections—had moved to Des Moines to open a similar place, leaving this one to be run, rather incompetently it seemed, by hired hands. So she'd approached Tree and his Family friends with an offer to buy controlling interest in the place, and she had really made a go of it. She was, it turned out, a natural businesswoman.

And that was the surprise, really; all those years she was working in a beauty shop, waiting for some rich fucker to come along and make her life easy, it never occurred to her that she might want to work, that a life of luxury was a bore and the challenge of making money was almost as good as spending it.

Oh, she liked eating well and living well; she liked her fancy house and her antiques.

But what she really liked was her role as owner of the Paddle-wheel; she liked that as much as the money that came with it. And she wasn't going to give it up. She'd be back. She would be back.

She headed down the stairs, a stairway enclosed only from the railing down, and crossed the small casino room, with its card tables and several craps tables and one roulette wheel, and slots off to either side, and walked toward the bar, off to the right of which was Harold's cubbyhole office.

He was sitting behind his desk; the money was on top of it. Stacks of money packets, still in their bank wrappers.

"Put that in something," she said.

His eyes looked sad, like a basset hound with glasses. "I don't have anything."

"There's a paper sack lining your wastebasket. Use that."

He nodded, emptied his wastebasket on the floor, removed the sack, and started filling it with the packets of money; he looked like a bag boy at a supermarket.

"What about Ron?" he asked.

"Dead," she said.

He flinched, but he kept dropping packets in the sack. "What happened?"

"The kid got away. I don't know how he managed it. He killed her before he left. Put the gun in her hand to try to make it look like suicide."

"My God. So they're both loose?"

"I wouldn't sweat the kid. He's probably wandering around a cornfield somewhere. It's Nolan who's the threat. Okay, that's good. Hand it here."

He handed her the sack. The desk was between them.

"I have to go," she said.

"I'll miss you," he said.

"I'll miss you, too," she said. Meaning it.

"You *will* be back?"

"I'll be back," she snapped. "I'm no idiot. This is a good gig."

"Yes. Right."

She leaned across the desk and gave him a big, long kiss on the mouth. She smiled at him. She really did hope he could live through whatever Nolan might do to him. "I'll be back before you know it, lover."

He mustered a pathetic, self-pitying smile. "Do that," he said.

"Are you going to stay here for a while?"

"Yes. I'm going to work on the books."

"He's liable to show up any time. Nolan, I mean."

"Okay."

"You have a gun?"

"No."

"Good I don't want you to. I don't want you getting into it with him. You have to be just some poor innocent sucker I involved in this, as far as he's concerned, understand?"

He nodded.

"Okay, then. Take care of yourself."

"You too."

He was still standing behind the desk when she left him.

Approaching the stairs, she heard the sound of footsteps above. Faint, but definitely footsteps. She ducked around the side of the stairs, knelt so that the enclosed part of the stairway hid her. She put her sack of money down. She still had the automatic in her hand.

Somebody was coming down the stairs.

It seemed like a year before the figure emerged at the bottom. He'd been looking around the room, slowly, as he came down, apparently.

It was Nolan, of course.

She wished she had a bigger gun, but the automatic would have to do. She grabbed it by its short barrel and clubbed him on the back of the head with the butt, and he went down.

18

Nolan eased into the Paddlewheel lot. Over to the left a Porsche was parked; a Pontiac was parked up near the front door. No one in either car, apparently. Nolan put the Datsun in park, leaving the motor on, the car turned sideways so that it blocked the exit of the lot. The rain wasn't coming down hard, but it was insistent, pattering the roof of the car as if the sky was slightly leaky.

"I'm going in," Nolan said.

"I'm going with you," Jon said.

"No."

"Nolan..."

"I know. You're pissed. You been put through the mill, and you're pissed. That's just what I need right now: you—acting like a psychopathic nut."

Jon didn't say anything; he affected a sort of scowl; it came off more like a pout.

It was deceptively peaceful, sitting in this car in the rain, rain shadows from the streaky windshield throwing abstract patterns on their faces. Rain dancing on the car roof. Contemplative. And underneath it, a current of something not at all peaceful.

Leaning up from the back seat, the girl said, "How do you even know they're in there? Maybe they took some other car and left these behind."

"You're right," Nolan said. "They could even be outside there in the bushes, waiting for us to get out of the car."

"Oh, nice thought," the girl said, her sarcasm not quite masking her fear.

"Going in after them is probably a bad idea in the first place," Nolan said. "The smart thing might be to wait outside for them. If they're in there, they'll have to come out sooner or later."

"Then why not wait?" the girl asked.

"Impatience," Nolan said, shrugging. "Also, as you say, we don't know for a fact they're in there. You know what's on the other side of that building? The river. Which means they may have hopped in a boat and gone to Iowa already."

"Or," Jon said, "they might be inside, getting that money together I heard her and Ron talking about, and *then* go for a boat ride."

Nolan nodded. "Except I think Julie'll go and leave that big boyfriend of hers behind for me to play with."

"Yeah," Jon said. "You're probably right."

"I think she's in there," Nolan said. "This has all been breaking too fast for her to be anywhere else."

"Won't that place be locked up?" the girl asked. In the rain, with its sign off, the building across the graveled lot looked much more like a warehouse than a restaurant.

Nolan reached in his pocket for the ring of keys. "I got these at that farmhouse," he said. "Jon said that Ron was a night watchman of sorts at the Paddlewheel. With any luck at all, these'll get me in."

"You want this?" Jon asked, holding the long-barreled .38 out to Nolan in his palm, like an offering.

"You hold onto that," Nolan said, picking up the 9mm from the seat between him and Jon. "I've got over half a clip left in this, and a spare, so if I have to exchange a few rounds with 'em, I can."

"Jesus," the girl said.

"But if you hear gunfire, you'll know it's them, not me,"

Nolan went on, pointing to the silencer attached to the automatic. "So you may have to come in and back me up."

"Where does that leave me?" the girl said.

Nolan turned and looked at her. "Just get behind the wheel and stay with this car blocking the way as long as you can. If Julie and her boyfriend come piling out of there with guns in their hands, before us, you got my permission to haul ass out."

"Why don't we just leave?" the girl said. "Why don't we just go home? This is crazy."

"I'm sorry you're involved in this," Nolan said. "But I told you I could drop you at a bar or motel or something, and you said no. So just keep your eyes open, and pitch in if you're needed."

Nolan got out of the car. So did Jon. He came around to Nolan's side. Nolan was looking around, looking for movement; he hadn't been kidding when he'd told Toni somebody might be waiting in the bushes. The rain was coming down harder now— not a downpour, but they were getting wet standing there.

"You're going to have to do it this time, Nolan."

"Kill her, you mean? Yeah, I know. I'm not nuts about shooting a woman, even if it is Julie. But that bitch is the fucking plague."

"It has to be done. You're sure you don't want me with you?"

Nolan smiled, put a hand on the kid's damp shoulder. "You're my insurance policy. Come in if you hear shooting. Otherwise, stick with the girl. Let's get her out of this alive, what do you say?"

"I'm for that," Jon said, smiling.

"I'm going in a side door," Nolan said, pointing off to the left of the brick building. "Bob Hale gave me a rough layout of the place. The kitchen should be over there. I'll leave the door open, in case you have to follow me in."

"Right."

"See you in a few minutes, kid."

"See you."

Nolan headed across the gravel at a slow jog. The gravel extended around the side of the building, where he found two doors, the first having no window, the second, down a ways, having a window with a grillwork through which he could make out what seemed to be the kitchen.

He started trying the keys on the ring; the fifth one opened the door. The Yale lock made a click that sounded loud as a gunshot to him, but he went on in, not hesitating, standing just inside for a while, leaving the door ajar, listening to see if his coming in had attracted anybody's attention. He stood there a good three minutes and heard nothing.

He was in a kitchen, all right, a big room with natural brick walls, but appointed white; it seemed spotless, too, though there wasn't much light in here to tell, just a small fixture on the wall inside the door, left permanently on, apparently. He moved past a row of stoves and pushed open a door that led into a small service area; he managed to avoid bumping into the trays on stands lining the wall, full of silverware, condiments, and the like. At the next door he listened for another minute or so, heard nothing, then pushed it open and went on into the big dining room.

There were some lights on. Just enough to get around without stumbling into things. And enough to get a look at the place, and see what it was that Julie was trying to hold onto. It was a nice layout, reminding him just a little of the Pier. The steamboat mural and the river view made this dining room a natural; with decent food, you couldn't fail here.

He walked as softly as he could, but the floor wasn't carpeted; it was a waxed wood floor that wanted to echo your footsteps.

He knew there were two other levels, but Hale had told him he thought Julie's office was upstairs, and her boyfriend's down. Since they'd be together, most likely, it seemed to Nolan a toss-up as to which office they'd be in. Hers seemed slightly more likely, so he decided to check the downstairs first and get it out of the way.

He went down the stairs slowly, looking the casino room over—nothing elaborate, a small setup designed probably for the weekend trade. And he listened. Across the room, down by the bar, to the right, a door was partially open; lights were on within.

This was it, then; soon it would be over.

He stepped off the last step and stood there, looking toward that partially opened door, and something slammed into the back of his head.

He went down, not out, but while he didn't lose consciousness, exactly, he wasn't exactly on top of things, either.

By the time he knew what was what, he was sitting up, rubbing the back of his head, and Julie was pointing two guns at him, one of them his. Or Sally's, actually: the silenced 9mm. The other gun was a little .22 automatic that looked like a toy, the sort of toy the PTA would like banned.

She was smiling, and he'd never seen anything quite like it—nothing as beautiful, or as ugly, as that smile.

She was standing over him, just a few paces away, wearing designer jeans and a suede coat, open in front to reveal a pale green blouse and the shelf of her breasts. There was a purse tucked under one arm, and a paper sack at her feet; the top where the sack had been twisted shut had loosened up, and packets of money were peeking out.

She was stunning: the brown hair frosted blonde; perfect features, with subtle makeup; tits he wanted to touch, even as he sat there knowing she would kill him, any time now.

Well, he thought. *Might as well play out the hand…*

"Where's Jon?" he demanded.

She shrugged. "He got away from me. He's wandering around the countryside, as far as I know."

"I don't believe you."

"I don't care."

"Listen. I don't give a damn about you, or the money you took that was partly mine. I just want that kid back." He started to get up.

"Stay put," she said. Pointing the 9mm at his head.

From the doorway down by the bar, the boyfriend came out and walked across the empty casino room, moving slowly between the various tables; a big, sandy-haired man with glasses, and a face that was the saddest thing Nolan ever saw.

Julie turned and smiled at him as he came up beside her; she handed him the toylike .22, keeping the silenced automatic for herself.

"Harold," she said, "I don't think I'm going to be leaving after all."

"You're going to kill him?"

"I'm going to take him up to the kitchen," she said. "It'll be easier to clean up afterwards."

"What about the boy?"

"Jon? He'll show up, probably. Eventually. I'm not worried about him. I'll handle it when the time comes." She looked toward Nolan with respect in her smile. "This is the guy to worry about. But not for much longer."

Nolan said, "Isn't it a little messy, a little dangerous, shooting me on your own property? In your restaurant? Why not take me out in the boonies somewhere?"

"You'd do anything to buy a little time, wouldn't you, Nolan?" she said.

"You killed Ron, didn't you?" Harold said to her.

"What?" Julie said, not following him.

Nolan picked up on it. "That's right. I just came from there, that farmhouse. She wanted Ron to kill the kid, but Ron wouldn't do it, let him go instead. Then your princess here shot Ron in the head and faked it up like suicide."

She looked at Nolan, just a little amazed.

"Get up," she told him. "We're going to the kitchen."

Nolan rose. "She's the plague, Harold. Haven't you figured that out yet? Everything she touches turns to dead."

She turned to Harold and smiled like a madonna. "You stay down here. I can take care of this myself."

Harold said, "I love you, Julie."

"I know you do, Harold."

He shot her in the right eye.

It knocked her back, left her sprawled across the bottom few steps of the staircase, a tear of blood tracing her cheek under where her eye had been. She looked at Harold out of the remaining one, or seemed to, anyway.

Nolan let out some air. Cautiously, he reached down and picked up the 9mm, which Julie dropped when she died.

"Thanks," Nolan said.

"Don't mention it," the big man said, and turned the toy .22 on himself and looked down the barrel and watched death come out.

19

Cracking sounds, first one, then another, seconds later; gunshots, Jon was sure of it. Faint, but gunshots.

Despite his turned ankle, he ran, .38 in hand, Toni calling out behind him, telling him to be careful. He found the door to the kitchen open and almost ran into Nolan, coming through the service area beyond the kitchen.

"Nolan! Are you all right?"

"I'm fine."

Nolan had a paper bag in one hand.

"What's that?" Jon asked.

"A sack full of money."

"No kidding? How much?"

"I don't know. Want to sit down and count it?"

"Maybe we ought to get out of here."

"Yeah."

Going through the kitchen, Jon said, "What happened?"

Nolan told him quickly; he was finishing his story by the time they reached the Datsun in the lot. When they got in, Nolan taking the wheel, Toni climbing in back again, Jon started telling her the story and was finished by the time they were going over the old rumbling metal bridge into Burlington.

"Killed himself?" she said, not quite believing it.

"That's right," Jon said. "Poor bastard killed himself."

"No, he didn't," Nolan said.

Jon looked at Nolan.

So did Toni.

"Beauty killed the beast," Nolan said.

Nolan handed the guy in the toll booth the round-trip token and drove on.

The
NOLAN
Novels

by **MAX ALLAN COLLINS**

Skim Deep

The first new Nolan novel in 33 years! The veteran thief finds
himself in hot water when he's entangled in a plot to steal the
skim money from a Las Vegas casino.

Two For the Money

Back to where it all began: after years on the run, would Nolan
bury the hatchet with the Mob…or would they bury him first?

Double Down

Stealing from the criminal Comfort clan is risky enough without
a skyjacker complicating matters.

Tough Tender

Their cover blown, Nolan and Jon must pull a job a second time
for a blackmailing bank exec and the femme fatale behind him.

Mad Money

Can even Nolan pull off a heist of every store in a shopping mall
at once? If he can't, the woman he loves is going to pay…

Available from your favorite bookstore.
For more information, visit
www.HardCaseCrime.com